GW00455912

Side Effect

Dr Paul Shepherd

ISBN - 13

This book is dedicated to my wife Jan without whose encouragement it would never have been written.

Side Effect, although based on many regularly occurring events within the NHS in the UK is entirely a work of fiction. Any resemblance to actual persons, living or dead, is entirely coincidental

The author gratefully acknowledges the helpful advice and support of the following people:

Sophie Baverstock, Dr Gary Calver, Isobel Cawelti, Judi Green, Michael Lang, Trevor Larkin, Sue Marson, Ian Mootz, Dr Graeme Smith

and

Professor Alison Baverstock

Side Effect

PROLOGUE

One year ago

It should have been just another routine operation being carried out by forty two year old surgeon Richard Davies at the Royal Brighton and Hove Hospital.

Richard had decided to be a surgeon when his appendix had burst aged fourteen. The memory of being rushed to hospital with acute pain in his stomach, the ambulance siren, the worried look on his parents faces, hearing talk of the word 'perforation'. He had been certain he was going to die.

And laying in a hospital bed after the operation he was convinced his life had been saved by the surgeon. He had read the consultant's name, 'Mr W. Beard', on a card displayed over the end of his bed. He knew who Mr Beard was but had never spoken with him. The consultant looked distinguished but he was aloof and unapproachable. Immaculately dressed in suit and bow tie he was followed around the ward by a train of junior doctors and students, appearing in awe of the great man. Richard heard questions and instructions being barked out in equal measures with fearful, tentative answers given in reply.

He decided he would become a surgeon, but not like Mr Beard. He would be kinder, he would be more friendly. Richard was going to be different.

He was a bright, determined boy from an ordinary background and through working hard had earned himself a place at Guy's Hospital Medical School in London.

Medical school challenged and stretched Richard but he had loved every minute. He had even found time to shine on the sports field. He was captain and central defender in the first eleven football team. Instead of medicine he could have chosen to pursue a professional sporting career. Just as well he hadn't, his knees reminded him constantly of the many knocks they had taken.

He sailed through his final exams and was accepted onto a junior doctor rotation for specialist training to become a surgeon.

The schoolboy patient had become Mr Richard Davies FRCS.

He was now doing the job he had aspired to and had risen to be appointed as Consultant at the Royal Brighton and Hove Hospital. His chosen speciality was vascular surgery and he excelled at it, respected by colleagues and more importantly liked by his patients.

Compared to some of the surgery he performed, especially the acute trauma work, today's operating list in theatre eight had been straightforward and routine. He was now undertaking an operation to correct the damage caused by three pregnancies to a forty year old lady's legs by removing her varicose veins. The Trendelenberg Procedure.

Some surgeons might regard procedures such as this to be trivial, beneath them, but Richard gained immense satisfaction from using his surgical skills to improve the lives of his patients, whatever their problem.

And he could perform this particular procedure virtually with his eyes closed.

He had already spent thirty minutes working on the ugly, worm like varicosities affecting the right leg around the back and sides of the calf. Just a series of small cuts to expose the offending vein, apply traction with surgical forceps, tie off with thread and excise with a scalpel blade. He felt he hadn't had to concentrate that hard. But unusually he had missed one or two veins and the scrub nurse had needed to point out the previously marked sites for his attention.

He was feeling tired today, on call duty the previous night had been busy, and he would be relieved when this case was finished. It was the last of the day on his operating list.

The superficial surface veins had been excised and all that remained was for him to deal with the deeper underlying problem. The unsightly and painful varicose veins were present because of damage to the valves in the connections to the deeper veins, in this case the long saphenous vein. It needed to be stripped out in order to prevent the varicosities from returning.

Richard glanced at the tray of surgical instruments being carefully and a little jealously guarded by Theatre Sister. He would normally not even need to look up, he would just issue a request for the appropriate instrument to be handed over. But he found himself unable to recall the name of the instrument he now needed. He lifted his head and gazed blankly at the instrument tray. Theatre Sister Shirley never missed anything.

'Is everything OK Richard? You seem to have stopped moving.'

Richard's attention returned. 'Oh yes fine. I just need those forceps we use during the next part of the procedure. For some reason the name has totally escaped me, it's been a busy day.'

'You mean the Spencer Wells?' she said.

'Yes of course, Spencer Wells please.'

He proceeded to make the small incision through the skin on the inside of the ankle which would enable him to locate the distal end of the long saphenous vein. He dissected the tissues, identified the vein and closed it off by clamping on the Spencer Wells.

His next job was to identify the proximal end of the vein high up in the groin, a trickier task; some important structures there, like nerves and arteries, that he needed to stay well clear of.

He suddenly realised he was struggling. His heart was racing and he had come out in a cold sweat. He couldn't remember exactly where to make the incision.

Relax, just keep going, don't let Theatre Sister know you are in trouble. This is what you do, you've carried out this operation hundreds of times before.

He closed his eyes for a moment and tried to subdue the fine tremor that had worryingly started in his hands. Surgeons cannot have shaking hands but the harder he tried to stop the tremor, the worse it became.

'Are you sure you are alright Richard?' she repeated.

'Yes, yes I'm fine, we'll be done in a few minutes, no problem.'

Richard was not fine and he knew it, but his pride and training would not allow him to call for help. Not for something as simple as this anyway. During training he had always been told he must cope, whatever happens. Never show weakness.

A few seconds passed, his mind started to clear and he was able to steady himself sufficiently to make the four centimetre long oblique incision over the pulse of the femoral artery and was relieved to find he was in exactly the right place to identify the saphenous vein. He took a few deep breaths.

'Could I have another Spencer Wells please Shirley,' he said. 'Nearly finished.'

Shirley handed over the forceps, taking a close look at Richard. He didn't seem right to her, but he was the consultant, he was in charge. But was he in control?

Richard applied the forceps to close off the vein. He concentrated hard and remembered that the next step was to cut through the vein below the forceps and then run the long stripping wire up through the vessel from the ankle. Simple. He introduced the wire and ran it up to the groin where it popped out through the cut end of the vein. He tied the wire to the vein using strongly knotted thread. Working back down at the ankle he grasped the handle on the stripping wire firmly and with considerable effort pulled downwards. The long saphenous vein was turned inside on itself as it was torn away from the surrounding tissues before being pulled out through the incision at the ankle. Brutal but effective. He handed the metre long excised vein and wire to Shirley. Thank goodness for that, job almost done.

He knew the operation was nearly at an end but his mind clouded over again and he became aware he wasn't thinking clearly. He had experienced episodes like this before but never while operating. Surely just little lapses in concentration. He had been so busy lately.

The vein is removed, what next? He paused for a moment, struggling to remember. Yes that's it, I just need to remove the forceps from the vein in the groin and sew up.

Richard unclamped the Spencer Wells from the blood vessel and was immediately confronted by a torrent of dark red deoxygenated blood surging from the end of the severed vein. He had forgotten to tie off the vein before removing the forceps. Blood was draining out of the inferior vena cava, a direct route from the heart.

'Richard you haven't tied the vein off, quick get the forceps back on,' cried Shirley, but Richard was standing there trancelike, oblivious to the crisis unfolding around him.

Blood was gushing from the operating site in the groin and had started to drain onto the floor of the theatre, splattering over Richard's operating boots. The elastic like vein had recoiled, he couldn't see the end of it and there was blood everywhere.

'Richard, Richard, do something,' shouted Shirley.

The sound of panic in her voice seemed to spark Richard back to life. 'Suction quickly Sister I cant see a bloody thing. I can't see where to put the forceps back on.'

Loud bleeping noises of alarm from the monitoring equipment jolted the anaesthetist from his happy thoughts on his family's summer holiday.

'Blood pressure is falling rapidly,' he shouted. 'What the hell's going on?'

'I need to get the forceps back on the vein and there's so much blood I can't see a damned thing.'

'Get the head end of this table down now,' screamed the anaesthetist to the operating room technician. 'Has she been cross matched? We need to get some blood inside her asap.'

Shirley was pressing gauze swabs to the wound to try and control the blood loss while at the same time using the suction in an attempt to clear the operating field.

'Richard, the saphenous vein, it's just there, quickly before it retracts again.'

But Richard had returned to his motionless, unresponsive state.

The anaesthetist, seeing what was playing out, shouted. 'For God's sake get the registrar in here, we are going to lose this woman, her blood pressure is down in her boots and her heart rate is sky high.'

The technician pressed the red panic button and screamed. 'Emergency, code red, help needed stat, theatre eight, patient about to go into cardiac arrest.'

A few seconds later the doors of the operating room exploded open with the arrival of Mannish Patel the surgical registrar and the crash team. 'What's happening?' he said.

'You need to get the forceps on the end of this patient's saphenous vein before we lose her,' shouted Shirley. 'Mr Davies has come over unwell, just move him out of the way Mannish.'

'Sorry Mr Davies,' said the registrar as he pushed Richard to one side.

Shirley applied more suction, the wound cleared. Mannish spotted the end of the severed vein and applied the forceps with a swift and reassuring click. The haemorrhaging stopped.

Shirley took several deep breaths. 'Can somebody please take Mr Davies to the surgeon's room and get him a cup of tea or something.'

'Patient is stabilising,' said the anaesthetist. 'BP coming up, pulse slowing down. What's the estimated blood loss?'

'We can weigh the swabs and we've got the contents of the suction jar but there's a heck of a lot more on the floor,' replied Shirley.

'Four units of blood on the way,' said the theatre technician.

Shirley added, 'Can you finish up here Mannish? She just needs sewing up but for Christ's sake don't forget to tie off the bloody vein first.'

Richard was drinking a strong cup of coffee and starting to recover in the surgeon's room under the watchful eye of Ruth, one of the theatre staff nurses.

'Are you feeling any better now Mr Davies? I hear you had a bit of a problem in theatre a few minutes ago but Sister has just called to say the immediate panic is over. Apparently Dr. Patel saved the day.'

'I don't know what happened, I think I must have forgotten to tie off the saphenous vein before I took the forceps off. How could I have done that? I'm a Consultant Surgeon.'

'These things happen to the best of us Mr Davies, don't worry. Sister has asked that you stay here. Apparently Professor O'Brien, the Head of Surgery, is on his way down to check things over. I think he wants to have a chat with you.'

Richard thought to himself that was the last thing he needed. There was so much rivalry in the department. Some of his so called colleagues would be delighted to hear about this afternoon's event.

He worried about what had just happened, but thank goodness the patient was going to be alright.

Richard worried about himself as well. He knew this was not the first time his brain had failed him recently, it had just never happened like this.

Richard was right to be worried about himself. He had no way of knowing, but deep inside a structure of his brain called the hippocampus, a region responsible for functions such as memory, emotion and sex drive, changes were taking place. Toxic proteins were forming and being laid down in plaques around his brain cells. Proteins which were starting to interfere with the normal smooth passage of the electrical signals that enabled his brain to carry out those functions.

These changes were not natural and should not have been happening in a person of his age. And they would ultimately lead to the complete disintegration of the life of Richard Davies.

CHAPTER 1

The present day

The sound of November Rain, by Guns N' Roses, filtered through into the early morning world of Dr Sam Preston.

There are worse ways to be woken up than by Slash playing a guitar solo, thought Sam as his Monday arrived with a noisy start. The seven o'clock radio alarm was bringing his working day into sharp focus. As usual he felt the stirrings of nervous flutterings in his stomach. A combination of hunger and apprehension of the day ahead at his practice. No point in hanging around in bed, it still felt like a lonely place. Even after five years.

He dragged himself up and started his attempts to look presentable for the day. He stared at his reflection in the mirror a little too deeply, as if judging himself. A contest impossible to win first thing in the morning. Unwelcome streaks of grey in his messed up brown hair and more worry lines than his forty two year old face deserved.

Just need to smile more and worry less, he thought. Probably will give me the same lines, just in different places.

From the bedroom along the hallway he could hear the sounds of his daughter Ella starting her day. She was more of a morning person than her father.

He dashed to the bathroom to stake his claim in front of his daughter. If he didn't get in first he might not get in there at all. They had moved to a smaller house five years ago and a single bathroom now had to be shared. But the modest size of the house had helped in keeping them close together as a downsized family.

His visit to the bathroom was necessarily brief with Ella indicating her need was greater than his. He didn't take long to dress himself either. Strictly casual wear for work, best not to intimidate the patients. Well maybe just the odd one or two. Black denim Levi's and a pink cotton Oxford shirt. Same as on Friday.

Early mornings were always on a tight and well rehearsed schedule. A hurried breakfast of coffee and double buttered toast for Sam while Ella sipped at her superfood smoothie. They left the house together, Sam for his short drive to work and Ella for the bus ride out to university at Falmer.

Sam arrived at his practice, parked in the space marked Doctor and entered through the main door of the building just as it was approaching eight thirty. The first few patients were already sitting nervously in the waiting room. He noticed one or two regulars who he would rather have faced later in the day. Best grab another coffee, instant would have to do. He greeted his reception team and popped his head round his Practice Manager's open door.

'Morning Anita, all well? Good weekend?' She spared him the details, he really wouldn't want to know. Sam took his coffee into his consulting room and readied himself for the challenges ahead.

'I'm sure that all you have is a simple viral infection Mrs Bradshaw. I have had a good listen to your lungs and they sound completely clear, no noises that shouldn't be there, and your temperature is fine. There really isn't any reason to worry that it might be anything more serious. It will get better on it's own. Old Father Time and Mother Nature are all that's needed.' Sam found himself saying these words, or words very similar, several times a day to over concerned patients.

'But I've been coughing for more than two weeks doctor, that can't be right. My husband has been the same and he was given antibiotics by his GP, I'm sure that's what I need too.' Mrs Bradshaw wasn't about to give up easily.

Sam was used to that kind of response. Some patients had the unrealistic expectation that antibiotics would cure every infection. And no prescription written could be taken as the doctor thinking there wasn't much wrong with them. He hated being put in a position where he would either upset his patient, or risk breaching one of the prescribing guidelines laid down by the government. Guidelines designed to reserve antibiotics for more serious infections but which never seemed to include advice on how to manage demanding, stroppy patients like Mrs Bradshaw. Fortunately after fifteen years as a GP Sam had developed various strategies for self preservation. But which rather too often seemed to include giving in and letting patients have exactly what they wanted. The last thing a busy GP needs is an unhappy, complaining patient.

'What if I get worse and develop pneumonia?' Followed by, 'I've paid National Insurance all my life doctor.' Sam had heard enough.

Having a quiet life was high on Sam's agenda these days and Mrs Bradshaw departed with her prescription for Amoxicillin. Happy with her medication and happy to have won the anticipated battle with her GP.

Sam even had a sneaking feeling that Mrs Bradshaw's husband hadn't been around for several years. Some you win, some you lose and a draw isn't such a bad result.

He finished typing his notes into the patient's file taking care to ensure that the medical record, if checked during a practice inspection, would justify his actions in line with the national guidelines. Antibiotic resistance was an increasing problem and with drug companies not having produced anything new for thirty years Sam understood the reasons why the guidelines were in place. Even if he didn't always agree with them.

He closed the patient file and returned to the appointment screen. He was running several minutes late and felt under pressure, as he often did after episodes like that.

Another six patients to go on his morning list of twenty four. Just ten minutes per consultation were allocated, hopeless for the patient and stressful for Sam. Surely there had to be a better way of working.

The next patient was in for review of her anti depressant therapy. Gail had been on medication since the break up her marriage two years previously. Several times Sam had tried to persuade her that perhaps now was the right time to start reducing her medication. The anti depressant she was taking was not physically addictive but she had developed an emotional dependence and was convinced she wouldn't be able to cope without her pills. The end of a surgery session with lunch beckoning was not the best time to exhaust any more energy persuading a reluctant patient. He signed the prescription and said, 'When you come back for review in two months time Gail, we really are going to have to talk again about getting you off these pills.'

'Yes of course Doctor. Thank you,' she said hurrying out of the consulting room door.

The rest of the morning surgery passed without major incident and Sam started to deal with the pile of paper and electronic admin that now faced him. He checked and signed several dozen repeat prescriptions. Medications taken long term by patients who didn't need to be reviewed in person by the doctor every time. Sam worried about these patients, how could he be sure they were OK and not suffering from side effects? He had to rely on his patients telling him if they were worried something might be wrong.

But sometimes they didn't realise something was wrong until it was too late.

Memories had been stirred which gave him feelings of both sadness and anger as he tried hard to stop his mind replaying the events of five years ago that had left him as the sole carer for his daughter Ella.

If only he had known, if only his wife had known.

Sam hated phones but that didn't stop them ringing and his desk phone was now demanding his attention, bringing him abruptly back to the present. The display showed it was Anita, his Practice Manager. She had known Sam for a long time, had worked with him in his previous practice, before the tragedy and the issues that followed.

Although Anita was then known as Andrew.

'Sorry to trouble you Sam, I know you've had a bit of a morning but there's a drug rep in reception, He says you know him, name of Malcolm Grant. Apparently you met at a meeting a few weeks ago and told him it was fine to pop in after surgery sometime. He wants to talk to you about his company's arthritis drug, he thought you would be particularly interested.'

Sam suppressed his immediate reaction, which was to tell Anita to tell Malcolm to bugger off. He couldn't quite remember who Malcolm was but the name did ring a slightly unpleasant bell.

'Just so you know he's brought cakes for the girls in the office,' added Anita.

Sam groaned, cakes, the reps entry ticket. He wasn't going to get out of this one.

'Best send him in then Anita. If he's not out within five minutes come and rescue me.'

Malcolm the rep was ushered in.

'Hello Sam, how are you and how's that lovely daughter of yours?' said Malcolm as he brought his overwhelming personality into the consulting room.

Sam thought. How come he sounds so familiar and how on earth does he know anything about my daughter?

He made a deliberate point of staring at the offered business card before saying, 'Ah Mr Grant, I'm aware we've met before but I'm having a little trouble remembering when. Forgive me, it's been a busy morning and I'm feeling in need of some lunch.'

'Call me Malcolm, please. We did meet briefly at the Postgrad Centre a few weeks ago. I was sponsoring an educational meeting about drug addiction management. Hope it was helpful.'

'And I can help with your hunger problem as it happens. Shall I nip out and rescue one of the cakes I brought in for your gorgeous receptionists?'

'No it's fine thanks Malcolm, cakes don't form part of my diet at the moment.' He let the issue rest for the moment about how the drug rep appeared to know details of his private life.

'So Malcolm I can give you five minutes tops because I have a couple of house calls I need to make.' He hadn't really but it was Sam's attempt to maintain some control over the length of the conversation. Sam had the feeling that once Malcolm got talking there would be no stopping him. Time was precious.

'No problem and thanks for seeing me, I won't take up much of your time. I just wanted to find out how you are getting on with my company's anti inflammatory arthritis drug Napralgia. I've got data that shows it's highly effective in controlling joint pain and it's side effect profile, especially from a gastric point of view, is better than anything else on the market.' He leaned over and started to take out some glossy looking brochures from his briefcase.

Malcolm Grant had no reason to anticipate that he was about to be shown out of the door by an upset and angry Dr Preston. What on earth had he said to be treated like that? This was something he was going to have to record in his 'doctor information database' along with all the other personal details he had found out about Sam. And about most other GP's in town too.

Sam had finally settled himself down after a practice based lunch with Anita. He had even eaten one of Malcolm's cakes, partly because they looked as if they would give him the sugar rush he needed but also because he felt a little irritated from time to time about the role of 'sensible person' in the family that his daughter Ella had taken on since he had lost his wife. Cakes would not be on her approved list.

'The drug rep wasn't to know what happened,' said Anita. 'Or even if he did, he really couldn't have known it was his drug.'

'Well he seemed pretty well researched about everything else. He really is a most insensitive man. If he pitches up here again asking to see me I think you know what my answer would be.'

'Like most drug reps he's pretty thick skinned Sam. Cant think he'll be back any time soon though,' replied Anita. 'Shame, these cakes are really rather good.'

The afternoon promised to be more satisfying for Sam than the morning had turned out to be.

His practice was in the Kemp Town district of the trendy seaside resort of Brighton, thirty miles or so due south of London. Famous for its colourful lifestyle and laid back tolerant attitude, it was the unofficial gay capital of England. A young population with two large modern university campuses just up the road at Falmer.

Sadly it also had a large homeless population along with areas of intense deprivation in the sprawling estates of social housing across the city. Inevitably, and in common with many seaside towns, Brighton had a huge drug problem. Back in the eighties and nineties it had also had a major HIV problem. A problem at which governments and pharmaceutical companies had thrown large amounts of money in their attempts to solve. And solve it eventually they did. In part, at least, through the opening of a specialist clinic, the Claude Nicol Centre. The doctors at the clinic prescribed large quantities of newly developed anti HIV drugs. Patients diseases controlled, drug companies made wealthier, governments kept happy.

But the addiction problem didn't have the high profile and celebrity support accorded to HIV and as a result was woefully underfunded. There had been a drug addiction clinic in town for some time which did it's best in difficult circumstances, but the clinic was overwhelmed with long waiting lists for treatment and maintenance therapy. Drug addicts needing help are not renowned for being prepared to wait. Their need was always immediate, there would be no tomorrow for some of them.

So the addiction problem bounced back to the bottomless pit of General Practice. Most GP's feel under qualified to work with addicts; some are terrified by them, and not entirely without good reason. Addicts live chaotic lives with multiple medical and social needs and can be very persuasive in their attempts to obtain the drugs fuelling their addiction. They do not easily take no for an answer, abuse and threats are commonplace.

Sam was not like most GP's and although he wasn't an addiction specialist he felt he couldn't just do nothing. He had found time to educate himself by attending suitable courses and had become convinced that he at least needed to try and help those patients on his list who had become addicted to opiates. Many of those patients had just made some bad life choices, but an increasing number were addicted to prescription drugs. Painkillers which were initially prescribed for the right reasons but the development of addiction had led to continued prescribing long after the original clinical need had gone. It often seemed to Sam that the addiction had, in a way, been caused by the doctor not taking enough care. And that made him feel more than a little guilty.

So he had set up a twice weekly addiction clinic in his practice and was determined to do what he could. And it would stop the addicts from causing stress and disruption during his regular surgeries. He quickly realised he couldn't carry out that type of work alone and Anita had employed a specialist mental health nurse to help with emotional support and sample testing.

Sam looked forward to his drug clinic afternoons. He enjoyed the challenge of helping those at rock bottom in their attempts to climb out.

After all Sam knew what it was like to be at rock bottom.

Unlike most other non specialist doctors, Sam was prepared to prescribe the drugs needed by the addicts. There were no government guidelines for addiction treatment he was obliged to follow. Of course addicts had to be sample tested regularly to ensure they really were users and not just dealers looking to peddle his prescriptions to others. But he prescribed opiate drugs like methadone, buprenorphine and oxycodone in situations where he and his nurse felt it appropriate. At least it would help keep his patients away from trouble with the police. Drug addiction and crime inevitably feeding off each other.

In a community like Brighton word had quickly spread among interested parties when it became known controlled drugs were being made available. Sam's patient list was growing quickly and he had to admit he had more than his fair share of drug addicts to manage. A victim of his own success he liked to think.

It probably depended on how you defined success and who was judging it.

The afternoon had been more inspiring and rewarding than the morning. Drug addicts can be more grateful than other patients. So long as they continued to get what they wanted. Some addicts were prepared to engage in lengthy reduction programmes in desperate attempts to overcome their addiction. Others were what might be best described as hopeless cases and the sole purpose of prescribing was to control the cravings and stop them resorting to other methods of obtaining what their bodies needed.

'So long as they get what they want.' Sam reflected to himself.

Anita knocked on the door and knowing Sam was on his own, opened it without waiting for a reply.

'Just checking you are OK Sam. I'm about to clear off home and thought I would bring this into you before I go. It might just cheer you up at the end of a long day. A rep, not your friend Malcolm, dropped it off for you earlier this afternoon.'

She handed Sam an already opened, expensive looking cream coloured envelope and waited to see his reaction.

Sam slipped out the enclosed gold embossed card and read the inscription. He looked up at Anita.

'It seems I have been invited to an awards ceremony. That doesn't exactly happen everyday. Rheumatology Specialist of the Year presented by Valerian Pharmaceuticals. It's being held at the Cafe Royal in London the week after next.'

'Yes I thought perhaps you might have won something,' Anita suggested hopefully but not optimistically.

'After all those drug side effect report cards I've been sending back I very much doubt it,' laughed Sam. 'They're probably just trying to make up the numbers. Can't think why else I would be invited.'

'Well, in any case, it sounds like it might be fun, an evening out in London. And the invite says bring a partner.' He paused for a moment. 'So Anita, if you happen to be free, I would love for you to be my partner for the evening. That might raise a few eyebrows.'

'Indeed it might,' said Anita with a smile. 'Let's hope so. And yes, thanks, how exciting, can't wait. Any chance of a pay rise for a new pair of heels.

CHAPTER 2

The sound of a wine glass being firmly struck with a knife eventually brought silence to the gathering of two hundred people assembled around tables of eight in the Pompadour Ballroom of the Hotel Cafe Royal in London. Valerian Pharmaceuticals certainly knew how to impress it's guests. Sam had not been in surroundings as opulent as this before.

They were seated in the elaborately ornate room which was decorated in an old French style. Rectangular columns projected from the walls of mirrored panels and gilded frames. The ceiling was partitioned and painted with classical scenes of love.

Sam was feeling uncomfortable and distinctly under dressed. He had put on his only suit, fresh back from the cleaners, and one of the few ties he possessed but most of the guests were wearing formal evening dress.

Thank goodness he had Anita with him. She looked fantastic in a royal blue, full length, silk dress. Her blond hair was pushed up and styled in an elegant chignon. She had spent a long time in front of a mirror applying her makeup, totally transforming her appearance. Sam, having taken the strong hint she had dropped, had treated her to a new pair of shoes. He was aware that Anita had been the subject of admiring glances from some of the other male guests and he couldn't help thinking, 'If only they knew!' He was proud she was there accompanying him as his partner.

'Ladies and gentlemen, thank you for joining us on this special evening where we are gathered to celebrate the achievements of some of the finest medical minds in the land. It is now my great pleasure to introduce you to the driving force and passion behind Valerian

Pharmaceuticals. Founder, owner and chairman Dr Hugo Thomson!'

After such an enthusiastic introduction it seemed only right and proper for generous applause to be accorded to the chairman from the assembled great and good, with some guests even getting to their feet as the man who was footing the bill for this extravagant evening made his entrance through the double doors at the far end of the room. A trumpeted fanfare would not have seemed out of place.

Sam couldn't believe it and couldn't believe he hadn't made the connection. This surely was his old medical school colleague Hugh Thomson; when had he become Hugo?

Sam ruefully remembered Hugh struggling in his early years as a doctor after an interesting route to qualification. He had heard that Hugh had left medicine in favour of the pharmaceutical industry, but had very much lost track of him. Not that he would have wished to keep in contact after what had happened back in his student days at Guy's Hospital. He wondered if Hugh or Hugo as he now seemed to be called would remember him? Did he know that Sam was among the guests for the evening?

After the episode at Guy's it would probably be hard for Hugh to forget Sam. He felt relieved that he and Anita had been placed at a table well towards the rear of the room.

Hugo certainly appeared to have done very well for himself even if his waistline and hair line seemed to have advanced in opposite directions at about the same rate. He was dressed to impress in white dinner jacket and bright red cummerbund with matching bow tie. And what hair he had left was stuck down in a comb over as part of a failed attempt to disguise the passage of time. The style looked faintly comical and interfered with the look of success he was probably trying to achieve.

Dr Thomson gestured with the palms of both hands to signal to his appreciative audience that he had been applauded enough and was ready to speak.

Hugh had always spoken with the sort of clipped tones learned only through attendance at one of England's finest public schools and if anything his voice sounded even more pompous than Sam remembered from the old days.

'Ladies and gentlemen, thank you for such a wonderful reception and thank you all so much for joining me and my team from Valerian to celebrate the success of my company and of course the achievements of our distinguished medical colleagues sitting here at the tables in front of me.' He indicated the doctors by spreading his arms wide. He turned to the man seated to his left. 'It's also a privilege to be joined this evening by my very good friend The Right Honourable Giles Barrington MP, our Minister for Health. It has been my pleasure to support Giles and the efforts of his government for a number of years and long may that cooperation continue.'

He paused for applause which the audience seemed a little reluctant to give.

'Thank you. Our success of course could not have been possible without the scientific brain behind the company, the man who discovered and developed the most innovative, effective and safest arthritis treatment on the market, Condrone. A round of applause please for Dr Peter White PhD.' Hugo turned to his right to indicate Dr. White, clapping his hands as he did so.

A gentle, polite round of applause rippled across the ballroom. A hesitant wave of acknowledgment was given by Dr White, clearly less comfortable in the spotlight than his chairman.

'Now I know you are all really only here to enjoy the food, and excellent it will be, so without further ado I am going to announce the winner of the Valerian Rheumatologist of the Year Award. This award is presented to the Rheumatology

Specialist who, in the opinion of the awards committee, has contributed the most towards advancing the successful treatment of their patients.'

Sam thought. In other words the biggest prescriber of Condrone.

Hugo was handed a large envelope, by a young woman seated directly to his right, which he opened theatrically. He took out a card and read from it as he held it out in front of him.

'And the winner is Dr Isaac Abraham, Consultant Rheumatologist at The North Middlesex Hospital. Well done Dr Abraham.'

Hugo led further applause, which quite rightly didn't reach the level accorded to himself earlier. The lucky winner rose from his front row table and moved forward to receive his award from Dr Thomson.

From the rear of the room it appeared to Sam that the award was a prosthetic knee joint, albeit a gold plated one. It seemed for a moment as though the recipient was about to make a speech himself but Hugo quickly took ownership of the microphone saying, 'A great believer in the benefits of Condrone and a great supporter of Valerian, thank you Dr Abraham,' while gesturing with his hand for the doctor to return to his seat. Dr Abraham retreated reluctantly raising the gold plated prosthesis in mock triumph.

'I would like to thank all you good doctors for your support over the last year,' continued Hugo. 'It is a very exciting time for Valerian. We are planning the launch of a major new product in the near future which will revolutionise the treatment of patients in a specialty new to us as a company. I look forward to telling you all about it. Watch this space!'

He sat back down and enjoyed the applause which was being led by the Health Minister who had taken to his feet in salute of his benefactor.

Sam whispered to Anita 'I used to know this guy Hugo at medical school, I could say he hasn't changed much but he's actually a lot worse. Don't know why he doesn't just give himself the award.'

'And I think I could suggest where he might like to stick it,' replied Anita.

CHAPTER 3

Twenty years ago Guy's Hospital

Sam Preston saw an opening and ran between the two central defenders of the King's College Hospital first eleven football team. He timed his run perfectly to avoid an offside flag and shouted to Richard Davies who was striding imperiously through midfield with the ball as if attached to his right foot.

'Now Rich. Through the channel.'

Richard had seen his friend making the run and threaded the ball between the defenders with pinpoint accuracy.

Sam ran onto the pass leaving the King's defenders behind him. He controlled the ball with his left foot before moving it to his right. He was thirty yards from goal and advancing rapidly with only the keeper to beat. He had come halfway off his line to narrow the angle.

Should Sam try to chip the keeper, always risky at speed, or dribble on and shoot past, or go round him? His brain automatically chose the latter having calculated the angles, distance and position of the keeper. He dropped his shoulder feigning to go right but took the ball the other way with the outside of his left boot, leaving the goalkeeper stranded and gently side footed the ball into the back of an empty net.

Guy's 1 King's 0.

'Great finish,' said Rich running forward with his team mates to congratulate Sam.

'You made it easy with that through ball,' replied Sam. And to his team mates shouted 'Come on Guy's let's take this game now.'

This was the first round of the annual Hospital's Cup and was being played at the Guy's Sport's Ground in Honor

Oak Park, South London. All London based teaching hospitals took part and there was intense and often fierce rivalry between the sides. Matches often ended up merely as opportunities for the students to take out their frustrations and anger on each other. Richard as the captain and central defender usually gave much better than he got but was often on the receiving end of aggressive challenges both on the ground and in the air.

Emotions in the match had risen to a higher level after Sam's goal, with King's stepping up a gear and they had been pressing for an equaliser for the last few minutes. A last gasp challenge by a Guy's defender on the edge of the six yard box had sent the ball behind for a King's corner.

Sam, as the centre forward, was good in the air, and was expected to come back to help the defence at set piece corners. His job was to defend the near post and try to intercept the corner kick before it got anywhere near the danger area in front of goal.

Richard was the leader of the defence and it was his role to organise the team and make sure every King's attacker was marked. The ball would likely come across in the air and it was Richard's responsibility to make sure it was headed away clear from goal. Tall, unshaven and wearing a headband in Guy's colours of gold and blue. You would rather not, as an attacker, be marked by Richard. There was a good chance you would be marked for ever.

The ball was swung into the penalty area from the right by the left boot of the King's winger, flying well over the head of Sam at the near post. Instinctively he turned to follow the flight of the ball and watched as Richard and the King's centre forward rose to meet it.

The sound of the two players heads crashing into each other was sickening. The forehead of the King's man had crunched into the right side of Richard's head just above the ear. Both players collapsed to the ground. The centre forward in the red shirt was able to get up soon enough, the blow being to a tough part of his skull, an area rarely seriously damaged.

But Richard lay still on the ground, immobile. Sam hardly heard the referee's whistle blowing to halt the match as he rushed over to his friend. He knew enough anatomy to realise that a blow to the side of the skull could be very dangerous. The middle meningeal artery coursed just below and a fracture of the bone in that region would tear the artery causing catastrophic bleeding around the brain. An extra dural haemorrhage, which would lead to pressure on the brain. Rapid loss of consciousness and unless treated quickly by surgery, death.

But Richard was unconscious for only a few seconds and by the time his team mates rushed to his aid he was coming back round. Plenty of under experienced and overconfident would be doctors eager to help.

It is usual in football matches for every injury to be treated by applying a 'magic' sponge soaked in cold water. A crude placebo but on this occasion seemingly effective as Richard was first able to sit up and then, against advice, rise unsteadily back to his feet.

Sam was relieved. It didn't seem like a fractured skull, so immediate bleeding around the brain was unlikely. But he was very probably concussed, and if so it would show itself as confusion and memory loss. Concussion was caused by the impact of the brain against the rigid box like structure of the skull.

The home goalkeeper fancied himself as a future neurosurgeon and took charge. He held up two fingers in front of Richard. 'How many fingers do you see captain?'

'Four,' replied Richard. 'I'm fine really.'

'Remind me, what's the score?'

'I'm not sure. I think we're winning though aren't we?'

'What did you have for lunch today Rich?' Our future brain surgeon thought this would be a good test of recent memory and, 'Who are we playing against?'

Richard didn't have a clue what the answer was to either question and it was obvious he was in no fit state to carry on.

Sam stepped in. 'Come on old buddy you've run your race in this game. Time to use our substitute, you're off for a lie down.'

'No I'm fine, just a bit wobbly that's all. Let me run it off'

At this point the referee decided it was time to reassert his authority on the match.

'I'm no medical man, unlike you lot, but even I can see he's not right. Take him off or I'll have to send him off for his own good. And if he won't leave the pitch I'll abandon the match.' Harsh words but ultimately effective, as Richard was led away to the sidelines.

The match resumed but the coming together of heads had taken the sting out of the game. The potentially serious injury had been enough to remind the players that it really was only a game. The fight and aggression had gone from both sides.

King's scored from a penalty kick shortly into the second half and the game petered out to a one all draw. A replay would be needed at the King's ground the following week.

The facilities provided for the students at the Guy's ground were comfortable and after a match, with hostilities at least temporarily over, the players joined one another in the clubhouse for refreshments.

Having got showered and changed, Sam wandered into the bar to find Richard already there. As a future doctor he was of course doing exactly what shouldn't be done after a nasty blow to the head. He was halfway down a pint of Young's Best Bitter and it probably wasn't his first.

'I gather my team couldn't cope without me,' said Richard, clearly feeling better after his liquid medication. 'But one all against King's isn't a bad result, we'll finish the job in the replay next week.'

'Well I can see your memory and sarcastic sense of humour is returning,' said Sam, 'What a relief.'

'But seriously you need to be careful, you aren't out of the woods yet as you well know if you've been paying attention to our surgery tutors.'

'Head injuries can lead to delayed bleeding in the brain and with alcohol causing blood vessels to dilate it would make any bleeding worse.' Sam listened to his own voice and realised he sounded as pompous as some of his teachers.

Good practice for becoming a doctor, his mother would probably have said.

But Sam wasn't going to be that kind of doctor.

A couple more beers and the traditional pie and beans later and Richard reminded Sam they had arranged to go to the weekly inflam back in the bar at the medical school. Inflam being the medicalised acronym for a drinking and dancing evening and was an abbreviation of the word inflammation. All medical students are taught that the cardinal features of inflammation are hot, red, swollen and painful. A fairly accurate description of a dance in the Guy's bar.

But they were popular. It was the one night of the week when the medical student's bar was thrown open to welcome the other students at Guys; the nursing students. A heady mix of alcohol, sweat, testosterone and oestrogen. Any release of emotion or passion not happening on the sports field could always be sought at the inflam.

Sam and Richard took the fifteen minute train ride back to London Bridge. It had just started to rain and they hurried across the connecting walkway from the railway station back to the hospital. They made their way through the subterranean network of tunnels under the Guy's campus to the students locker room, dumped their sports bags and made their way towards the student's bar.

Somebody else hoping that tonight's inflam would bring about a much needed and sought after release of passion was fellow student Hugh Thomson.

Hugh was in the same year group as Sam and Richard. Despite a more privileged education and wealthy family backing he was struggling with the work demands of the medical course. He was regarded by his teachers as being lazy and poorly motivated. Hugh had once been told by the Dean that without the privileged education and wealthy family he probably wouldn't have been at Guy's, not that Hugh would have cared much.

Student Doctor Thomson had been admiring and pursuing Student Nurse Jarvis for some time now. He had spotted her on one of the surgical wards, a vivacious girl of medium height with fiery red hair. Tied back during work hours and released, like an unfurled flag of danger, when off duty. Hugh was captivated by Gilly Jarvis, her smile, even by her name, but so far his advances had not been encouraged. Neither had they been completely rejected but it would seem clear to anybody who cared to notice that Gilly Jarvis was hoping to do a little better for herself than the squat, arrogant, plum voiced Hugh Thomson.

Gilly was sure to be at the inflam tonight with her group of friends. Hugh would keep a watchful eye and when the moment was right and the vodka tonics had done their job, ideally to both Hugh and Gilly, he would make his move.

Hugh was not a natural athlete, God how he hated natural athletes, but he had been closely studying a selection of videos on the internet and now felt reasonably confident that when the right pace of song was played by the DJ he would be able to perform a few routines on the dance floor. Once Gilly had seen his moves she surely would soon be feeling his hands move too. All over her! Hugh found himself getting a little too excited at the thought and had to pause and adjust his trousers before heading down to the bar.

The student's bar at Guys could best be described as a dive, situated on the lower ground floor, dark and dingy, definitely not the cleanest room in the hospital. But it was well suited to its purpose with low level lighting and vinyl flooring which would become covered with a slippery slick of beer as the evening progressed. The walls were furnished with cheap bench like seating behind long low rectangular tables. The table football games and pool tables had been removed for the evening to clear a space for dancing and a DJ had installed himself in the far corner where he was currently building liquid confidence behind his consoles of electronic equipment.

The bar was just starting to get busy when Sam and Richard made their way in. The effect of the post match beers at the sports ground had already worn off and they were eager to reintoxicate themselves as soon as possible. Richard was feeling better now and apart from the events immediately before the head injury his memory had returned. Sam was currently more worried about getting his next drink than he was about his friend's recovering amnesia.

There was a crush at the bar with eager drinkers competing to get served by a single struggling bar man. Sam recognised him as Phil who usually played in midfield for the seconds. Having pushed his way through the crowd Sam caught Phil's eye and shouted 'Two pints of lager please Phil'.

The barman seemed eager to serve the striker and the captain of the first eleven, and placed a pint glass under the Carling tap.

'Hey I was before him in the queue, I've been waiting ages.' Hugh just didn't have that required presence at the bar and always seemed to get ignored in the throng. He was already tense and nervous about the challenge he had set himself for the evening and he desperately needed a drink to steady himself.

'Sorry about that Hugh,' said Sam. 'I didn't notice you down there,' he added as an insult.

Instantly regretting what he had said and perhaps noticing the wild look in Hugh's eyes he quickly tried to remedy the situation. 'Best make it three pints Phil.'

'You should know by now I don't drink beer,' said Hugh. 'I'll have a vodka and tonic, a double seeing as you're buying.'

Hugh ungratefully took his drink away from the bar and looked around the room to see if Gilly and her friends had arrived. He soon spotted them, a group of four nurses looking strangely unfamiliar without their work uniforms on, seated around a small circular table just to the left of the bar entrance. They were engaged in animated conversation while surreptitiously scanning the room. Empty glasses sat on the table with a realistic expectation of being refilled.

The ceiling of the bar was supported by several round pillars to which circular standing tables had been attached. Hugh positioned himself behind one of these and established a good view of his target. He took a hefty swig of his drink and felt his nerves start to calm as the alcohol hit his brain. Tonight would be the night, he was sure of it.

Richard and Sam spent the early part of the evening drinking with friends and fellow team mates but, like most of the men present, always keeping an eye out for what might be available later. Richard seemed back to his usual lively self, he was the leader of the gang as well as leader of the football team. Pints of beer were being replaced by the customary Jager Bombs. Confidence levels were rising in direct proportion to blood alcohol levels.

The DJ pumped up the volume, deliberately making any normal conversation impossible, in an attempt to encourage the dance floor to fill. The mood lighting, loud music and alcohol were starting to lower the usual inhibitions and Gilly and her friends needed little encouragement. This was their chance to attract the attentions of all those future doctors.

It hadn't been that hard to attract the attention of Sam who had always had a bit of a thing for red heads. He had noticed her earlier, sitting with her group of friends. When he had quietly pointed her out to Richard he had seemed more interested in the dark haired girl sitting next to her.

They too were waiting until the moment was right.

One person Gilly was not keen to attract the attentions of however, was the squat man who seemed to be finding it increasingly hard to stand up straight, propped against the pillar. She had noticed him staring at her earlier and had become increasingly concerned as the evening had worn on. She knew who he was of course but she didn't quite know the extent of the unrequited feelings that he held about her. Unrequited because those feelings were unfortunately not shared by Gilly. Quite the opposite in fact. She actually found him repulsive but didn't want to cause trouble by upsetting an apparently well connected medical student.

A solution to Gilly's little problem appeared just a couple of minutes later as Sam and Rich made their approach towards the girl's table.

Gilly quickly looked up, keen to solve her problem.

'Hi there Sam. Hi Rich, how did the match go today?'

Sam thought. Crikey she knows who I am, how does she know about the match? Swiftly followed by. My luck could be in here tonight.

'Grab a couple of chairs guys, come and join us, let me introduce you to the gang.'

Sam and Richard didn't need to discuss the merits of the invite before finding two spare seats and dragging them over.

Hugh of course had been watching these events unfold from his hiding place and was finding it hard to contain his anger. His evening and ambitions were being ruined. And ruined by that bastard Sam Preston and his friend the footballer.

Hugh watched as Sam and Gilly along with Richard and the dark haired beauty Kate joined the crowd on the dance floor. To a hopeless dancer like Hugh the boys seemed to float around the girls, and they were responding by smiling and laughing. He knew he should just go back to his depressing room in the halls of residence but he couldn't tear himself away from his own suffering. He was drinking more and more and had been warned by Phil the barman that maybe enough was enough. Hugh was in a foul mood and looking for trouble.

Gilly was enjoying herself in Sam's company but felt a little guilty that she might be taking advantage of him in order to solve her Hugh problem. She had noticed the rapidly declining mood Hugh was displaying and he now appeared to be even more fixated than before. She wondered if she should say something to Sam but was worried about what might happen if she did.

Time to leave, thought Gilly. But no way I'm leaving alone.

'You boys must be feeling hungry after all that dancing, why don't we take ourselves off to the nurses home, the cafeteria is still open, we can grab a bite to eat.'

An invitation to the nurses home! That sounded too good to turn down. And Sam was feeling more than a little hungry, the pie and beans felt like a long time ago.

Rich was certainly up for that plan and he and Kate led the way out of the bar. As Sam and Gilly followed, she slipped her hand through Sam's arm and held on tightly.

The group made their way up the stairs and out into the freshness of the night air. They crossed the senior doctors car park and climbed the steps into the black and white marble floored colonnade.

Hugh had not been able to stop himself following and could see where the group was heading.

The nurses home, the fantasy place of Hugh's dreams where his passionate advances were to have been rewarded.

It was all too much for Hugh and, fuelled by vodka, he lost control and started running at Sam and Gilly.

It happened so quickly. Sam heard footsteps approaching rapidly from behind and turned to see what was happening. Sam's face was met by Hugh's balled fist and he was knocked to the ground. Out for the count.

Richard and Kate were about twenty yards in front and spun round to see Hugh standing over Sam shouting 'Bastard, bastard, bastard'. Richard moved quickly to the aid of Sam as Hugh ran off back in the direction of the bar.

Sam was lying unconscious on the floor of the colonnade, blood pouring from his nose. Gilly was moving him carefully into the recovery position and trying to staunch the flow of blood.

'Sam, talk to me mate. Are you OK?' said Richard.

There was a groaned response as Sam started to come round. 'What the fuck just happened?' he muttered.

'What just happened is that complete idiot Hugh Thomson has punched you,' said Gilly. 'I'm so sorry Sam this is all my fault. He had been eyeing me up all evening and he's taken it out on you. I can't stand that little fat shit.'

'Can you manage to sit up,' said Rich. 'We're going to need to get you sorted out in Casualty. Come on old buddy,' he pulled Sam to his feet. 'We'll deal with Hugh some other time.'

'Sorry girls, not your fault Gilly, let's do this another evening.'

A visit to Accident and Emergency had seemed inevitable earlier in the day and that visit was now taking place. Just with a reversal of roles, as Rich helped Sam stagger through the sliding doors of the entrance to be met by the triage nurse.

Rich gave a quick summary of what had happened and Sam was led away to be assessed.

Sam had been knocked unconscious and this head injury was taken going to be taken much more seriously than the one earlier in the day. The consultant was summoned and he carried out a full neurological exam before ordering an immediate CT scan of the head. Whatever the outcome of the scan Sam was going to be detained for the rest of the night in the observation ward.

Richard returned to the bar, looking for Hugh, with vengeance on his mind, but Hugh was nowhere to be found.

Probably just as well, he thought. His head injury, with the drinking and dancing, had taken it's toll and it was time to call an end to an eventful day.

Sam had not slept at all in the casualty ward. Not really surprising bearing in mind a nurse had appeared every twenty minutes to shine a light in his eyes and to assess his conscious level. He had a nasty pain in the side of his head where he had been struck and he felt nauseous. He just wanted to get out of the ward and back to his room. He would decide what to do about Hugh later, he wasn't going to let the attack go unpunished.

Sam's hopes of a quiet start to the day were ruined with the arrival of the A&E consultant Dr. Watson.

'Ah Mr Preston. I trust you've had a comfortable night. Your observations have been satisfactory and I'm pleased to say your CT scan was normal. Even your rather elevated blood alcohol level appears to have reduced,' he added pointedly.

'That's good news sir, I'm sorry to have troubled your department overnight. I'm feeling fine now, thank you,' he lied. 'Am I OK to leave now? I'm anxious to get back to my studies,' he lied again.

'Yes, I am signing you off as fit to be discharged. You will not be surprised after such an incident, that it was my duty to inform the Dean of the Medical School,' said the specialist and he added a little ominously. 'He has given instructions for you to go straight to his office from here.'

The Dean had deliberately kept Sam waiting on an uncomfortable wooden chair in the corridor immediately outside his office. He was eventually instructed to go through by the Dean's personal assistant.

'I have already spoken to the two student nurses involved in last night's unfortunate incident Mr Preston and it would appear you were not at fault,' said the Dean of the Medical School, Professor Mellor.

I should bloody well think not, thought Sam.

'That is correct sir,' said Sam instead.

'I was relieved to hear from Dr Watson in casualty that your CT scan showed no evidence of serious injury and you appear to be recovering well enough.'

'Just a nasty headache sir, thank you.'

'Well from what I hear about your blood alcohol level last night that may not be entirely down to the fist of Mr Thomson,' the Dean said rather unnecessarily.

'I have also spoken with Richard Davies, he seemed a little less clear than the nurses, but given his nasty head injury in the match yesterday that is perhaps understandable.'

The Dean appeared to have another concern on his mind.

'You have clearly been the victim of an entirely unprovoked assault by Mr Thomson and I shall be talking with him and dealing with the matter shortly.'

'Incidents like this, if made public, don't do the medical school or the hospital any good at all, especially at times when funding is so tight.'

'I'm not sure what you are trying to get at here sir,' said Sam, knowing exactly where this conversation was heading.

'I was wondering if you have made a decision about going to the police on this matter? Obviously that decision is entirely yours and who could blame you if you did?'

'But before deciding, I think you should take a little time to reflect on whether that would be the best course of action. Naturally I am only thinking about what's best for you, after all finals are fast approaching. Do you need that distraction?'

'Thank you for your concern sir,' replied Sam. 'I'm aware of my legal rights and I will do what I consider to be the right thing. As you say the attack was unprovoked and I think my attacker was very drunk. Do you intend to take any action on behalf of the Medical School sir?'

'Well I shall see Mr Thomson in a moment. While I appreciate what you have said, it would not be appropriate for me to discuss disciplinary matters with you. But please do talk to me again before thinking of making any rash decision about police involvement.'

It was apparent the interview was over. No apology on behalf of the medical school and no promise of any specific action being taken against Hugh. Sam felt irritated.

If the medical school wasn't going to do anything maybe he should go to the police, Hugh certainly deserved some sort of punishment and it was clear that now the Dean was involved he wasn't going to be able to settle the score himself.

As Sam left the Dean's office he saw Hugh Thomson sitting, waiting for his turn to be summoned. He looked somewhat worse for wear as if he had been dragged out of his bed inconveniently early. Sam heard him being called in as he walked off down the corridor.

'Have you anything to say for yourself Thomson?' said the Dean. 'You appear to have followed another student out of the bar last night, quite clearly drunk, and you carried out an unprovoked attack. What on earth got into you man? Do you think that sort of behaviour is what is expected of a future Guy's doctor?'

Hugh assumed the Dean was being rhetorical and felt it best not to reply.

The Dean continued. 'Let's face it you are as guilty as hell of common assault. Anything in your defence, any mitigating circumstances?'

Hugh didn't think it would go down too well to describe his thoughts and intentions of the previous evening towards Miss Jarvis.

'No sir, I would like to apologise for my actions. They were completely out of character and I can assure you they won't be repeated,' he eventually said after an awkward silence.

'Damn right they won't be repeated,' said an increasingly exasperated Professor Mellor.

Privately the Dean would have liked to have given Hugh Thomson the push from his medical school but he remembered the degree of influence Hugh's father had exerted for his underperforming son to have been admitted in the first place. He calmed himself down.

'Your apology is accepted by the medical school,' said the Dean. 'But I rather think with regard to Mr Preston you are going to need to do a little better than that.'

'How do you think this is going to make the hospital and the school look if Preston reports the incident to the police? Which I think he may very well do.'

'You will of course be punished by the school for your actions but before deciding on your punishment I strongly suggest you get together with Sam Preston and see how you can make it up to him. I would like you to make this incident go away.'

He added, almost as an afterthought. 'I understand you and your family have considerable resources at your disposal that might be helpful at a time such as this.'

As if any further threat were needed he added, 'I shall be reporting this to your father, as a matter of course, later this morning.'

Hugh wasn't really that bothered about being thrown out of medical school and this was clearly a possibility, but the likely reaction from his father was definitely not worth contemplating.

And he was only a few weeks away from qualification, always provided he could find a way past the examiners.

'I think I understand what you are saying sir. Perhaps you could just hold off the phone call to my father and give me a chance to make things good with Preston.'

'Very well, I will give you until tomorrow. Now get out of my office Thomson and fix this problem.'

The Dean really had had enough of sorting out fights between students. He just wanted to get on with the more important job of attracting fee paying students from overseas in order to balance the budget deficit.

Hugh had got the message very clearly from the Dean and he was prepared to do whatever it took to pacify Sam. Perhaps not surprisingly the incident had also had the effect of dampening his passion for Student Nurse Jarvis. Clearly her taste in men was appalling. Time to move on.

He had persuaded Sam to meet him for a free lunch and they wandered over with their trays to a quiet table in the corner of the student cafe.

'I'm not really sure why I am here Hugh. I've just had a night in casualty because of you. Thanks a lot.'

'Naturally the Dean wanted to speak with me, after he had dealt with you, in order to hear my side of the story,' Hugh lied.

'We had a discussion and the Dean felt it best we sort this out man to man with one another. He also seemed very concerned about the reputation of the medical school. He rather hopes, as do I, that you won't feel it necessary to involve the police. Just a drunken brawl after all.'

'I think you will find it takes two to make a drunken brawl Hugh. How many punches did I lay on you before you buggered off? I'm inclined to think that going to the police is exactly what I should do, I've suffered actual bodily harm because of you.'

'Well I am prepared to apologise for my part in what happened last night. I had been drinking rather too heavily and wasn't entirely responsible for my actions. You must have known the depth of my feelings for Nurse Jarvis. How did you think it would make me feel to see you disappearing off with her for a good time in the nurses home?'

'Hugh I have no idea what your feelings are or were towards Gilly Jarvis but I could give you a good idea what her feelings are towards you right now if you like.'

'And I don't think the police are going to accept that you weren't responsible for assaulting me just because you were pissed.'

Hugh realised he wasn't getting anywhere here. Really Preston was being most unreasonable.

He was going to have to resort to plan B very quickly. He wasn't surprised, he would have been straight off to the police himself.

He was aware that his and Sam's financial circumstances were very different. Hugh had always had plenty of money during his time at Guy's and in contrast to most of his student colleagues already owned a reasonably respectable car. It had taken quite a lot of financial persuasion from his father to make sure he had continued with his studies.

Sam however was evidently in a difficult financial state. Hugh knew that Sam had run up quite a large student debt. His own fault, he had spent far too much money on drinking.

'I have a proposition to make,' said Hugh. 'A financial arrangement that will keep the bank manager off your back and keep the bloody Dean off mine.'

Hugh laid out in some detail to Sam how his proposal would work.

The meeting had not gone in the direction Sam had expected but Hugh's proposal certainly had some merit. He abandoned his lunch plate with substantial food for thought.

CHAPTER 4

Eight years ago, Hugh

'I'm telling you Hugo, this is an opportunity far too good to miss out on,' said an excited Dr Peter White PhD. They were sitting together in the lounge bar of a Surrey pub not far from the English headquarters of Smithson Pharmaceuticals. They had both joined the drug company round about the same time and had struck up a sort of friendship. Peter had recognised certain qualities in his colleague which he had decided were going to be essential for his tentative plan to work.

They could see no sign of anybody else from Smithson in the bar but were keeping their voices low.

'My scientist colleagues in the research department gave up on a certain compound last year, they've all moved on to that new respiratory project. The entire work has been archived, never to see the light of day again,' said Peter.

'So would you be talking about the compound we were all so excited about three years ago,' enquired Hugo. 'The drug some of our colleagues thought was going to revolutionise the treatment of arthritis, heal the joints. It was called Piricoxib I seem to remember.'

'Yes Piricoxib, revolutionary certainly and not just because it had the potential to repair cartilage damaged by the arthritic process. It also would not have killed patients by giving them stomach ulcers. As you know all the conventional anti inflammatory agents cause ulcers and gastrointestinal bleeding, despite claims to the contrary by a few pharmaceutical companies less reputable than ours.'

'But if I remember correctly, it was decided at a pay grade well above mine, that further development of Piricoxib would be terminated due to concerns about the huge level of costs involved,' Hugo remembered correctly.

'Yes that was the case, the research costs were staggering, the company decided to cut its losses and concentrate on asthma treatment. But I think I might just have solved the cost issue, thanks to a novel technique I have developed, let's say, in my spare time,' said Peter a little cautiously.

'You mean in our company's spare time?' suggested Hugo.

Peter looked affronted. 'I wouldn't be bringing you into my confidence if I didn't think I could trust you Hugo. I think our philosophies on life are similarly aligned. I happen to think that as Smithson have washed their hands of the project that maybe you and I have an opportunity, that's all.'

'So what exactly are you proposing?'

'I think you and I should leave Smithson, take my research with us, and set up our own company. With my new technique I think I could could ensure this drug is ready for trials in a very short time, and at relatively modest cost. The potential here is massive. An anti inflammatory drug that heals joints and doesn't cause gastro intestinal side effects is the holy grail of arthritis treatment.'

Hugo certainly liked the idea of massive potential, although the modest cost would need some consideration, but that was what he was good at. 'We would need to be very careful PW. Less open minded individuals than myself might think you were stealing Smithson's research material. But I like the sound of what you are saying and I think you have made the right move in approaching me. You would certainly need somebody with my particular skill set to turn your research into a commercial reality.'

'My thoughts exactly. That's why we're sitting here. Me with my pint of lager and you with your vodka and tonic.'

The medical career of Dr Hugh Thomson had been, predictably, both delayed and short. Following the debacle back at Guy's, Hugh had failed his finals and been forced by a combination of Dean and father to repeat his final year for retakes. The medical school at least now had a new electron microscope. Less predictably he had somehow managed to negotiate a way past the examiners second time around and found himself working as a junior house doctor for his pre registration year. The Dean had arranged for him to be sent away to jobs in a provincial hospital far from his alma mater.

He had actually quite enjoyed being a bigger fish in a smaller pond and his new found status as a doctor had earned him more success in the nurses home than it had back at Guy's.

He had even found himself a wife. A pretty, nice, sensible girl who had been flattered by Dr Hugh's attentions. A redhead funnily enough. In fact she was so sensible that when she found out about her new husband's continued visits to the nurses home she made the decision to become his ex wife. No children, no harm done. And Hugh had realised he didn't really want to share his life with anyone, he rather enjoyed concentrating on his own needs.

Post entry to the medical register and a career had to be chosen. Hugh, by this time, had been cast adrift financially by his father but the strong paternal influence remained. It was decided that as Hugh did not seem well suited to dealing with patients while they were awake that maybe he should try anaesthetics. A more academic discipline his father had argued.

It sounded like a good idea at the time. Hugh, if motivated, had the potential to be a capable doctor and if he didn't have to deal with conscious patients so much the better. But it all went horribly wrong.

Hugh's idea of a general anaesthetic was to generally get things right most of the time and indeed there is some room for manoeuvre in the delivery of the exact cocktail of drugs required. Sadly he managed to overdo the muscle relaxant and underdo the sleeping agent halothane during a hysterectomy. The poor patient had not been fully anaesthetised but because her muscles were paralysed she wasn't in a position to inform anybody about her predicament. Post surgery the unfortunate lady had been able to not only describe colourfully the pain she had experienced but also recount most of the details of what had been done and said during her surgical procedure. It kept the hospital legal team busy anyway.

Hugh's medical career was only just still on track, but it was a single track leading to a terminus in that provincial town.

Hugh, however, was not completely without potential. It was really his father's fault that his latent talent had been channeled in the wrong direction. A career in the city, eating and drinking his way to prosperity would have suited him better.

He spotted his chance while reading the classified section of the British Medical Journal during a break one morning. It was in the section titled 'Miscellaneous' and had been placed by Smithson Pharmaceuticals. They were looking for young doctors with entrepreneurial skills for exciting opportunities. Hugh wasted no time in filling out and submitting the application form. He took great delight in taking the first available train out of town when he heard his application had been successful.

The rest had become history. Hugh had applied himself enthusiastically to his new found career and his employers seemed to agree with him that he was rather good at it his job.

The exciting opportunity was a liaison post acting along the difficult line that both joins and separates the pharmaceutical and medical establishments. A difficult line that is deliberately blurred by the lavish hospitality provided by the former to the latter. Hugh had a foot in both camps and was easily able to entertain and educate while at the same time managing to persuade and sell.

He had been seduced by a good salary plan, a nice new BMW 5 Series and a generous unaudited expense account. Almost as good as his father had provided for him at medical school. And he was still, officially, a fully registered doctor so Thomson senior was satisfied.

Hugh's position in the company advanced, he had risen to the position of Senior Medical Adviser and his liaison skills had developed and expanded into networking skills. He found himself rubbing shoulders with increasingly powerful and influential people. Not just consultants and specialists but financiers and politicians.

In an attempt to make his shoulders more expensive to rub, Hugh had decided on an upgrade and it was at that stage that Hugh rebranded himself as Hugo.

CHAPTER 5

Five years ago, Sam

Mrs Preston said to her husband, 'Have a good morning at the surgery darling. Don't forget you've found room in your busy diary for us to have lunch at Browns. I've booked the table for twelve thirty.'

Gilly Jarvis, the redhead, had become Gilly Preston not too long after that fateful evening at Guy's. Something to do with them being the proud parents of Ella, now aged fourteen.

Sam had followed his dream of becoming a GP and after completing house jobs and a GP training scheme in his chosen city of Brighton he had been invited to join his training practice as a partner. It was early days but he was settling in well and already challenging what he saw as the old fashioned ways of his more senior colleagues. With mixtures of encouragement and tolerance things were moving along nicely in the career of Dr Sam Preston MRCGP.

Sadly the same could not be said for the career of Gilly. When they had moved to Brighton she had been snapped up to work as a Staff Nurse at The Royal Brighton and Hove Hospital. She had always been fascinated by diabetes and she was making a career for herself as a liaison nurse working between the hospital diabetes clinic and General Practice. Life had been looking good for the Preston family, but sadly for them it was about to change.

The first signs of what was to come displayed themselves as painful, swollen joints in the fingers of both of Gilly's hands. She thought little of it, she had been using her hands a lot updating the decor in their newly purchased house in Kemp Town. But swollen hands had been joined by swollen wrists and then elbows followed by knees. She had started to lose weight and she was so stiff could barely move in the mornings.

It was clear something was badly wrong. Gilly had been forced by the pain to go off sick from work. Sam made some phone calls, pulled a few strings and had arranged for the local rheumatology specialist to see her urgently.

Sam accompanied Gilly to the appointment and they were sitting on uncomfortable plastic chairs in out patients waiting for Gilly's turn to be seen. They were both feeling tense at the thought of the likely outcome of the consultation. Gilly broke the silence.

'I'm not stupid Sam, I think we both already know what the specialist is going to say. I've got rheumatoid arthritis haven't I.'

This had been a diagnosis unspoken between them for a couple of weeks, both knowing, neither admitting, hoping they were wrong and that the disease would just go away.

Despite doctors and nurses being notoriously bad at self and family diagnosis, on this occasion they were not wrong. Blood tests were organised, X rays and scans carried out and the following week they returned to the specialist who confirmed their worst fears.

'Well you were quite right with your diagnosis Sam,' said Dr Sykes. 'I'm afraid the diagnosis is indeed rheumatoid arthritis. The blood tests such as ESR and CRP confirm there is a lot of active inflammation going on and the X rays show evidence of early damage to both bone and cartilage in many of the joints.

Gilly muttered, 'It was my diagnosis too and it's my illness.' She was feeling irritated that the specialist had addressed her husband instead of her.

'Yes of course, sorry Mrs Preston, I was forgetting about your nursing background,' said Dr Sykes.

And Gilly realised at that moment that her nursing career would only ever be just that, a background.

'The important thing now is to manage the condition aggressively, suppress the inflammation and treat the disease process itself before too much joint damage is done. So I'm going to recommend you start treatment immediately with a combination of Methotrexate, a biological agent called Etanercept and of course an anti inflammatory drug such as Napralgia. You will need to be monitored closely for side effects such as bone marrow suppression with regular blood tests.'

'Well that certainly sounds like block buster treatment,' said Sam and added to his wife a little fearfully, 'I just hope the drugs don't upset you too much darling, that's quite a potent combination.'

'What has to be has to be,' said Gilly stoically, 'I'm going to be positive about this, it's just another challenge that I'm going to overcome. The drugs are going to work and I'm not going to allow them to upset me.'

Sam felt so proud of his wife, he wasn't sure he would have been able to put on such a brave face if he were in Gilly's place. He felt tears welling up in his eyes and quickly tried to blink them away. He was a doctor, never show weakness!

After a few weeks of swallowing the prescribed pills and attending out patients for intravenous infusions of Etanercept, Gilly's joints were starting to settle. The pain and stiffness were less and the swelling was subsiding. At Gilly's command the brutal drug regimen had not caused any obvious upset or at least nothing so bad that Gilly had felt obliged to inform Sam. She was now feeling well enough to consider going out and today's lunch date back at a favourite old haunt was being used by Gilly as a sign that some degree of normality was returning to her life. Perhaps she could even start to reconsider those pessimistic thoughts about her nursing career.

The lunch date was so important to Gilly that she had called Sam's Practice Manager at the surgery and asked that his time keeping that morning be kept an eye on and perhaps he could have a day off from home visits?

She had revisited the contents of her wardrobe and chosen something smart and pretty but not too formal. Gilly had put back on some of her lost weight and the fit wasn't too bad. She had spent some time with her makeup, studied herself in the mirror and vowed that her next trip out would be to the hairdresser.

Gilly wasn't yet well enough to consider driving, she didn't feel her knees were reliable should she need to hit the brake pedal hard, so she had organised a taxi to take her down to Browns, in The Lanes area of Brighton.

She had been feeling hungry all morning but in the last few minutes her hunger pangs had started to turn into something less pleasant. They were real pains now, she felt them in the top of her stomach clawing their way up into her chest. Her appetite had disappeared. She took a couple of antacid tablets from the range of free samples collected by her husband.

The pains worsened, the tablets were not helping and Gilly was worried. She was feeling cold and had broken out in a sweat. Old habits die hard and she took her pulse. One hundred and twenty, that's not right, much too high. Probably just getting anxious. She started to feel faint and giddy and she was finding it hard to stay standing.

What should she do? She had forgotten about lunch, that was the least of her worries. She decided to call Sam at work on his mobile. Her call flashed up on his iPhone screen.

'Hi Gilly darling, I'm nearly finished then I'll be on my way,' he answered but could hear his wife breathing too heavily and quickly on the other end of the line.

'Gilly somethings wrong. What's up?' he was immediately worried.

'Sam can you come home now, something's not right, not right at all. I've got this horrible pain in my stomach and I think I'm about to throw up.'

Gilly never made a fuss about anything and Sam could sense the panic in her voice. Home was only five minutes away.

'Hang on there Gilly, I'm on my way right now. Leave the front door open for me if you can.' He ran through reception, out of the building, got straight in his car and tore home.

The front door was closed, why hadn't Gilly opened it? He fumbled with his keys in his anxiety, he threw the door open and rushed in.

He called for his wife but there was no reply. He rushed from room to room with increasing anxiety until he got to their bedroom where he found Gilly collapsed on the floor, writhing in pain. She had vomited bright red blood over the carpet.

'Oh my God, oh my God. Gilly stay with me.'

Gilly was only just rousable. Sam had been trained to deal with emergencies, but this was different, the patient was his wife. She needed hospital and fast.

Instinct kicked in and he dialled 999. The line was answered quickly and Sam said, 'This is Dr Sam Preston, I have a code red emergency, I need an ambulance now, right now, to 67 Arundel Road, please hurry the patient is my wife.'

Sam grabbed a towel from the bathroom and rushed back to Gilly. He had the bizarre thought that Gilly would want to look her best when the ambulance arrived and he wiped the blood from her face and hair. 'Stay with me, stay with me Gilly darling.'

By now Gilly wasn't responding, she was barely conscious, just emitting a groaning sound.

Sam knew exactly what was happening and he knew exactly why it was happening.

The paramedics arrived and took control of the situation. They quickly inserted a cannula into a vein in Gilly's arm and started to run fluid into her. 'Her BP's down in her boots, as much fluid and as quickly as you can. Squeeze the bag if you have to.'

They had wired Gilly up to a heart monitor and Sam watched, stunned, as he saw her heart rate rise to 180, three times the normal rate. He knew that if her blood pressure didn't pick up and her heart rate didn't slow she would go into ventricular fibrillation, the condition immediately before death when the heart muscles just quiver instead of contracting and pumping.

Sam certainly knew what was happening. His wife had a perforated stomach ulcer and she was bleeding heavily internally. The haemorrhaging was causing her blood pressure to fall and her heart rate to rise to critically dangerous levels.

And that stomach ulcer had been caused, as a side effect, by the very drug being given to ease her pain and suffering, the anti inflammatory drug Napralgia.

'We need to get her to hospital, there's no future in keeping her here,' shouted Sam, emotion causing his voice to crack.

The paramedics loaded Gilly onto a stretcher and carried her down the stairs with Sam lifting the IV bag as high as he could.

They wheeled her out of the front door and lifted the stretcher through the double doors at the back of the ambulance. Sam jumped in before the doors were shut. The paramedic looked at him enquiringly.

'I think you might be needing another pair of hands before we get to the hospital,' said Sam.

Gilly was just about holding her own. At least she hadn't vomited any more blood. She had already been given two bags of fluid and this appeared to be just enough to keep her blood pressure and pulse stable, albeit at critical levels. Sam knelt by her side, stroking her face, making sure his wife knew how much he loved her.

The vehicle's blue light was flashing and the siren was doing it's best to clear the road ahead. It was only a short distance to the hospital. Every second was crucial. They needed to keep Gilly alive long enough to get fresh blood back into her circulation. It would be the blood loss that would kill her. And she would need emergency surgery to stop the bleeding from the stomach ulcer that Sam knew she had. All these thoughts were going through his mind as the ambulance sped through the lunchtime traffic.

The hospital was just ahead on the left and the ambulance screeched round a corner and up the hill to the Accident and Emergency department. The paramedic had been in constant communication with base and a reception team of doctors and nurses was waiting for Gilly outside the main doors of casualty.

The ambulance stopped and the doors were thrown open. Gilly was taken out on the trolley and wheeled quickly into the department. Sam watched from the back of the ambulance. There was nothing more he could do now except hope and pray. He knew his wife was in good hands but he realised it was going to be touch and go.

He thought of their daughter Ella, at school, totally unaware of what was happening to her mum. If the worst happened how on earth could he tell Ella. 'No stop that, stay positive,' he said to himself.

The paramedics had played their part. They had kept Gilly alive. Sam thanked them profusely before walking in to the hospital. All seemed quiet in reception, Gilly had obviously been taken further back into A&E. He didn't know what to do, he felt completely hopeless. He didn't even want to ask anybody what was happening. Surely no news was going to be good news. He took a seat in the waiting area and putting his head in his hands leaned forward trying to compose himself. He decided to put a call through to his practice to tell them about the crisis. His senior partner came on the line and told him to not worry about the rest of the day. They would cover his surgery for him. He had seemed more concerned about the surgery than he had about Sam and his wife. The conversation left Sam feeling angry. He stood up and paced around, his adrenalin levels would not allow him to be still.

A door to the side of the reception window opened and a doctor in green surgical scrubs came through. There were splatters of blood down her front. Gilly's blood. She looked around and identified Sam as being the likely husband of her patient. She walked over towards him with a serious look on her face and introduced herself as Dr Libby Armstrong, an A&E registrar.

Sam didn't know her and felt he needed to say that he was a GP. He needed the doctor to explain in medical language what was happening.

'How is my wife? Is she OK? Has the bleeding stopped. What's happening?' So many questions to ask.

But the registrar had only one answer to give.

'I'm so sorry Dr Preston. Your wife hasn't made it. We did all we could, but the bleeding wouldn't stop and we couldn't get fresh blood into her fast enough. I'm afraid she passed away a few minutes ago.'

CHAPTER 6

Gilly had lost her life and Sam and Ella had lost a wife and mother and the lives they once had. Normal would never be normal again.

The early days passed by in a sterile blur, so many arrangements that needed to be made. Sam wasn't eating properly and sleep was only possible through sheer emotional exhaustion. He had been offered Diazepam to keep him calm. He took a few but they were just making him numb and preventing the grief within from pouring out. He knew he had to let the tears flow.

The days passed into weeks and Sam tried hard to hold his life and family together. His priority was to care for his daughter but it became apparent to friends that it was really Ella who was propping up her dad, stopping him from drowning. But her efforts were in vain, she was fighting a losing battle, Sam was descending on a downward spiral towards his breaking point.

He had returned to work after just three weeks, before the numbness had worn off and the shock had set in. Stupidly he had even felt guilty about taking time off sick from his practice. And his GP partners did little to discourage his guilt. He had thought that maybe if he just threw himself at his job he would be distracted. Give one part of his life some sense of normality.

'Concentrate on the parts of your life you can control,' he had been told by his work colleagues.

But he realised that work was making him feel worse. Gilly had been killed by a drug prescribed by a doctor and he was potentially doing the very same thing to patients dozens of times every day. He had always been aware of the risks of side effects of the drugs he prescribed, but he had been able to take a detached view and reason that the benefits outweighed the risks. But his altered view was not detached any more, it had all become very personal. He lost confidence and found himself unable to make decisions about his patients. Often he couldn't stop himself breaking down in tears in front of them. He began to realise he wasn't coping.

Word of the tragedy quickly spread among the patients and as would be expected, they were initially very sympathetic towards Sam but with time it became apparent that their doctor wasn't there for them in the way they needed. Their needs hadn't changed just because of Sam's bereavement.

His surgeries were no longer filling up, while those of his partners were overflowing. Patients were starting to mutter and gossip.

At first it was 'Poor Dr Preston is having a breakdown, I hope he gets some help,' but gradually it became, 'I'd rather see another doctor than Dr Preston at the moment.'

Breaking point arrived when a patient complained to the Practice Manager that he was sure he could smell alcohol on the doctors breath and that his voice sounded slurred.

The relationship between Sam and alcohol had always been a tricky one. At medical school and after qualification, at difficult times, Sam had found himself needing to drink in order to relax, and sometimes just to enable him to cope. But never when on duty.

Until now.

The Practice Manager was obliged to take immediate action. She needed to talk with the senior partner, this was not for her to sort out alone.

Sam was ordered into a crisis meeting with two of the other partners. The Practice Manager was in attendance, taking notes for the record. This was official. But was the meeting to try and help Sam or was it the other partners trying to cover their backsides?

'Sam, as you know, you have our sympathies, we all care about you very much. We are as shocked as you are at what happened to Gilly,' said the senior partner, inaccurately. 'We would like to support you as much as we can at such a difficult time.'

Why did Sam feel there was a "but" coming.

'However it's clear to us you are not coping and the practice is starting to suffer as a result. You aren't keeping to time. Patients are complaining that you are being sharp with them. Apparently you are not listening to their needs. All very understandable of course. Given the circumstances.'

He continued. 'But it has been reported to the Practice Manager, by a patient, that yesterday you smelled strongly of alcohol and that your speech was slurred. He said he thought you were drunk. You need to be honest with me Sam. Had you been drinking?'

Sam didn't try to deny it, what was the point? He had been drinking heavily for several weeks, he had to have some way of escaping from his dreadful new reality. But what a shame it had needed to come this far before his partners were apparently concerned enough to step in and offer help, if indeed that's what it was.

Sam was suspended from the practice by his partners, with immediate effect, and told that unless he got the help he needed without delay they would have to report him to the General Medical Council. It was their duty, they had no choice.

'Sorry Sam, but the patients must always come first.'

But hadn't the doctor become a patient too?

Ella was sent to stay with her grandparents and Sam checked himself into a private clinic in Wiltshire for detox and counselling. He travelled down by train alone submerged in his feelings of grief and shame.

Sam was stopped from drinking immediately on admission to the clinic. His addiction to alcohol was replaced by addiction to other drugs before eventually being weaned off those too. His physical state of health had declined along with his mental state, but he was slowly improving, the shakes and cold sweats had gone. He had regained some of the two stone in weight he had lost through not eating. And he at least felt safe in his sanctuary, hidden away from his new world.

He was prescribed bereavement counselling, initially on his own and then as part of a group. Therapy had helped, but he had been unable to rid himself of the anger within. Anger at his wife for falling ill, anger at the drug companies for making such dangerous drugs but mostly anger at himself for just not having known what was going to happen. Surely some warning signs must have been there and he hadn't noticed.

He was eventually declared well enough to be discharged home and outreach support was arranged. Not one of his work partners had made the effort to visit him while he was ill and as far as he knew nobody had even enquired about him. All too busy with their precious work. Nobody except Ella of course. 'Just the two of us now honey.'

He knew he would need to return to work some time soon, although he was no longer sure in his mind where that would be. But when he did go back he was determined to make sure that no patient had to suffer side effects from drugs, especially arthritis drugs, in the way that Gilly had.

CHAPTER 7

The present day

Sam looked out of the consulting room window at his new practice building and gazed across the road at the row of Regency era houses. After a bleak winter, spring was arriving and the cherry trees were just coming into blossom. But Sam was gazing beyond the trees and houses into a distance that only existed in his mind.

How things had changed. He recalled having returned to work, in his former practice, hoping to make the fresh start that he had feared might be impossible. And impossible it had turned out to be, it was never going to happen in that practice, with those partners. Sam was a changed man and, he accepted, probably difficult to work with. He had developed a fixation with medical problems caused by doctors and the drugs they prescribed and his partners had felt resentment when he challenged them about their prescribing habits. The truth was that Sam had never been able to forgive them for their lack of sympathy and support after Gilly's death. The best they had been able to do was tell him they would report him to the General Medical Council 'for his own good'.

So it was with relief all round when Sam had announced his intention to resign from the partnership and set up a new practice a few streets away. They had not objected when he asked for permission for his patients to be allowed to leave with him. Those who had stayed loyal to him anyway.

And Andrew from the reception team, having had some life events of her own, elected to join Sam in his new practice. She became his Practice Manager and to reflect her new circumstances changed her name to Anita.

Sam snapped himself out of his trance, returned to his desk and started work on the pile of admin waiting for him. Generally he hated paperwork but one thing he didn't mind was work connected with the government funded group he had joined, The Post Marketing Surveillance Group. It was the group's mission to monitor for side effects, specific new drugs that had recently been released to the market.

At least he felt he was now able to take some positive action about the side effects caused by drugs prescribed by doctors. He was realistic to know that there was always a pound of flesh to give when it came to drugs, none of them were free from potential adverse effects. But his thoughts and emotions were now getting back under control and the monitoring was helping with that.

The group provided a mechanism for the government's health regulatory body, the MHRA, and through them the pharmaceutical companies, to be informed immediately of any concerns about a new drug.

One such drug that Sam had very strong reasons to show a particular interest in was called Condrone or, to give it it's generic name, Piricoxib. It was a novel anti inflammatory drug for arthritis with, apparently, a complete lack of gastric side effects. It had been released onto the market by Valerian Pharmaceuticals with a massive fanfare and it promised great things. The "Joint Booster Drug". An anti inflammatory drug that didn't cause gastrointestinal bleeding and that repaired worn out, damaged joint cartilage. If the drug was as good as the pharmaceutical company claimed then it was a major breakthrough. And the owners of the drug company would become obscenely wealthy.

Fantastic, Sam had thought. If only this drug had been there for Gilly. But maybe too good to be true?

In fact Sam had seen one of his many patients who were now established on long term Condrone therapy during the surgery session he had just finished.

The patient, Mary, was in her mid fifties and like so many people who had led active sporting lives she had developed osteoarthritis in her knees and hips. He had asked her how she was doing.

'I'm fine thanks doctor,' Mary had replied. 'Not sure my brain's getting any younger but the Condrone seems to be making my joints better with every passing day.' She was actually being semi serious in her light hearted response.

Sometimes, Sam knew, patients were too frightened or embarrassed to admit to other problems when things seemed to be going so well, and her knees were definitely less painful. She could even walk her dog for a couple of miles along the seafront now.

But her husband had been remarking to her for a few months that she sometimes seemed a little forgetful. Nothing serious, silly things like forgetting exactly where she had parked her car when she went shopping, or forgetting where her keys were.

We all do that sometimes don't we?

She had dropped a little hint to Sam and he was very astute at picking up these little asides during consultations.

'What do you mean by "your brain's not getting any younger"?' he asked and glancing at her notes on the screen said. 'You are only fifty four years young. Anything in particular you've noticed?'

Sam was given the stories of car and keys and after a little more prying he did start to wonder if maybe there was more than his patient was admitting to but he didn't want to alarm her by enquiring too much.

'We'll keep an eye on things, perhaps you could make a note of anything that doesn't seem quite right. I'm sure it's just one of those things that happens occasionally but we'll keep an open mind. I can't think it's likely to be anything to do with your medication.'

She was happy with that, her husband shouldn't be pointing things like that out to her anyway, he was hardly perfect himself. Why couldn't he tell her about all the things she got right instead of the things she got wrong!

Sam was feeling less convinced than he had sounded and made a note in her records to ask her delicately about the issue when he saw her next. Perhaps he could carry out a little memory test without her realising what he was doing?

At times Sam had wondered if he actually wanted to find something wrong with Condrone, the drug really did seem too good to be true. Was it because it hadn't been available for Gilly? She would probably still have been alive had she been taking Condrone instead of Napralgia and that made him feel cheated in some way. Or more worryingly was it because this drug, made by Valerian Pharmaceuticals, was making it's owner, his old adversary Hugo Thomson, a very wealthy man.

Goodness that almost sounds like jealousy, he thought guiltily.

But he really did have a thing about drug side effects, that was OK, he should be concerned. What was it he had said in his Hippocratic oath after he had qualified? 'First do no harm.' A good principle to go by.

So Sam decided that he would call in a few of his patients who were taking Condrone long term for routine checks and as part of that he would carry out a quick 'mini mental' examination. They would probably be fine, it would at least put his mind to rest and he could use that to reassure Mary next time he saw her.

But no rush, he would do it when he had time. He had a busy few days in front of him.

Sam was feeling hungry after a morning of too much stress and coffee. He just had time to pop round the corner to a Little Waitrose to pick up something for lunch. They did rather nice crayfish and rocket baguettes. Ella, as always, would ask him later what he had eaten for his lunch. He thought that would be acceptable. Best not mention the Mars bar that would probably follow.

It had now started to drizzle with rain, a typical English spring day, and Sam, having no coat with him, hurried on his way to the shop. He generally tried to avoid eye contact with fellow pedestrians. So close to his surgery they could possibly be patients and he didn't want to get involved in a street corner consultation.

As he entered the shop he had to walk past the tills and he noticed an upset customer in conversation with the check out girl. He overheard something about PIN number.

'You've put your number in three times so the card will be blocked now,' said the girl with the badge. 'Have you got another card or maybe cash?'

It would appear not. Sam didn't want to seem nosey but he took a second glance anyway and immediately saw it was Mary, the woman with the ungrateful husband whom he had seen half an hour ago in surgery.

'Hello Mary, is the credit card playing up?'

Mary looked at him, her face empty of recognition.

'Oh you're my doctor aren't you,' she said eventually. 'I didn't recognise you without your stethoscope.'

'Yes, Dr Preston,' he replied and just managed to stop himself saying 'You were in my consulting room half an hour ago.'

'Has Mrs Murray had a problem with her card?' Sam enquired of Kayleigh, reading her badge.

'I'm her GP,' he added.

'I think she's forgotten her PIN number.'

'Let me sort it out if I can. How much is her bill?'

'£15.49' replied Kayleigh.

Sam reached into his pocket, took a credit card from his wallet, and settled the transaction.

'Problem sorted,' Sam said to Mary. 'Perhaps you could drop the cash in sometime when you're passing the surgery.'

He handed Mary the receipt, suspecting he wouldn't get his money back. He didn't care about that but he suddenly cared a lot more about Mary's mental state.

He had better call those other Condrone patients in sooner rather than later.

CHAPTER 8

Sam kept the promise he had made to himself and within a couple of weeks he had managed to call in six of his many Condrone patients for review.

Surprisingly he had also got his money back, Mary's husband had dropped by the surgery and paid up a few days ago.

Well that must be a good sign, he had thought.

He had been very careful not to reveal the exact reason to his patients why he had called them in.

'Just routine,' he had said. 'Part of the monitoring process when new kinds of medication are being prescribed.'

He told them a brief physical exam would be needed. Nothing terrible, blood pressure, pulse, reflexes that kind of thing.

'And one or two questions which I hope you won't mind, just intended to check the grey matter is still working OK.'

They were simple questions to test short term memory and orientation. A bit insulting potentially, but only if you knew the right answers.

'I want you to remember the names of these three flowers for me. Tulip, rose, daffodil,' he said slowly. 'I'm going to ask you to name them again in a couple of minutes.'

'What month of the year are we in at the moment?'

'What's the name of our current Prime Minister?'

That one sometimes got an interesting answer!

'Please start at one hundred and keep subtracting seven from it.'

'Now what were those flowers called?'

Five out of the six patients sailed through but one of them had struggled with a couple of the questions. He could only remember two of the flowers and his arithmetic wasn't too good, he got as far as ninety three before getting stuck. But he was seventy six, so maybe not that surprising.

Generally Sam felt reassured, but if the seventy six year old had a memory problem, and with Mary being a concern as well, then that made two patients out of seven with a potential issue.

Sam went online to the website of the drug surveillance group. Like many hastily arranged government websites it was not straightforward to navigate and Sam had to admit that computers were not his strong suit.

He entered his medical registration number and name followed by his password.

'drugskill'

He had liked the double meaning but admitted he felt a little embarrassed every time he entered it. A bit juvenile. He wondered if anyone responsible for administering the website noticed that kind of thing. He was then forced to read through a couple of alert messages before he was able to enter and submit details of the possible problems with his two patients.

The system worked by entered information finding its way via the medicines regulatory authority to the relevant drug company, in this case Valerian, and you would then expect a call back from somebody in the company for a more detailed discussion. Usually one of the medical officers or maybe a scientist. Generally it seemed to work well enough and Sam had enjoyed some of the intellectual conversations that followed. It was definitely in a pharmaceutical company's best interests to detect and correct any problems before patients were harmed. Or worse still share prices affected.

Unusually in this case nothing happened, no email acknowledgment, no call back, therefore no discussion.

Maybe I messed things up when I made the submission through that useless website, thought Sam.

He wanted his intellectual discussion about Condrone and certainly didn't want his concerns to be ignored. He decided that he would give Valerian Pharmaceuticals a call. He looked up the number on the Valerian website and couldn't help noticing the images of the very impressive building that Hugo Thomson had commissioned for his company, located with many of the other major players in the industry on The Cambridge Science Park.

'Valerian Pharmaceuticals, manufacturers of the ground breaking drug Condrone, Monica speaking, how may I help you?'

Blimey, thought Sam. Talk about self publicity.

'Yes, hello, it's Dr Sam Preston speaking, I'm a GP in Brighton, I hope you can help me. I submitted some data about your drug through The Post Marketing Surveillance Group a couple of weeks ago and been expecting a call back but I have heard nothing, so I wonder if you could put me through to somebody so we might discuss my data.'

'Well I'm sorry you have heard nothing doctor, I know the research department has been very busy recently. I will just see who I can find to speak with you. Dr Preston did you say?'

'Yes that's right, Dr Sam Preston, I was at medical school with your chairman Dr Thomson.' Nothing like a bit of name dropping to get himself treated properly he thought.

'I'm just going to put you on hold sir, won't keep you waiting too long, I'm sure you must be very busy.'

That sounded better thought Sam but he was kept on hold none the less.

'Sorry to have kept you waiting Dr Preston, this is Dr Peter White speaking, I'm the chief scientific officer here at Valerian. I understand that you tried to submit some data through the PMSG. Can't seem to find anything on our system here, so thank you for taking the trouble to call us.'

'No problem,' said Sam. He hadn't been expecting to be talking with the Chief Scientific Officer, perhaps he shouldn't have used the Chairman's name after all.

'I have had some concerns with a couple of my patients who have been taking Condrone for a few months and I wanted to make sure, firstly, that you are aware of that and secondly whether any other doctors have reported anything similar.'

'Well thank you for your concern doctor and I am happy and interested to listen to what you have to say but naturally I wouldn't be able to share any confidential or sensitive information with you. I'm sure you will understand.'

'Yes of course, that's fine, I'm not looking for company secrets but I thought you ought to know that two out of seven patients I have checked up on appear to be showing early signs of memory problems. I think I would probably refer to it as cognitive impairment,' Sam said.

He continued, 'I have used Condrone in quite a large number of my patients, it appears to be an excellent drug and is doing very well for their joints. But I would hate to think that I might be prescribing a substance that could be causing them harm in some other way.'

There was no immediate reply and Sam wondered if the connection had been lost, but Dr White's voice returned, 'Thank you for your kind comments about Condrone doctor and I'm so pleased your patients are benefitting from our endeavours here at Valerian. It makes all the hard work seem so worthwhile.'

'I'm sure I wouldn't be divulging too many secrets if I told you that we have had no reports from other doctors of that kind at all. Interesting, but of course there is no theoretical reason why our drug would have any effect on brain function.'

'How old were these two patients doctor?'

Sam replied 'Fifty four' with confidence and 'Seventy six' with less confidence.

'I see, so not exactly young then,' said Dr White rather defensively. 'Sounds like you have a tiny cluster there in, of course, an extremely small sample size.'

'Our data bank contains hundreds of thousands of patients now Dr Preston and we have seen no trend over and above what one would expect to see in patients who are usually getting a little older,' he added.

Sam did feel reassured and also relieved. Dr White seemed interested in what he had been told but not overly concerned.

'OK, well thanks for taking the time to listen and for your reassurance. I felt you would wish to know at the earliest opportunity if there was any hint of a problem.'

'Indeed we would, of course we would, it's our job to do good not harm and I'm grateful you felt enough concern to call. Your patients are clearly lucky to have such a caring doctor.'

'Thank you for calling today Dr Preston, I will send you a couple of adverse event forms by email and perhaps you would be kind enough to fill those in and we will add the details to our database. Good morning to you.' And with that he was gone.

The receptionist, Monica, came back on the line and said 'I hope that was helpful doctor, if I could just take your email address and I will send those forms out to you tonight.

CHAPTER 9

The schoolboy Hugh Thomson did not have many
friends. He wore the look of privilege too easily, and gave
out an aura of being untouchable. It put other boys off. His
father was a wealthy man, a fortune obtained by having
been born into the right family. And he carried
considerable influence in the corridors of Hampstead Boys
School. Hugh Thomson could get away with most things
and the other pupils were well aware of that. Hugh was
somebody best ignored or avoided.

Except by Giles Barrington. Giles was from a completely
different family background. His parents were certainly not
poor, his father was a high street bank manager, but they
were not in the full school fee paying league. Giles was a
bright boy and had impressed his teachers at the local
primary school in Islington. They had suggested to Mr and
Mrs Barrington that their gifted son should sit the
scholarship examination for Hampstead. Success in the
exam would mean a huge reduction in the normal school
fees.

'And an education at somewhere like Hampstead would
give your son the best possible start.'

Giles had received extra coaching from his teachers and
his parents had managed to find money for additional
private tuition. It came as no surprise to parents or
teachers when Giles easily topped the rankings in the
scholarship examination. He was offered a full academic
scholarship to Hampstead which would continue until he
left school at the age of eighteen.

They were not natural potential friends when Giles joined
the school aged eleven. But Hugh had been a pupil since
he was five and his parents were keen for their son to form
some sort of friendship with this bright new boy. Mr and

Mrs Thomson perhaps hoping that some of the brilliance of the scholar would rub off on their underperforming, lazy son.

And Giles of course came from a different world to that inhabited by most of his new peers. Many of whom didn't take too kindly to the arrival of a new boy whose sunshine put their modest achievements in the shade. He quickly had become known as "Boffin", except to Hugh who knew what is was like to be called "Porky".

So a friendship of mutual benefit developed between Hugh and Giles. The former was able to benefit from the assistance of the latter with his homework and the latter benefitted from the purchasing power of the former's family.

But they were like chalk and cheese. Giles slender, gifted and athletic. Hugh chubby, lazy but cunning.

They progressed through school, Giles winning the academic prizes and Hugh's family generally paying for them.

Towards the end of their penultimate academic year it was clear to everybody at the school that it would be inevitable for Giles to be chosen as Head Boy. He had no realistic competition.

But of course he did have competition in the shape of Hugh, even if it didn't seem realistic at the time. His parents would see to that. All those donations to the school were not to be wasted. If Hugh was to have a useful career, preferably as a doctor, he would need all possible assistance. And Head Boy on the medical school application would do no harm at all.

The choice of Head Boy was to be made by the Headmaster and the Chairman of the Governing Body. Mr and Mrs Thomson had felt that a relaxing evening enjoying the opera at Glyndebourne accompanied by the decision makers and their wives would be helpful.

The decision was made during the long interval of "The Magic Flute", just after the fourth bottle of Moët et Chandon had been opened by the Thomson's private butler.

It was of small consolation to Giles that he was made Deputy Head Boy. The friendship was damaged but not beyond repair. Giles suspected that he had been used by Hugh but was clever enough to know that his turn would come, he just needed to be patient.

CHAPTER 10

The Right Honourable Giles Barrington MP, Minister for Health, and Hugo Thomson the Chairman of Valerian Pharmaceuticals were now enjoying an early evening drink in a quiet corner of their private members club in St James, London. This was their usual place for discreet discussions about old times or any potential mutual business interests. This particular club had been a popular haunt of politicians and business leaders for centuries and Hugo had only recently managed to gain membership. It was one of those clubs where money didn't automatically unlock the front door; it was who you knew but importantly what you could do for them that counted. Giles had been pleased to be of some assistance to his old school friend Hugo and club membership had been one of his favours. Whenever Hugo looked at his gold membership card he knew that he had finally arrived where he belonged. He hoped that maybe at last his father would be proud of him.

They were seated in ancient but comfortable leather upholstered club chairs that had supported the backsides of the great and good over many years. The club was already moderately busy and some serious conversation and drinking was taking place at the surrounding tables. The country is run from places such as this.

Hugo had his customary vodka and tonic, a double, but Giles was being more restrained with his choice of mineral water. He was due back in the house for an important vote later and possibly he would be interviewed for the late evening news programmes. The viewers might not be able to smell the alcohol on ones breath but the BBC political editor Laura Carter certainly would.

'How's progress on the new building at our old school coming along?' enquired Hugo.

'Very nearly completed,' replied Giles. 'Really just the internal fitting to be done. It's amazingly generous of your company to have provided the funding for the creation of a state of the art science block.'

'Least I could do for our alma mater after the amazing success of Condrone. Makes sense for us as an expanding company to nurture the scientific development of the next generation.' Hugo reasoned. 'Any thoughts from your governor colleagues regarding a name for the building?'

Giles had recently been appointed as Chairman of the Governing Body at The Hampstead Boys School.

'How does the Valerian Science Centre sound?'

'I think the Sir Hugo Thomson Science Centre would sound better,' said Hugo hopefully.

'That might sound a little odd with you having failed your A level chemistry first time round. As for the 'Sir' bit, keep playing your cards right and you never know.'

Intended in humour of course but comments about failed exams were best avoided these days and Giles quickly changed the subject.

'I really would like to thank you for all the help you have given to me personally and to our party Hugo, it really is most appreciated.'

'I've always followed your career closely Giles and when I started up Valerian I just felt that the ambitions of your party were closely aligned to our own values. It's in our best mutual interests and I've been pleased to help with donations when I could,' said Hugo.

'The pharmaceutical industry is very important to us and to me personally Hugo,' replied Giles. 'We don't want you taking your company off to Switzerland, not with all those taxes you pay. I hope our long friendship will continue to be of benefit to us both.'

Giles' career progression had been rapid. After graduating with a first in politics from Magdalen College Oxford he had been talent spotted by the party and encouraged to share the vision they had for him of a glittering career in politics. Giles had thrown energy and enthusiasm at the challenge and had turned down numerous offers of far more lucrative jobs in the city. Politicians in Great Britain are not well paid, far less than a reasonably competent tradesman. He was a high flyer, but a rather impecunious high flyer and bills were starting to turn red in colour. Not a situation he would want any of his political rivals to be aware of.

He had become Member of Parliament for Maidstone at the age of just thirty and had risen quickly through the party ranks to become the country's youngest ever Minister for Health, despite of course knowing very little about medicine, or health, in general. A point not lost on former doctor Hugo.

The moment at which Hugo had realised Giles could be of benefit to him was shortly after he and Peter White had founded Valerian. After a couple of bottles of decent claret he had felt it right to share with Giles the slightly less than ethical method by which he and Peter had obtained the ability to further develop the Condrone molecule from their previous employer. As a gesture of mutually assured destruction Giles had shared his little secret, the one that failed to appear in the Declaration of Members Interests Register in the House. It was a secret Hugo had not forgotten.

There had naturally always been an element of risk in starting up a new company based purely around the potential of an unlicensed drug, Hugo knew that, but he had poured all he had, and quite a lot he didn't have, into the enterprise.

He definitely could not have afforded for anything to go wrong with the Condrone project and had been quick to spot that having the Minister for Health on ones side could only be a good thing.

Once more Hugo's excellent networking skills had been put to very good use.

Giles' mobile vibrated and he glanced at the screen.

'Vote in the house is expected shortly, my presence is required,' and he rose stiffly from his chair and left Hugo to finish his drink alone.

CHAPTER 11

'I had an interesting phone conversation the other day with someone who might be familiar to you Hugo,' said Peter White.

Since taking the call it had been nagging away on Peter's mind and although he knew he needed to tell the chairman about it, he didn't know how best to and had been putting off the moment.

He had eventually decided on the direct approach and now was that moment during their weekly official meeting. As was their established custom minutes were not being recorded. After all they had no share holders to answer to. And minutes recorded made potential future evidence.

'Not sure I liked the way you used the word interesting there Peter. Anything I should be concerned about?' said Hugo. 'And who was the person I might have been familiar with, there have been quite a few over the years.'

'The call was from a doctor down in Brighton, a GP, he told me he had been checking up, as he described it, on some of his Condrone patients and was concerned a couple of them might have developed an element of cognitive impairment.'

Hugo's brain was faintly starting to make a connection between GP and Brighton. It didn't feel like a good connection.

'What was this GP's name?' asked Hugo, fearing the answer.

'A Dr Sam Preston,' he said referring to a note on his iPad while at the same time sensing it might be best to carry on referring to his iPad a little longer.

'Sam Preston, Sam bloody Preston! I am indeed familiar with him, we were at medical school together. Always a bit too clever for his own good. In fact he fucked me over quite badly.' The memory was clearly still a painful scar in Hugo's mind.

'Well he didn't mention anything about fucking you over Hugo. Anyway I imagine you would have given as good as you got,' said Peter trying to both calm and flatter his boss.

Hugo took a moment and Peter was wise enough to be still finding his iPad interesting. Hugo managed to regain his composure.

'I am sure you handled the situation well Peter and were able to reassure Dr Preston that we have lots of data, that he's not welcome to inspect, that clearly demonstrates the impressive safety profile of Condrone.'

'Yes I think he was actually quite impressed with having spoken to the Valerian Chief Scientific Officer. Seemed to go away happy enough.'

'Good, Sam Preston can be a persistent bugger once he's got a bee in his bonnet. We don't want the possibility of any adverse publicity that might put at risk our new and exciting development project.'

Hugo felt uneasy that at such a sensitive time for Valerian his old adversary should have popped up again. He would have to give the matter some thought.

Might be best to deal with Sam Preston before he becomes a problem. One or two potential strategies started to come to mind. Carrots and sticks. He decided to start with the stick.

CHAPTER 12

'Can you let me know when you've finished with your last patient please Sam,' said Anita on the office phone. 'I need to come and talk with you about something that's come up this morning.'

Sam thought that sounded rather ominous, Anita had seemed more formal than her usual relaxed style. He finished up with his last patient as soon as he could and decided to go through and meet with his Practice Manager in her office. He didn't want to discuss what might be bad news in his own room, he had to do that often enough with his patients.

'Hi Sam, I was happy to come through to you but take a seat, can I get you some coffee?'

'I'm fine thanks Anita, had too much caffeine already. I'm guessing from the tone of your voice you don't have good news for me this morning.'

Anita held out a letter that had been received by recorded delivery that morning.

'Would you like to read it or shall I summarise?'

'Best just get on with it Anita,' said Sam feeling distinctly uncomfortable.

'Well I won't beat around the bush then. I'm afraid it's a letter of complaint against you Sam. Of course I'm sure there's nothing to it but you know how seriously we are expected to take these things.'

Letters of complaint always had to be taken seriously and had been a major cause of stress to Sam on the infrequent occasions they had been received.

'What am I supposed to have done wrong? Have I missed a diagnosis or something?'

'The letter is from a lady by the name of Ms. Amanda Collins. I've checked our records, you saw her as a temporary resident the week before last. She was staying down in Brighton for a few days. Does it ring any bells with you?' Anita seemed a little reluctant to tell Sam what the complaint was about.

'No bells ringing Anita, tell me what's going on.'

'She apparently came in to see you regarding a cough and while you were examining her chest she is alleging you touched her breast inappropriately. The left one,' added Anita trying to lighten the atmosphere.

Sam felt his heart sink immediately. He had certainly never had a complaint of this kind and this was definitely the worst kind.

Sam steadied himself and tried to stay calm. 'Have you had a look at the record of the consultation?'

'I have, there's not much to see really, I've printed a copy for you, best read it for yourself.'

Anita handed over the letter and a copy of the medical note Sam had written.

The letter was quite brief but shocking. It was alleging that Sam had pushed his hand inside her bra while he was using his stethoscope to listen to her lungs. The complainant had apparently been too shocked to say anything about it at the time but later decided she needed to complain 'in order to stop this sort of thing happening to any other women'.

The medical note was brief and to the point. 'Diagnosis. Cough. Gives a history of coughing for the last two weeks, no sputum, no dyspnoea, non smoker. Apyrexial, oxygen sats 98%, lungs clear on auscultation. Treatment. Patient advised likely viral, antibiotics not required, see again if worsens or fails to improve'.

He had this type of consultation several times every day and he had no reason to particularly recall any further details.

'This is complete and utter nonsense Anita, I've never touched anyone inappropriately in my life, patient or non patient, female or male. I would never do anything like that.'

'Try and stay calm Sam, I knew you would be upset and I'm hating being the bearer of bad news. I know it's nonsense as well and I've been both male and female,' she added helpfully.

'Well there are only two explanations here,' said Sam ignoring Anita's warped sense of humour. 'Either she has completely misinterpreted a perfectly normal examination, or she has some sort of axe to grind. But what could I have done to deserve this?'

Sam was feeling anger and bemusement in equal measures.

'Would you have offered her a chaperone? Did she ask for one?'

'You just can't offer a chaperone for every single patient you see. Only if you are planning to do a breast or genital exam and I wouldn't do any sort of exam like that without having the practice nurse in the room with me.'

'And we've got posters up, offering a chaperone, to anyone who wants one. There's a poster in the waiting room and one in my consulting room in full view of the patient.'

'Point taken, yes of course, sorry I asked.'

'Look Sam, I know you haven't done anything wrong here and I don't know what's going on but I'm afraid we do have to go through the usual process. Needless to say there is an official pathway we have to follow.'

Sam's day had been completely ruined, he didn't fancy any lunch, he'd have to make something up to tell Ella, and he certainly wasn't going to tell her about this.

The pathway was duly followed. Between them Sam and Anita composed a letter of reply to Ms. Amanda Collins. A copy of the medical record was sent along with the letter, which was composed in the standard format used for all cases of complaint.

Sam admitted he had no personal recollection of the consultation and apologised 'because a misunderstanding clearly must have taken place'. He had examined her lungs (he avoided using the word chest) in an entirely normal and appropriate manner which had certainly not involved interfering with her bra. He wished to reassure Ms. Collins that he had never received any complaint of this kind in the past and he had certainly never touched a patient inappropriately. He hoped this reassured her and answered her concerns etc etc.

Correspondence was sent and Sam was able to relax a little. Anita had reassured him that it was a good letter and the likelihood was they would hear nothing more. Sam wondered if this was maybe just another patient upset at not being prescribed antibiotics.

As part of the process, it had been required of them, in the event of Ms. Collins remaining unhappy, to offer either an informal meeting between her and the practice, or to suggest that she could escalate the complaint to the local area of NHS England.

Three weeks passed and Sam had pretty much assumed the complaint had gone away when he received a phone call. It was from the Area Medical Director for NHS England.

'Hello there Dr Preston, it's Dr Andy Vaughan here from NHS England, I think we might have met at a meeting a couple of years ago,' he said. 'I just wanted to give you a heads up that you will be receiving a letter within the next couple of days requiring your attendance at a hearing to further investigate a complaint we have received from a Ms. Amanda Collins. I imagine you are familiar with the complaint.'

Sam was lost for words, he thought this had all gone away.

'All part of the process I'm afraid. Just one of those things we doctors have to put up with.'

'But this is nonsense, utter rubbish, it must be some kind of set up.' Sam stopped himself, he knew he was wasting his breath. 'Sorry I know it's not your fault Dr Vaughan but false accusations like this are incredibly stressful.'

'Yes I do understand but unfortunately there are formal processes that have to be followed. Ms. Collins may well have legal representation at the hearing and I would strongly suggest you contact your medical defence organisation for advice.'

'Anyway the letter will detail what will happen next doctor.'

Thanks a lot, thought Sam.

He had talked things through with Anita and they had decided it would be a wise move to seek legal advice and today he was meeting with representatives of The Medical Defence Society. He was thirty eight floors above the River Thames at Canary Wharf in London and the view outside was a lot more appealing than the view inside. He had never had a serious complaint before and had certainly not been sued, so this was his first personal encounter with the MDS.

He had been to doctors meetings arranged by the MDS and had always listened to the message of 'Just leave it to us doctor, follow our advice and everything will be fine'.

Sam wasn't so sure. As well as providing legal advice to doctors in various spots of bother they were also the representatives of an insurance company. As such they were very keen to avoid paying out ever increasing sums of money to litigious patients. So how could you be sure the advice you were getting was truly in your interests and not theirs? Often of course the interests were the same but not always. As far as the MDS was concerned every complaint was a court case in the making, with the potential to cost them tens of thousands of pounds. 'Cut your losses and settle doctor.'

Fine but whose losses were they?

Not that court was on the agenda for now, a kangaroo court maybe, he thought.

'So Dr Preston you have a complaint against you, by a female patient, of inappropriate behaviour of a sexual nature. We are here as your friends and advisers to help you and to act in your best interests,' said a female lawyer who had introduced herself as Veronica Davey. 'Have you any questions before we get going?'

'No, not really, but I do just want to say that I would like to remain the judge of what is in my best interests, thank you.'

'Yes of course doctor. I should also say at this point that the worst case scenario here is that if this case does not go in your favour you would automatically be reported to the General Medical Council by NHS England and your registration would then be at risk. You could also be reported to the police who have the power to investigate with a view to bringing a charge of sexual assault.'

Sam didn't think the meeting was starting too well. He was being told his career was at risk, his freedom could even be under threat.

But it was a process that had to be gone through, as they kept on reminding him. It was so unfair, why would somebody do something like this to him? Guilty unless you can prove yourself innocent seemed to be the nature of the process he was being put through.

The meeting dragged on for a couple of hours and Sam wasn't sure it had achieved very much for him.

It seemed to be entirely a case of Sam's word against that of the complainant. Whoever came across to the panel, at the hearing, as most believable. It seemed in Sam's favour that he had followed all the rules, but 'Maybe you should have verbally offered a chaperone if you were examining a ladies chest?' was an unspoken accusation. Even his legal advisers didn't seem on his side. He had been expecting some support and reassurance. He paid several thousand pounds every year in fees to the MDS and he had been hoping for better.

Sam thought. Have these people any experience of actually working in General Practice?

He was, in any event, assured of the "total support" of the MDS and one of their trained advisers, a former occupational health doctor, would attend the hearing to offer on the spot advice.

Sam made the lonely journey on the train from London Victoria back to Brighton. He aimlessly watched the countryside passing by. How he missed the support of Gilly at times like this. She would have been so positive and upbeat. He would probably have had to stop her seeking out the complainant and giving her a piece of her mind, or worse. Sam smiled at the thought. He had come to terms with the loss of Gilly and had adjusted to his new life but he still missed her terribly.

He now felt as if he was in a kind of limbo while waiting for the hearing to take place. Every patient he saw felt like another potential complaint. The doctor patient relationship was one of mutual trust and Sam felt that trust had been badly let down.

The hearing was set for the following week. A complaint of a sexual nature was of special interest to NHS England and they had expedited proceedings. The hearing itself was to be held in a committee room in Brighton just off the Old Steyne, the one way system that takes visitors from the main routes entering Brighton down to the seafront, past the Royal Pavilion.

Sam had been warned that the hearing was to be open and it would be possible members of the public could be present and if he was really unlucky, a journalist.

Privately the MDS rep had thought it quite likely the press would be there but hadn't wanted to be the one to tell Sam. Somebody in the know was very likely to have tipped off at least one of the local papers, and they just loved this kind of story.

At least the hearing was to be non confrontational, in the sense that Sam and his accuser would not be meeting face to face. Ms.Collins was to be invited to present her side of the story first, the panel would then hear from Sam and he had been told to expect some cross questioning.

'Stay calm at all times Dr Preston,' his adviser had told him. 'Don't let them get under your skin and remember to remain professional, no matter how cross you might feel. You must always show respect for the complainant, she was your patient if only for the day.'

'Sure, a patient seemingly intent on ruining my career,' said Sam angrily. 'No problem.'

The group of three had met for a light lunch beforehand to discuss strategy. Sam, MDS rep and Practice Manager Anita there to offer her support. They were now being held in a side room waiting for their moment in the headlights. Everything that had needed to be said in preparation had been said and it was now feeling painfully quiet. Sam gazed out of the dirty window across the busy road. People in cars, people walking, going about their normal daily lives. And his life felt on hold right now. He was already in jail before the trial, before sentence had been passed. With the prevailing politically correct climate he had no confidence he was going to be believed rather than his accuser.

Sam had been through stressful professional situations before, like finals and job interviews, but this was different. His career, his livelihood were potentially at stake. He took some long slow breaths and deep within his mind he was sure he could hear Gilly's voice. 'It will be OK Sam. You are a fine man and a good doctor, and we will always have each other whatever'.

If only that was the case. Right now he missed her more than in a long time.

A stern looking woman came to collect the accused and his supporters. She ushered them into the sparsely furnished hearing room. Sam, Dr MDS and Anita were positioned together at a table directly opposite the seated, unfriendly looking, panel.

The panel consisted, he was told, of the local area NHS Chief Executive, a senior doctor from the local medical committee and a lay member - she was sitting in a wheelchair. Seated with them was the area NHS solicitor to offer legal advice. Sam thought he was now facing the kangaroo court he had feared.

There were some chairs to the right and Sam was relieved to see only two were occupied. One by a baby faced man who looked of Eastern European origin and the other by a young man with notebook and pencil poised.

Anita nudged Sam and said, 'I think that's Peter Weller, he's a journalist with the Brighton and Hove Herald.'

Sam had no chance of hiding this from Ella now. Why were the bloody press allowed in? And who was the other weird looking guy?

In fact proceedings went a little more easily than Sam had been expecting. He was given an opportunity to describe the events of the consultation. There wasn't really much to add to what he had already submitted in writing, he had no definite recollection of the consultation. Maybe if he'd caught sight of the complainant his memory might have been jogged, but it was probably just as well that he hadn't.

He thought maybe the female lay member, who had turned out to be chairperson of the local disability action group, would be difficult. He was wary because he knew how hard it could be for people with disabilities to access NHS services, and that sometimes led to bitterness, but she was all sweetness and light, she seemed to be on his side.

The local medical committee doctor was a pain. He had come across all high and mighty and had audibly tutted when Sam admitted he had not actually verbally offered a chaperone. Sam didn't know the doctor, he apparently worked in Lewes, a town a few miles away. He looked close to retirement and Sam hoped he wouldn't meet him again anytime soon. Doctors sticking up for their colleagues was a complete myth, this guy was enjoying feeding on the discomfort of his more junior colleague. Sam found it difficult not to tell him what he thought of him but remembered the instruction he had been given to remain professional.

The Chief Executive was wrapping things up when Anita suddenly got to her feet.

'I would like to say something please,' she said. The MDS rep turned round sharply as if to say 'This isn't a good idea'. but Anita was not to be denied her chance to stand up for her Sam.

'Hello members of the panel. My name is Anita and I am Dr Preston's Practice Manager. I have worked with Dr Preston for a number of years. In our practice we have never had a single complaint against Dr Preston, he is a wonderful GP and completely dedicated to his patients. He would never ever touch a patient, male or female inappropriately. This, in my opinion, is a ridiculous complaint, with no evidence and totally without foundation. It should be dismissed without delay. Thank you.'

And with that she sat down defiantly and Dr MDS stopped looking at his shoes.

'Thank you, er Anita, for your character reference. Your loyalty to your employer is noted.'

The hearing was over. Sam was told that having heard evidence from both sides, discussions would take place and external advice sought if thought necessary. It might be a few weeks before they heard anything more.

Shame the press had been there. The journalist had been scribbling away furiously throughout and there seemed little doubt a sensational news item would be appearing shortly in the Herald. What would his patients make of that?

But Sam was really proud of Anita, it was as though she too had received some words of advice from Gilly.

CHAPTER 13

'Hey Laura,' said Peter Weller. 'I've got something you might be interested in. Not really my cup of tea but you being the feminist you are I reckon you could get your teeth stuck into this one,' he added a little rudely.

Such was the nature of the banter in the office of a provincial newspaper.

This was the office of The Brighton and Hove Herald, the proud bringer of news to first the town and more lately the city of Brighton and Hove, for more than a century. Well placed offices in the centre of the city just up the road from the Brighton Dome, the concert hall where Abba first found fame in the Eurovision Song Contest back in 1974.

Laura looked up enquiringly from the computer monitor she had been staring at intently for the last hour.

'More footballers been misbehaving then?' she said. She had made something of a name for herself a year back with a story about an irregular and indiscreet after match party attended by two of the stars of the Seagulls, Brighton and Hove Albion, the local football team.

'Not footballers this time, but could be just as juicy. Some local GP who might not have been exactly keeping his hands to himself.' Paul was sure he was destined for greater things very soon, preferably at one of England's finest tabloids.

Laura listened with mild interest to what Paul had to say about his visit to the medical tribunal the day before. It was currently her kind of story but not really the kind of story she wanted to write. She fancied herself as more of a serious investigative journalist. But bills had to be paid.

In any case the public loves reading about the antics of high profile footballers but surely nobody wants to think badly of their local GP. Do they?

Sounded interesting, somebody needed to take a look, but she would tread carefully.

Laura was sitting in her car across the road from the GP surgery, keeping an eye on the comings and goings at the front door. Foot traffic was getting lighter now, morning surgery must be coming to an end.

She had done some background research online about Dr Sam Preston, even found a photo of him. Not bad looking she had thought. Scruffily handsome, light brown hair, blue eyes. Didn't look as though he would have too much trouble getting his kicks in the usual way without having to touch up his patients. But there you go, Dr Harold Shipman had looked just like your favourite uncle.

Laura knew about the death of Dr Preston's wife. There had been an article in her own paper after the tragedy in which Sam had tried to warn readers of the hidden dangers of some drug or other.

She felt that she needed to get to know Dr Preston and that was why she was sitting in her car with three hours of parking already paid for.

She had no trouble recognising him as soon as he came out of the building. He appeared much as he had in the photo, perhaps a little older, certainly looking tired, but the guy had just finished his morning surgery. She was guessing he was probably also more than a little stressed about the patient complaint.

Sam crossed the road and walked directly past Laura sitting in her ageing green Audi TT. She managed to stop herself instinctively ducking down to avoid his eye, but she felt sure Dr Preston had not noticed her. She reminded herself she was a journalist not a detective and knew she would have a steep learning curve if she was ever to succeed in investigative work.

Get on with it girl, do the best you can, what to lose?

Dr Preston was disappearing rapidly down the road as Laura stretched out of the drivers seat and headed off in pursuit. At least he would have no reason to think he might be being trailed, no furtive glances in shop windows or doubling back on himself for her to worry about. Laura shook herself out of the fiction she had created and walked after him. Sensibly she was wearing trainers and had dressed casually in jeans and a top covered with a blue cotton jacket that matched the colour of her eyes. She had decided against the dark glasses despite it being a bright June day. She didn't want to seem too obvious.

Sam looked like a man on a mission and Laura thought she knew why. Like most men round about 12.30pm he was hungry. Could he be meeting somebody for a lunch date? That might add something to a story.

She followed him along Eastern Road past the austere buildings of Brighton College on her right. Sam crossed the road and turned left. He was heading down towards the seafront. She wondered if he was going to duck into one of the little bistros they were passing but he kept going until he reached Marine Parade, the upper level of the seafront.

Laura was keeping a discreet distance and was sure that Dr Preston had not noticed her. Would it matter if he had? She was good at thinking quickly on her feet and she hadn't really worked out how she was going to intercept him and engage in conversation.

The prey and the hunter took a set of rusting iron stairs down to the lower sea level, Madeira Drive and walked along beside the old Volks electric railway, in the direction of the pier.

A lunch rendezvous on the pier? Surely not.

But that was exactly what it seemed to be when, to Laura's surprise, he crossed the gaudy forecourt of what had once been called the Palace Pier.

The pier was busy for a weekday, it wasn't even the school holidays, and there were plenty of people milling about, some like Sam apparently in search of lunch.

She followed Sam along the wooden boarded pier until he stopped at a kiosk aptly named 'The Fat Plaice'. The smell of fish and chips cooking was overwhelming and suddenly her own hunger motivated her to form a plan.

She joined the short queue right behind Sam and listened when he made his order of large cod and chips. She thought his voice sounded kind, he even told the counter girl to keep the change. His wrapped up fish and chip lunch was handed over.

'What you having love?'

Goodness she hadn't had time to think and said the first thing that came into her head. 'Large cod and chips please.'

Laura tapped her credit card to pay for the unplanned treat and quickly turned round, worried she might have lost Dr Preston.

Of course she needn't have worried. A hungry man with fish and chips in his hands sits down as soon as he can and gets on with it.

Sam was sitting on a bench a few yards further along. He was facing west along the seafront toward the ruined structure of the old West Pier and the more recent addition of the British Airways Viewing Tower. In the distance the bay stretched out far beyond, past Shoreham to the prominence of Selsey Bill. You could see for miles and miles and miles as the old Who song went. Today was a very clear day.

It felt like it was make or break time and Laura was just figuring out a way to approach Sam when a large and aggressive seagull, having seen the potential treat, swooped down to launch an attack on Sam's lunch. The look of surprise and horror followed by disappointment on his face almost made Laura burst out laughing. The battered fish had been seized by the gull and it was now doing it's best to fight off it's dining rivals on the slatted wooden flooring of the pier. In different circumstances she would have laughed but she seized this totally unexpected opportunity and stepped forward.

'Don't you just hate it when that happens,' she said, fiercely guarding her own lunch package. 'You obviously don't eat fish and chips on the seafront too often.'

Sam looked up and found himself instantly drawn to the smiling, brown haired girl looking down at him.

'Yes I obviously need more practice. You however seem to be an expert,' he said noticing how she was protecting her still wrapped lunch.

'Not so much of an expert that, for some reason, I mistakenly ordered a much too large portion of cod and chips.'

'I'm sure I can't manage it all alone so, rather than share mine with the seagulls too, could I suggest we might solve each other's little difficulty?' She couldn't believe she was saying this to a man she had never met. Was it just journalistic instinct or something else?

Sam smiled as Laura sat down on the bench next to him. 'Well if you're offering to share your lunch with me I'm happy to help out. Perhaps I should keep guard while you get started.'

CHAPTER 14

Sue Anderson had moved her long term address to a genteel part of Hove, high up on the hill, with views down across the sea towards the hundreds of wind turbines that had recently been installed in the Channel. To be more precise her address had been moved for her.

The house was a large Victorian building, formerly some well off family's residence but now converted for multiple occupancy and renamed as Forever Autumn.

It was one of a large number of care homes that had been opened up in recent years to cater for the ever increasing numbers of dementia patients along this part of the South Coast of England.

Sue had lived in Brighton with her husband John, just the two of them since their daughter and son had left home, until he had died suddenly two years ago in a car crash on the M23 while returning from a business meeting in London.

Sue had not coped well after her loss. At first her children, and her medical advisers, had put Sue's difficulties down to the shock and the bereavement. Given time and support they had all hoped she would pull things together and start to adjust to a new way of living.

But instead her mental state had rapidly worsened and it became clear that neither bereavement nor depression could explain Sue's confusion and personality change. She started to wander away from home, unable to find her way back. The police had returned her once or twice and inevitably Social Services had become involved. They arranged extra support for Sue at home but after a few days the carers were harshly told to go away. She wasn't looking after herself, not eating properly, her house had become a mess. Her social worker decided she was becoming a danger to herself.

A case conference had been called bringing together Social Services, her daughter and Sue's GP. After discussion it was decided that a psychiatric assessment was required.

It was of no great surprise to the professionals when a diagnosis of dementia was made. Sue's husband had been covering for her and his sudden absence had unmasked the underlying illness.

But it was an enormous shock to her daughter. Mum was only sixty, surely dementia happened to people a lot older. Apart from an old back injury Sue had always been fit and healthy. Not a surprise according to the psychiatrist, she said was seeing increasing numbers of patients at a much younger age than a few years ago. Maybe dementia was becoming more common or perhaps diagnosis was just a lot better now.

Sue could not be left alone in her current state. There were only two options given to her daughter. Either she had to move back home to look after her mother or Sue had to move permanently into a dementia care home. She chose the former, she owed it to her mum. Her career in London was put on hold and home she came. Just as well she was single.

But she soon realised she couldn't be a full time carer, she had to admit it wasn't in her nature and Mum was becoming increasingly difficult and rude. In any event money was tight. Dad had made some bad business decisions in the months before his death, leaving his wife with really just the house. The care allowances paid by the government were pitiful. For reasons of finance and her own sanity Sue's daughter had to find herself a job.

A further attempt was made to bring in carers during the day, while the new job was started in town, but after just a couple of weeks Sue stopped letting them in the house.

Why did she need interfering busy bodies in her home? It was bad enough having her daughter there so much of the time.

The new family dynamic was not working for Sue or her daughter and it was becoming clear that alternative arrangements were going to be needed.

Her daughter knew there was no way her mother would have been prepared to move into a dementia care home. Even mentioning the matter would have provoked a furious response. She would not accept there was anything wrong with her at all. She had no recollection of having got lost on the streets or of leaving the gas cooker on. But something had to be done, Social Services were insisting on it as a matter of what they called adult safeguarding.

Her daughter felt terrible at what she knew she had to do as she formed a plan to move her mother into care.

'It's just for two weeks Mum, while I go on holiday, you know you can't manage without me,' she said. 'I've found a lovely hotel for you to stay in, perched up on the hill with views all the way down to the sea.'

The reassurance of a mini bar in the room eventually did the trick and Mum had been duly loaded into the car along with her suitcase and taken on the twenty minute journey up the hill.

Sue was greeted at the front door of Forever Autumn like an old friend. 'You've just missed lunch Sue, but let's get chef to rustle you something up. How does an omelette sound?'

As Sue was being ushered in and led away, she turned round to her daughter, who had stayed behind in reception, and said in a surprising flash of insight, 'Am I doing the right thing?'

Emotions of many different kinds flooded through her daughter and she had to rush out of the building to the sanctuary of her car. The tears ran freely down her cheeks after the outpouring of adrenalin and her bodily shaking gradually subsided.

'Look who's come to see you today,' said Sue's key worker, as she and the visitor stepped into Sue's room.

Sue was sitting in her old wing backed chair by the window, one of just a few pieces of personal items she had been allowed to bring with her from the old family home. Despite the stunning views outside she was gazing at the favourite childhood doll she was holding in her lap. She looked up.

'I'm sorry I don't know who you are,' she said.

'My name is Laura,' said her daughter.

Sue continued to look blank until a memory glowed faintly inside her brain.

'I've got a daughter called Laura.'

'Yes and I've got a mum called Sue,' said Laura.

Conversations, if that's what they could be called, often started like that. Laura had found it very upsetting initially but, after a few minutes of talking about times long past, some degree of recognition usually occurred. It was strange, thought Laura, how her mum could often remember quite intricate details of her daughter's childhood, while at the same time be unable to remember what they had spoken about just five minutes before. The short term memory loss inevitably led to their conversations being constantly repeated as if on a continuous never ending loop.

Same old things time and time again. 'When's Dad coming to see me?' And 'When am I going home?' Upsetting and frustrating for Laura and she had to admit, boring and soul destroying. But Sue seemed to get some sort of benefit from talking. And within a few minutes of Laura leaving, it was as if her daughter, that nice young lady whoever she was, had never visited.

She often wondered if her mum had any insight into what was happening to her. Was she happy or was she sad? Does she even see, hear and smell things in the way she once did?

Surely she must know her mind was not working properly. Why does she keep asking 'What have I done wrong?'

She must think she is a prisoner. Which of course she was. The doors to the home were all protected with coded locks and visitors instructed never to let any resident pass through the front door with them.

The day after she had been admitted to the care home, management had applied for and been granted a Deprivation of Liberties Safeguarding Order by Social Services. She was being legally detained, and it was a life sentence. Nobody gets cured of dementia.

Laura didn't enjoy her visits. She wasn't sure if that was down to her feelings of guilt or whether she just couldn't bear to see her mum like this. At times she wondered if it would be better if her mother just faded away and died and then she thought, better for who? Mum or me?

She hated the care home. She had visited several when choosing one for her mother and she had disliked them all. She had been assured by the social worker that Forever Autumn was about as good as it got and Laura readily admitted that the care given to her mum was fantastic. She had no idea how people, mainly women, could do that sort of work. Most of the staff were recruited from abroad, usually from countries where old people were valued and treated with more respect and love than was often the case in England.

The sights and sounds of the care home depressed her. Repeating loops of music play lists curated from the fifties and sixties competed in the communal living area with Sky News in the vain hope of stimulating some interest or memory. Residents, patients, inmates, mothers, fathers sitting around the edge of the lounge in high backed chairs, some lost in their own worlds and some moaning and groaning, occasionally crying and shouting. Attention demanded from Mummy.

But the biggest assault on the senses were the smells, they made Laura feel nauseous. Relatives were encouraged to come and share lunch with their loved ones in the dining room. The stench of long cooked meat and two veg mixed with disinfectant and urine did nothing to stimulate the appetite. And the sight of old people hopelessly failing in their efforts to feed themselves, dribbling and drooling into their food.

Lunch with the seagulls was definitely better than that.

CHAPTER 15

It had been mutually decided that their second meeting would have the benefit of a ceiling and a roof. They had enjoyed sharing food with each other but, having helped with the introduction, the seagull had been an unwelcome guest. Perhaps acceptable at lunch time but definitely not in the evening.

As such Sam and Laura were now sitting at a small round table in the Victoria Lounge of the Grand Hotel which took pride of place along Brighton's seafront. The ceilings looked fine. Some of the walls had taken a bit of a pounding though in 1984 when the provisional IRA had attempted to assassinate then Prime Minister Margaret Thatcher.

The hotel had been recently refitted in a classical style and was the best Brighton had to offer its more discerning visitors.

Sam was sitting there because he had been instantly attracted to Laura. Not just because she was in his opinion beautiful, but because of her infectious smile and light hearted approach to life. He had enjoyed sharing her lunch and had prolonged the chance meeting when he bought two ice creams with chocolate flakes for dessert. He felt relaxed in her company and found her easy to talk to. A welcome relief after all the tensions of the last few weeks.

Laura was sitting there, she hoped, because she had a story to investigate and thought that after a couple of drinks maybe Sam's secrets would be prised out of him and her story of the GP pervert would be half written. Or at least that's what she thought she had been hoping but sitting there in Sam's company she wasn't so sure. In any case the first part of the plan had already gone wrong when Sam had ordered himself a mineral water to go with her glass of Sauvignon Blanc. Why was he not having a drink?

It was a bit tricky for Laura not being sure how much of what she knew about Sam it was OK to know, and how much she needed not to know. Very confusing having the benefit of inside information and it might get even more difficult if she had another glass of wine.

Sam had already told her he was a GP and that he had a grown up daughter. She knew of course about the death of his wife and there was no outward sign of a replacement having been found. She had made a point of noticing no evidence of a recently removed wedding ring.

Laura had been deliberately vague with Sam. Told him she worked for the Herald and had jokingly suggested she was a food critic on a mission to find the best fish and chip shop in Brighton. She had considered coming clean to Sam about her pursuit of him from his surgery but was worried that, not unreasonably, he might just get up and leave. She would deal with that issue later if she had to. It depended on which direction things went in tonight.

As it turned out Sam made things ridiculously easy for her. He felt comfortable enough in her company to talk about his work, with only gentle prompting from Laura.

'I had reason to come across one of your colleagues, I think, last week,' said Sam. 'Bloke by the name of Peter Weller, ever heard of him?'

Laura felt herself flushing and thought. Oh no. I've been rumbled already. How can he have found out about what I'm up to?

But it was just Sam wanting to be open and honest with Laura, especially now he knew she was a journalist. He didn't want her finding out about the patient complaint through a probably very unflattering piece in the local rag.

'Sure I know Peter, bit of an arsehole really. Has his eyes on a career with one of the tabloids, always looking for salacious gossip,' replied Laura, providing an opportunity for Sam to expand.

He happily took the offered bait. 'I have the misfortune to be currently going through just about the worst thing that can happen to a GP, a male GP anyway. A female patient, somebody I'd never seen before, and hopefully never will again, has made an allegation of improper conduct against me. I was giving evidence at a hearing last week and your colleague Mr Weller was there with his notebook. Best you hear that from me rather than him.'

Laura pretended to look shocked and lost for words. She paused before asking cautiously, 'So what are you alleged to have done Sam? I hardly know you but you don't seem like the sort of man who would act inappropriately.'

'I wouldn't be here otherwise,' she added, desperately hoping that Sam wasn't setting her up and about to confront her. She wasn't like Peter Weller. He wouldn't have given a shit!

'The lady has accused me of touching her up while I was examining her lungs, she had a cough. It's complete and utter nonsense but the way the NHS sees things like this is that it's just her word against mine. It's a question of who they choose to believe. That's why she and I were at the hearing. Perhaps Mr Weller could enlighten me as to what she told the panel.'

Laura's decision was made in an instant. She had a strong and reliable instinct for when to trust somebody and her perception was very much that Sam was a good man. Her story of doctor scandal was going to be a non starter.

'I'm so sorry you are having to go through something like that Sam. It sounds completely ridiculous to me. Surely there has to be some sort of evidence to back up accusations like that? I'll make sure next weeks headline in the Herald, written by Peter, is 'Brighton GP is completely innocent'.'

Sam laughed, feeling more relaxed now he had been able to get the complaint issue out into the open.

'Probably best not, but a word in his ear to the effect that there really isn't a story on offer would be nice.'

'Consider it done,' said Laura. 'Time to go and eat?'

It was early days in any potential relationship but hunger on both sides was already a major driving force for Sam and Laura and they had found their way out of the hotel bar and were walking along the seafront past crowds of excited, mainly young, people on their way to a concert at the Brighton Centre. The posters and advertising hoardings outside the venue announced the band to be Elbow.

'I love Elbow,' said Laura and Sam realised that was another shared interest they had, after fish and chips.

'Next time they're here then.' said Sam with more feeling of hope than he would care to admit to.

They turned left, into Ship Street, away from the seafront, into the district known as The Lanes. Sam had booked a table at 64 Degrees in anticipation the early part of the evening would go well. He thought it would be fun to take a short detour through the Lanes, they were a little early for their reservation. The area was busy with people looking for somewhere to eat or perhaps just enjoying the atmosphere provided by the trendy boutiques and bars in the intricate maze of alleyways and twittens. He had eaten at 64 Degrees before, although not with Gilly, it had only recently opened.

'Now's not the time to think about you Gilly. Sorry,' he said to himself.

'They do a great tasting menu here,' said Sam as they walked into the tiny restaurant.

'Yes I know,' said Laura. 'I was here last month. Don't forget I'm the food critic for the Herald. But they change the menu every week, so I can't wait.'

They were seated at a window table and happily watched couples and groups of people making their way along the street. It had been a hot, sunny day and was just starting to cool down as day was being gently nudged aside by night.

They failed to notice a baby faced man of apparent Eastern European origin take a quick glance through the window of the restaurant as he wandered casually past.

Inside, the restaurant was all activity and they were able to watch the chefs busily in action just behind a seated counter. The aromas from the cooking food were drifting over. They were eagerly awaiting their first course of hot smoked sea bass with horseradish and dill infused cucumber. The sounds were a mixture of excited chatter along with glasses and cutlery being put into action.

Laura decided it was time for her to share one or two secrets about her own life, she already knew a few things about Sam that she shouldn't have known and she was keen to get chatting and gain her knowledge of him officially. Less chance of being being caught out that way.

She started by telling Sam about life in Brighton as a child. She had a happy upbringing along with her younger brother who she said now worked in the security services, although she didn't elaborate further. After school had come University, at Bath, where she had graduated with a first in computer science. It was at Uni that she had had her first experience of journalism, she had been editor of the student magazine.

She talked about moving to London and a job with an investment bank which she hadn't liked much. She had been in a serious relationship or two but had never felt tempted to commit to marriage or think of having children.

She described her father dying suddenly and her mother being diagnosed with dementia. Sam was a good listener, and he seemed to take a close interest in her mothers diagnosis.

'I thought doctors hated talking about people's illnesses when they're off duty,' said Laura.

'Some doctors hate talking about people's illnesses when they're on duty,' replied Sam with a smile.

'But it's a really big thing in your life,' he continued. 'You gave up your career to come back home to care for your mum. Not sure I could have done something like that.'

'I didn't mind too much coming back to my home town but I should have realised that I wasn't cut out to spend my life as a carer. No regrets though, I'm not going back to London.'

'It just seems so unfair for Mum to develop dementia at her age. But the psychiatrist did tell me she has started to see a lot more younger patients in the last couple of years and I have to say there are far more people in the home of my mum's age than I would have expected to see.'

'Well there are certainly more people developing dementia now than ever before,' said Sam. 'For the older people it's hardly a surprise really. Modern medicine has become so much better at treating all the usual causes of death. Things like heart attacks, strokes even cancers. Some of the money I'm paid by the NHS is actually based on my success rates in treating conditions like heart disease, high blood pressure and diabetes. It's a political thing really. The politicians love to tell the voters how well they've done in helping the NHS to reduce death rates. Sometimes it feels as though people aren't actually allowed to die. We all have to die of something and if we live longer then we develop things which are common in old age, like dementia. There's no treatment for old age and no effective treatment for dementia.'

'Sorry that probably sounded like a bit of a lecture but it's a hobby horse of mine. I think most people are more keen on living a happy and enjoyable life than trying to live forever. And who wants to end up in a care home like your mum?'

'Can't think anyone would choose to live so long that you end up in somewhere like that,' said Laura.

'But it's funny what you say about younger people with dementia,' continued Sam. 'I've got a couple of patients in my practice with dementia who are quite young and it made me wonder why. I checked through their medical records and found that they are both taking that new arthritis drug called Condrone. I expect you've heard of it, there was a lot of mention in the press when it was released. The papers called it the 'joint booster drug'.'

'I do remember,' said Laura 'I've got a sneaking feeling that Mum could actually be taking it. Do you think it might cause dementia then?'

'The thought had crossed my mind,' said Sam. 'But there are really quite rigorous mechanisms in place to pick that sort of thing up. Any potential side effects have to be reported to the Medicines and Healthcare Regulatory Authority, they are the people who give a new drug a licence in the first place. I even gave the drug company who make Condrone a call to double check. I spoke to their chief scientist and he reassured me there are no problems. Obviously it's only a small sample of patients, things like that happen just by chance all the time.'

Sam for his part had shared with Laura that he had a daughter, Ella, and that she was studying sociology at Sussex University.

'She lives at home with me, I can't get rid of her,' said Sam. 'I think that since she lost her mum a few years ago she feels a need to look after me. I'm definitely going to have to report back about tonight I'm afraid.'

'She sounds like a good girl,' Laura commented. She felt it was a bit too soon to talk about sensitive matters like nineteen year old daughters.

She changed the subject, feeling a little awkward. 'So apart from Elbow and fish and chips what else do you like? I know next to nothing about you.'

'Well, I like to go flying,' said Sam. 'After what happened a few years back I needed some distraction so I learned to fly light aeroplanes. I joined a flying school at Shoreham Airport and gained my wings. Flying gives you a great sense of freedom and the views from up there on a clear day are fantastic.'

'Good for you,' said Laura. 'I like your sense of adventure Sam. Don't suppose you need a co-pilot do you?'

CHAPTER 16

The last patient of the day was his old friend from medical school. It was a happy coincidence that had found them both practicing in the same town. Sam always saw his patient Richard Davies at the end of his working day. The formality of the medical consultation often continued to the informality of a quiet drink and a chat about the old days in the Thomas Kemp pub just around the corner from Sam's surgery.

It wasn't generally considered good practice to be the doctor to a friend but Sam had become Richard's GP because he knew he would be able to do provide him with the best possible treatment. And poor Richard really needed the best treatment, as well as Sam's friendship, because his life was in the process of falling to pieces.

The incident with the varicose vein surgery had been the first outward sign to his colleagues of what was to come. His chat with the Head of Surgery, Professor O'Brien had been friendly enough and his boss reassured him of the full support of the department. In fact his boss had felt somewhat guilty about the workload that Richard had been shouldering over the previous few months. It had been agreed Richard would take a month off from work. Relax, take a holiday, recharge the batteries.

The break had seemed to help and when Richard returned to work his colleagues worried about him a little less until a further incident occurred when he was found wandering aimlessly around the gynaecology ward. The Ward Sister had wondered what on earth the vascular surgeon was doing on her ward and Richard had not been able to make her any the wiser. She had felt duty bound to report the incident to the hospital Chief Executive.

He wasn't quite the same person either. Normally so easy going and relaxed, unusually for a surgeon, he had become anxious and irritable. On one occasion he shouted and swore at Theatre Sister Shirley when she handed him the wrong surgical instrument. Richard had never had much of a temper, not even when provoked on the football pitch, but his colleagues now lived in fear of his volatility.

Maybe Richard was depressed? Professor O'Brien certainly didn't have the expertise to make such a diagnosis but he had been given the task by the Chief Executive to deal with the problem before any embarrassment was caused to the hospital.

With some reluctance and under threat of suspension, Richard had agreed to be assessed by a psychiatrist in a neighbouring town. Discretion and confidentiality had been paramount for all concerned. A careful medical history was taken and cognitive tests carried out.

The conclusions were worrying. There were clear deficits in Richard's short term memory and he had undergone significant personality change. The psychiatrist feared that organic brain disease was likely and he recommended a neurological opinion should be sought. He was put on gardening leave while being further investigated.

The neurologist had been equally concerned. In a man aged forty three there was a high likelihood of some kind of physical brain disease as the explanation for his symptoms. The specialist was aware of Richard's history of repeated head injuries from his footballing days. An MRI scan of the brain was ordered. The result was distressing.

Richard was told that his memory loss and episodes of confusion were likely being caused by a condition called Post Traumatic Encephalopathy, a condition being seen with increasing frequency among former professional sportsmen. The scan had suggested the presence of multiple areas of damage to his brain, probably caused by micro haemorrhages as a result of the repeated head trauma. The prognosis was not good, there was no treatment available. Once established gradual deterioration to a state of advanced dementia was inevitable. There were many causes of dementia and PTE was one of them.

As far as the hospital was concerned the diagnosis of PTE was the end of Richard's career as a surgeon. He was provided with an adequate pension and retired on medical grounds. He had been forced to surrender his licence to practice medicine. The schoolboy's dream had come to an abrupt end.

'So how have things been Rich?' enquired Sam during the formal part of the meeting. 'I saw you six weeks ago and I thought you were struggling a bit. I hate seeing you like this old buddy.'

'Not as much as I hate being like this,' replied Richard. He had turned up today wearing his replica Arsenal shirt, mainly to annoy Sam, a lifelong Chelsea fan. 'My life has fallen apart, surgery was my life and that's been taken away from me. I know they had no choice, but the NHS just chucks you out on the scrap heap when you're no use to them anymore.'

'And your replacement's hopeless,' said Sam trying to lighten the atmosphere a little. 'But I do understand what you mean. The worst part for me is that they say your illness is all down to the football we played together. I almost feel responsible for what happened to you.'

'Yeah it's all your fault Sam. If you'd scored a few more goals I wouldn't have had to try so hard to head the ball away at the other end. Football has buggered up my brain now as well as my knees. Who would have thought I had something in common with the likes of Jack Charlton and Nobby Stiles?'

'You were pretty good Rich but maybe not quite up to their standards,' said Sam. 'Much better looking though.'

Sam brought the consultation back to serious matters.

'So how do you see the future Rich?' A casual sounding question which often provided a revealing answer.

'Well I hope my team win the league this year instead of your lot.' Richard was avoiding the question as well as failing to remember the name of either team.

'I was hoping for a serious and more realistic answer,' said Sam.

'The reality is that there is no future for me Sam. I'm basically fucked, as you know if you've read the bloody neurologist's report. My brain may not be working well enough for me to be a surgeon anymore but I can at least remember to wipe my own arse.'

Sam was distressed to hear the obvious frustration in his friend's voice.

'And if and when the time comes that you detect I'm not able to do that please just give me something to take so I don't end up in some dementia care home dump.'

'Well that probably tells you how I'm feeling. Just hand over the prescription for my buggered knees and that pointless anti depressant and we'll get off to the pub.'

Sitting in the pub with Richard always reminded Sam of the old days back at medical school. Sitting in the bar or a pub had been a regular part of life back then. As young medical students they were seeing all manner of things that were shocking. Dead bodies were OK, it was the ones who were living, but only just, who were the problem. The patients brought into Accident and Emergency after car crashes. Limbs missing, faces burned beyond recognition. Drinking had become part of their established culture, to help relax and forget the horrors they had seen.

And old habits died hard as Sam had found out after the death of Gilly. Although he had been in rehab he didn't consider himself to be an alcoholic, despite all those meetings where it had been obligatory to confess to your weakness, your condition, your illness.

Sam didn't not drink but he always stayed in control. He liked to enjoy a beer or glass of wine in social settings. He never drank alone or to calm himself down.

And it felt good to be sitting there with Richard, he was just sorry about his friends plight. Having a beer or two with him was probably better than any medicine he could provide. Sam didn't think Rich had much support from anybody else. He had been married once, to a lawyer who had helped defend him successfully on an occasion when he had been sued.

But they both had busy professional lives, which they seemed to value more than their marriage and they had found their lives drifting apart in different directions. There was a daughter but when the divorce had inevitably become less than amicable she had sided with her mother. They had moved away and apart from providing financial maintenance for them he had lost touch.

Apart from Sam, Richard was very much on his own.

CHAPTER 17

'I call on the Right Honourable Giles Barrington, the Minister for Health.'

'Thank you Mr Speaker,' said Giles as he rose from his seat on the front bench in the House of Commons. He buttoned his suit jacket and swept his gaze around the chamber.

'For far too long successive governments have failed to address the issue of providing adequate funding for social care. The right honourable gentleman on the bench opposite had many opportunities while his party was in government to come up with a long term solution. Plenty of first aid plasters as short term fixes but the glue on those plasters was not sticky enough Mr Speaker and they kept falling off,' he paused for effect.

'It is now my intention and that of this government that the issue of funding for social care and in particular for those increasing numbers of patients afflicted by the plague of dementia, that the costs of their long term residential care will be fully funded. Mothers and fathers will no longer have to sell the family home and deprive their children of their rightful inheritance.'

'So I announce today the formation of a cross party steering group to ensure that this government's intentions are brought to reality at the earliest possible opportunity. This is great news for dementia sufferers, their families and those people who provide such crucial and excellent care in the many residential dementia homes across the length and breadth of this country.'

He retreated from the lectern and sat back down to a mixed chorus of cheers from his own benches and braying from the other side of the house.

A few days later and Hugo was meeting with Giles again. This time in the well appointed surroundings of the Chairman's office at Valerian HQ on the Cambridge Science Park.

'I've just spoken with my Head of Security about that little problem I mentioned previously to you Giles. I've decided an additional and different approach might yield the desired result,' said Hugo.

'You mean that GP in Brighton who was asking questions about Condrone? Your love rival wasn't he?' Giles rarely missed an opportunity to put down his wealthy friend.

Hugo ignored the sarcasm of the minister.

'We neither of us want awkward questions nor any hint of adverse publicity right now Giles. It's not in my interest and don't forget my interest is your interest. Pressure has been applied to him, he should be feeling very uncomfortable. But I think some carrot as well as stick would now be helpful. He will get the message one way or the other.'

'Anyway I've invited you up from London to discuss how I can best help to further your political ambitions. I'm sure you are keen to keep a high profile.'

'I saw you on the news the other day making your speech in the house. Your calls for increased government funding for residential social care sounded very impressive. Always popular with the voters that one, shame no political party has had the guts to deal with the issue properly. Your chance to make a bit of a name for yourself.'

Giles knew that Hugo was not being entirely sincere with his remarks.

'As you should know Hugo it's a subject very close to my heart, I'm determined the issue will be resolved during this parliament,' said Giles defiantly. 'Anyway do tell how you plan to help further my political ambitions. And you might need to tell me what you expect in return.'

'Very cynical of you Giles, you are my long term investment, let me explain what I propose.'

Hugo adjusted his posture in the comfortable leather swivel chair and looked at Giles seated on the other side of the impressive walnut desk.

'I understand that the government books aren't exactly balancing at the moment Giles. The NHS sucks more and more money away, new drugs don't come cheap do they? I also understand that the government has had to renege on its legal commitment to the overseas aid budget. Those third world countries are going to make a bit of a fuss when they can't afford medicines for their citizens. Just as well most of them don't have the same electoral systems in place as we do.'

Giles was listening patiently, not quite sure where Hugo was going with this.

'As you know Condrone is doing incredibly well for Valerian. It's a great drug and I feel it should be more easily available for as many people as possible, all over the world as well as here in the UK.'

'So I am proposing that as part of Valerian's wish to be recognised as a philanthropic company, you and I hold a joint press conference where you will announce a groundbreaking agreement between my company and your government. You have negotiated for the price of Condrone to the NHS to be halved and for my arthritis treatment to be provided free of charge to whichever African country you like to choose. Probably one of those you are about to reduce the funding to I would imagine. It will give the opportunity for tens of thousands more patients to benefit from a medicine that will change their lives. And you might like to mention all the extra money the NHS will be saving by not having to replace so many worn out hips and knees.'

Hugo leaned back in his chair and waited for the well deserved gratitude of his old school friend and business partner.

CHAPTER 18

The co-pilot had collected the pilot in her little Audi TT and they made their way west along the coast to the officially named Brighton City Airport, known to everybody locally as Shoreham Airport.

Laura parked the car outside the Art Deco style terminal building and she and Sam exited the car. Sam feeling the buzz of nervous excitement he always got before a flight and Laura feeling, just nervous. Well, terrified in fact.

She had been full of bravado when she had dropped the not too subtle hint about being prepared to be Sam's co-pilot but she had also been just a little full of wine. But Laura was not the type to show fear. She had been reminding herself of that for several days now after Sam had called to invite her out for a spin. She had to agree the setting was fantastic and the weather was set fair, a gloriously sunny day with not a cloud in sight.

'Should be a nice smooth flight today Laura, no clouds, nice stable air, not too much turbulence,' said Sam.

Any turbulence is too much turbulence, thought Laura.

'What kind of plane are we flying in Sam?' she asked. 'How many propellers does it have?'

'Just the one,' said Sam. 'But it does have two wings. It's called a Piper Warrior.'

Sam had arranged to hire the plane for the afternoon from his flying club. They walked into the old white painted building, it had a real sense of the 1930's to it. They made their way up a wooden staircase onto the wide walk around balcony of the whispering gallery, and on through into the offices of Sky Leisure Aviation.

Laura enjoyed the panoramic views from the windows across the airfield back towards the South Downs with the imposing Lancing College chapel beyond the far end of the runway. Sam meanwhile was filling out the required paperwork for the flight. He collected a couple of headsets and handed one of them to Laura.

'We're going to need to wear these during the flight. It's very noisy in the cabin and we talk to each other using them,' he said. 'I, as Captain, also get to talk to air traffic control through them.'

'Yes Captain,' said the co-pilot. 'Just tell me when to shut up.'

They took the outside metal staircase from the office down to the apron of the airport. They walked across the tarmac and Sam pointed out their aircraft. A white and blue low winged plane which Laura thought looked rather old.

'It is rather old,' said Sam. 'It's just had its fortieth birthday I believe. Don't worry it's gone forty years and hasn't crashed yet so we should be OK today.'

The words plane and crash didn't go together too well for Laura but she wasn't about to back out now.

Sam had in his hand a small book, which he said was called a check list.

'Before every flight there's a whole list of safety checks you need to make, so we use a list like this to make sure we don't forget anything.'

Laura followed Sam around the aircraft as he inspected every surface for signs of wear and tear or damage. He checked the condition of the wheels and landing gear. He made sure the ailerons on the wings moved freely up and down and the rudder on the tail from side to side. The engine canopy was lifted and the oil level checked. Then Sam went under each wing with a small measuring cylinder.

'What are you doing there Sam?' said Laura seeming a little puzzled as Sam appeared to be draining fuel into the cylinder before inspecting it.

'Just making sure there's no water in the fuel tanks, sometimes you can get condensation forming. It's heavier than the fuel so goes to the bottom of the tank. Planes don't run too well on water.' Sam had sensed Laura was a little apprehensive and was trying to use humour to lighten the tension she obviously felt.

With the external checks completed they clambered over the wing and into the little bucket seats inside. Pilot on the left and co-pilot on the right.

'Just a few instrument and control checks now and we'll be ready to get the engine started.'

He checked the control column was moving as it should and turned around to watch the ailerons and elevator moving properly.

'The rudder is controlled with your feet,' he said pressing right then left. 'And you steer on the ground using your feet, not that little wheel in front of you.'

Laura had noticed that she was sitting behind an identical set of controls to Sam and wondered if she needed to do anything with them.

'Only if I pass out,' said Sam.

All was ready. Sam opened his small window and shouted 'Clear propeller'. 'It's going to get a bit noisy now so headsets on.'

'Can you hear me alright Laura?'

'Yes Captain.'

'No need to call me Captain, Sir will do nicely.'

Sam turned the key and the engine coughed. The propeller made half a turn and stopped.

'She is forty,' Sam reminded Laura.

Another couple of twists of the key and the propeller turned with intention, the plane shuddered and the engine roared into life spinning the propeller into a blur. Sam adjusted the revs with a small lever and put in a radio call to Shoreham Tower.

'Shoreham Tower this is Golf, Papa, Romeo, Sierra, India with information Delta. Request permission to taxi to two zero for a VFR flight to the east.'

'Golf, Sierra, India cleared to taxi to hold for two zero.'

Laura had got the message to keep quiet but hadn't understood a word of what had just been said. But a couple of weeks ago she had made her decision that she trusted Sam, she was about to find out if she was right or not.

Sam released the brakes with his feet, increased the revs and Sierra India taxied gently forwards. He started to steer the plane with his feet and they passed by the tower on their left before turning to the right, or starboard as Sam called it.

They passed by the Avgas filling station.

'We don't need to fill up with fuel, we've got plenty for what we're doing today.'

The plane speeded up a little as it trundled along the taxiway parallel to the runway before it turned ninety degrees to the left and came to a halt. Sam applied the brakes.

'One or two more checks and we'll be on our way,' said Sam. He increased the power and used the key to check both sets of ignition systems making sure there was no loss of revs with either circuit.

Power checks were completed and Sam pressed the small button on the control yoke to speak to air traffic control.

'Sierra India ready for departure.'

'Line up and roll when you are ready Sierra India, no immediate traffic,' came the reply.

The plane moved forward and turned left onto the runway lining up with the white centre line.

Laura felt surprisingly calm.

No turning back now.

'Here we go,' said Sam through the intercom.

The noise became deafening as Sam gently increased the engine revs to maximum. He released the brakes and the plane moved forwards, slowly at first but quickly accelerating.

Laura watched the dials in front of her moving as the plane sped down the runway. When the speed indicator was reading sixty knots Sam gently pulled back on the control column and the nose of the Warrior rose as the aircraft left the ground.

'You're flying!' said Sam. 'We keep the speed at seventy knots as we climb and when we reach six hundred feet we'll start to turn to the east.'

'Sam this is fantastic,' said Laura as she watched the ground recede beneath them.

'You can help us by keeping a good lookout for other aircraft Laura. Air traffic said it was fairly quiet today but we don't want any near misses.'

'Don't we have radar or something like that?'

'You are the something like that,' said Sam.

The plane banked in a climbing turn to the left, they had just passed over the coast line and were now above the sea, sparkling blue, dotted with sailing boats, several hundred feet below. Sam allowed the plane to climb to two thousand feet and then gently pushed the control column forwards while reducing the revs to establish level flight.

'Golf Sierra India has cleared the field to the east.'

'Roger Sierra India keep a close watch and have a good flight.'

They passed by the single remaining chimney of a retired coal fired power station and were soon abeam Brighton. Laura noticed a flock of seagulls milling around in front of them.

'Is this where we get our revenge on the seagulls?' she said.

'More likely their friends are getting revenge on us right now. On your car to be precise,' joked Sam.

They had already passed over both piers and could see the city of Brighton sprawling back from the sea onto the lower slopes of the Downs beyond. The main A23 was busy and looked like a shining river of steel flowing into Brighton.

Laura looked across to her left. 'There's the school I never got to go to,' as she pointed out the famous girls school Roedean.

'You need to have very wealthy parents to be able to go there,' replied Sam.

'Time to carry out a few more checks,' said Sam as he carried out the standard FREDA checks. Fuel, radio, engine, direction indicator, altitude. 'All good.'

'Are you feeling OK Laura? No air sickness? Bag under the seat if needed.'

'I'm fine thanks but I'm desperate for the loo, can we stop for a moment?'

Sam looked across in horror, saw Laura's face and realised she was winding him up. A good sign, she must be feeling more relaxed. He returned her smile.

'I've been meaning to ask, by the way, what happens if the engine stops?'

'What you mean while we're still in the air?'

'Funny man. Does the plane fall out of the sky?'

'It just turns into a glider,' said Sam. 'And you need to find somewhere to land fairly quickly. We could try the beach down there, it looks quite flat with the tide out.'

'Happy to take your word for it Captain.'

They had just crossed over the Greenwich Meridian Line, out of the Western Hemisphere and into the eastern half of the world, and Sam was allowing the plane to descend gently by reducing the power. He thought it would be fun to fly along just above the line of the white chalk cliffs on their left.

They passed over the port of Newhaven. A ferry had just slipped out of the harbour and started its voyage across the English Channel to Dieppe in France.

'Would you like to try flying it Laura? There's a full set of controls in front of you and I can just take back over whenever.'

'Thanks, maybe next time, I'm just enjoying the view.'

They were passing over the mouth of the Cuckmere. The river seemed to be literally cascading over the beach and into the sea, changing its colour from blue to brown. A few people were paddling and one or two braver souls had ventured out further to swim in the chilly looking water.

'See this row of chalk cliffs in front Sam. There are seven hills and they are called The Seven Sisters. If you count carefully there are actually eight hills. I guess the eight sisters doesn't sound as good though.'

'I had never noticed that,' said Sam. 'And I'm quite familiar with the coast just here. I help out from time to time with medical work on the local lifeboats.'

'Planes and boats, you lead an interesting life Sam. I'd like to hear more about your lifeboat work sometime.'

Sam had reduced the height further still and it gave Laura an exhilarating sense of speed as the ground rushed past. The plane was, after all, flying at nearly a hundred miles an hour. They were actually lower now than the tall cliffs on their left. There was a bright red and white lighthouse reaching up from the rocks below and Laura could see areas on the beach close by where large parts of the chalk had fallen away from the fragile cliff.

'Beachy Head,' said Sam.

A spectacular sight and one of the most famous stretches of coastline in England. And not just famous for its stunning beauty. It was the spot where people only too frequently chose to end their lives. Laura and Sam both knew that and neither felt it right to mention it. The moment was far too good to spoil.

Beyond Beachy Head the resort town of Eastbourne came into view just as the coastline retreated past the eastern end of the South Downs.

Sam warned Laura he was going to increase power in order to gain altitude.

'Don't want to go scaring all those nice old folks having a snooze in their deck chairs.'

The engine noise increased as the nose of the Warrior lifted and Laura could see only blue sky through the front screen of the plane.

Sam banked the plane to the left and navigated the Warrior in a northerly direction, away from the coast and glancing over his shoulder, back towards Shoreham, saw a bank of towering grey clouds rising in the distance.

'They look as if they could be thunder clouds forming. It can sometimes happen quite suddenly on hot days like this. We definitely don't want to have a close encounter with a cumulonimbus cloud.'

'So if it's alright with you we'll make our way back home.'

It was alright with Laura to head back home and she indicated her approval to Sam. It sounded like thunder clouds could lead to some of that turbulence Sam had mentioned earlier.

They were flying at three thousand feet and heading in a westerly direction. Laura noticed a large orange coloured passenger jet in front and above them, probably returning from some Costa back to Gatwick.

'Well spotted co-pilot, she's way above us, it's the reason we're not allowed to fly much higher than we already are in this part of the country.'

They flew over the conical shape of Mount Caburn and below them Laura could see as many as twenty brightly coloured parachutes pirouetting in the air.

'Paragliders,' said Sam, 'They won't come up this high.'
'I hope,' he added.

They passed to the south of Lewes, with its semi ruined castle in the middle of the town and started to follow the main A27 road.

'All we have to to now is follow the route of the A27 and it will guide us back to Shoreham. The thunder clouds are just off to our north so they shouldn't be a problem.' Sam, having enjoyed teasing Laura earlier, was now doing his best to reassure her. He had been more concerned than he had admitted to Laura when he had seen the towering clouds.

Sam listened to the automated airport information on the radio and then put in a call to Shoreham Tower.

'This is Golf, Papa, Romeo, Sierra, India with information Foxtrot returning to you for landing. Currently five miles east of the field at three thousand feet, heading two seven zero.'

'Roger Sierra, India. Join base leg. One Cherokee ahead of you, report finals.'

'It's going to get a bit busy now Laura, a few pre landing checks to make. If you can just keep an eye open for the traffic in front of us.'

Sam reduced the power to allow a descent to the field circuit height of eleven hundred feet. He pulled out a black knob on the dashboard in front as he eased off on the throttle. 'That's called "carburettor heat",' said Sam. 'It stops ice forming in the fuel intake when we're on low revs.'

Laura could see the airfield off to the left in front of them with its triangle of runways, two green and one black. They were flying at ninety degrees to the direction of the asphalt runway and still descending.

Sam pulled a lever to lower the flaps and pushed forwards on the control column. The view over the lowered nose of the plane improved considerably. More land, less sky.

As the runway on their left became closer Sam banked the plane and turned with ailerons and rudder, lining them up with the centre of the runway. They were still about two miles out.

'I think the traffic in front has just landed,' said Laura.

'Golf, Sierra, India finals to land two zero.'

'Continue your approach Sierra India.'

The plane in front exited the runway to the left.

'Cleared to land Sierra India.'

The runway was getting bigger and bigger in the view in front of them. The ground ahead seemed to be coming towards them more quickly as they got closer. Sam made tiny adjustments with his hands and feet on the controls to keep them straight on the centre line. The plane passed overhead the dual carriageway of the main road, crossed the field perimeter fence and the runway was directly beneath them.

Laura hadn't realised how tightly she had been gripping her thighs. The palms of her hands felt damp.

Sam cut the power completely and pulled the control column back to raise the nose and the plane touched down, with only a slight bump, on the main wheels under each wing. The Warrior slowed and the nose wheel gently settled down bringing the runway back into view. Sam allowed the plane to taxi to the nearest exit from the runway and steered their way back to park on the apron.

They were sitting in the Hummingbird Cafe back in the terminal building. For one of them relaxing after, and for the other recovering from, their flight.

'That was great Sam I really enjoyed it. Perhaps we could do it again sometime. I think I'd be keen to have a go at the controls,' said Laura from over the rim of her mug of tea.

'Anytime. You were an excellent co-pilot, and great company. Thanks for not needing the loo.'

Sam was quiet for a moment, he was about to change the subject. 'I've been thinking about what you said about those young patients in your mum's care home. It all just doesn't feel quite right to me, my instinct is telling me something's wrong.'

'I asked about my mum's medication when I went to see her last week and just as I thought, she is taking Condrone, that arthritis drug you mentioned.'

'If you think something might be wrong Sam then my journalistic instinct is telling me there might be a story to be written. I think you and I need to join forces and investigate this further.'

Although it had been five years since he had lost Gilly he found himself feeling a little guilty that increasingly he was liking the idea of joining forces with Laura.

CHAPTER 19

Sam had given some thought to what Laura had said about her mother and some of the other care home residents. He called three more of his Condrone patients in and carried out mini mental examinations on them. For their sakes he was relieved that they seemed to have no impairment of memory. But all three had only been on the new drug for a few months, Laura's mother had apparently been on Condrone for at least three years.

He had encouraged Laura to ask at the care home if she could be allowed to inspect the medication records of some of the other residents. He had hoped that, as a journalist with the local paper, she might be allowed access if she told the manager she was investigating a drug for possible side effects. After all Laura had said that the staff seemed genuinely concerned for the well being of their residents.

He was sitting at home with Ella who, since she had prised out some details about the mystery woman who had suddenly appeared in her father's life, had become more protective than usual. They were having an 'at home' evening together. Take away Chinese followed by a movie was the plan.

Sam's mobile rang. 'Hi Laura how are you doing,' said Sam as he got up from the sofa to search for a little privacy. Ella frowned, her evening with Dad had been disturbed.

'I'm good Sam thanks. I won't keep you, I know you and Ella have an evening planned. I just wanted to feed back to you how my enquires at the care home have gone.'

Sam thought that didn't sound very promising.

'I made a request to the manager of the home, a Mrs Prior, on behalf of the Herald, to take a look at the medication records of a few of the residents. I tried to make it sound official, an investigation on behalf of the Herald into possible side effects caused a drug some of her residents were likely to be taking. I even offered to approach their relatives to get consent. She said that sort of thing was above her pay grade but I persuaded her to ask the boss at head office. As you probably know Forever Autumn is part of a big national chain of care homes.'

'Anyway,' Laura continued. 'I've just called them back to enquire if there was any news. I was put on hold for ages and then somebody, apparently from head office, came on the line. Didn't say who he was, but left me in no doubt that I was definitely not going to be inspecting any medication records, with or without relatives consent. Said they were confidential and the property of the care home. He told me I wasn't to cause trouble or bother the staff. I think I've been warned off Sam.'

Sam wasn't too surprised at Laura being refused access to the records but he was surprised the care home hadn't appeared concerned for the safety of their residents. After all it was in their interests to keep their guests as healthy as possible. Keep the beds filled and keep the fees coming in.

'Well it was a good try,' said Sam. 'Any thoughts as to what we should do next?'

'Oh yes,' said Laura. 'I have an idea. Not sure you're going to like it though. Best you get back to Ella and we'll have a chat about our next move tomorrow.'

Sam returned to the living room to find Ella concentrating hard on her iPhone and tapping away on the screen at a speed only teenagers are capable of. She didn't look up when Sam sat back down next to her. Sam had the strong feeling she was ignoring him as punishment for taking the call from Laura.

He waited patiently until it seemed Ella thought he had suffered   enough. She put down her mobile and looked at her dad.

He was not going to apologise for having taken the call. He could do tantrums as well.

'So shall we get our order for Chinese take away in then Ells?'

They looked at the menu together on line using Sam's iPad. Half a crispy duck, chilli beef, sweet and sour prawns, mixed seasonal vegetables and special fried rice. Sam nearly forgot the prawn crackers, that would have been a disaster. He placed the order.

Tonight was the anniversary of Gilly's birthday and Sam and Ella always celebrated the occasion with Chinese food just as they had done when they were a family of three.

Sam opened a bottle of Prosecco and they started to watch their movie while waiting for the food to arrive. It was Gilly's favourite film. The Bridges of Madison County, it had always made her cry and Ella and Sam would probably continue with that tradition too.

Sam and Laura were out walking along the seafront. Summer was being typically English and after a couple of weeks of glorious sunshine the weather had broken. The thunder clouds had been a sign of change. The day was gloomy and cool with a light drizzle of rain. The sea no longer looked blue and had reverted to its more familiar grey green hue.

Sam had just sprung open a large umbrella and he was happy to have Laura close, both of them feeling comfortably cosy sheltering from the weather.

'So what devious plan have you been working on?' said Sam. 'I'm glad you're not the sort of girl to give up easily.'

'You don't get a scoop on premiership footballers by giving up,' Laura said.

'That reminds me,' said Sam. 'When you've told me your plan I have, in fact, a football related piece of news to share with you.'

'Well it's clear the care home owners are not going to just let us take a look at the residents medical records and I'm assuming, because it's not your part of town, that you have none of your patients there. So I think we need to be a bit more adventurous.'

'How do you fancy meeting my mum? Here's what I think we should do.'

Laura explained her plan to Sam who started to look a little worried at the part he was being asked to play.

'Don't worry Sam, nobody at the care home will know who you are. You're not going to risk losing your licence.'

Thoughts of Sam's licence made Laura suddenly feel a need to confess about her involvement in the matter of the complaint made against him.

'Talking about your licence Sam I really do need to come clean about something with you.'

Sam actually thought it was quite funny when Laura related the story of how she had been passed the lead by Peter Weller and stalked him to the pier looking for scandal. 'We must thank that seagull sometime for arranging to share your lunch,' he laughed.

Laura felt relieved to have been able to get her guilty secret out in the open. 'Well I'm glad I've got that out of the way Sam. I was really worried you wouldn't want to talk to me ever again.' She quickly brought the subject back to something more comfortable. 'So what football related news have you got to share with me then?'

'I was in surgery this morning when Anita put a call through to me. She said it was a Dr Hugo Thomson. I was in the middle of a consultation and I didn't make the connection at first, but of course it was my old adversary from medical school, the one who is now owner of Valerian

Pharmaceuticals, you know the company that makes Condrone.'

'He said he had been meeting with his Chief Scientific Officer and had just found out about my phone call. He said it was great I had got in touch and that we should get together. He wondered if I and a partner would care to join him and a few friends in the hospitality suite at Stamford Bridge next Saturday. Chelsea are at home to Liverpool in the season opener.'

'So I was wondering if you might be free next weekend?'

'Would love to come Sam, you know me and footballers. But doesn't it make you wonder what your old friend is hoping for in return?'

Ten thirty in the morning and Sam was having a planned recovery break in the middle of surgery. Sometimes he needed to use the twenty minutes as an opportunity to catch up on a patient list that was running late but today he had been working to time. He wandered into Anita's office with two drug company sponsored cups in hand. Strong coffee as usual for Sam and camomile tea for Anita. One needed stimulating and one needed settling. It's just that the drinks were the wrong way round.

'You know how sometimes you get a little tense Sam when I tell you there has been some correspondence that we need to discuss?' said Anita.

'I really don't need to hear about another complaint right in the middle of morning surgery Anita,' said Sam with a look of resignation on his face.

'Not a letter of complaint Sam. A letter about a complaint though. In fact two letters to be precise.'

It had been four weeks since the complaint hearing and Sam had been become increasingly tense about the prospect of hearing news of the outcome. He immediately felt a churning sensation in his stomach.

'Two letters Anita? Which shall I read first?'

His Practice Manager handed one of them over, the less official looking of the two.

The envelope was addressed to Dr Sam Preston, but as was their usual practice Anita had opened it already.

Sam read the type written letter inside.

Dear Dr Preston

I am writing to inform you that I have asked NHS England to proceed no further, at the present time, with the complaint I raised against you of inappropriate touching. I hope that your attendance at the hearing can be regarded as sufficient punishment for what you did to me.

As a GP I think you will now realise that you are in a vulnerable position and I strongly suggest you concentrate on becoming a better doctor rather than becoming involved in matters which are none of your business.

Yours sincerely

Amanda Collins

Sam inspected the letter and the envelope but found no sign of a return address. The only identifier was a postmark for Cambridge. He decided to make no comment until he had read the second piece of correspondence. He gestured for Anita to pass it over. It looked official, in a window envelope, with his name and qualifications as well as his surgery address.

Re Complaint Ms. Amanda Collins

Dear Dr Preston

I am writing to inform you that we have received correspondence from Ms Collins stating that she does not wish to progress any further with her complaint against you.

She has specifically stated that she does not wish for the original complaint to be withdrawn and as such the correspondence and minutes relating to the complaint hearing will remain on your file.

They may be referred to in the event of any similar complaint being made against you in the future.

Yours sincerely

James Finlay

Chief Executive

NHS Area Brighton

Anita looked at Sam waiting for his response. She wasn't sure what to expect. He said nothing. Anita sensed the tension developing in the room and felt obliged to break the silence.

'Well at least it's over Sam, your licence is not at risk anymore, but I can understand if you are feeling more angry than relieved. As I told them at the hearing the entire episode has been complete nonsense.'

'Yes Anita, thanks I am relieved of course but it feels as if I'm regarded as being guilty anyway. "The correspondence will remain on file." Bloody cheek.'

'I'm the victim here not that damned woman. And what did she mean about "matters which are none of my business"?'

Sam calmed himself down and thought for a moment.

'I think I will give the MDS another call Anita, this isn't fair, I should be able to clear my name completely.'

'You know me Sam,' said Anita. 'I always like to look on the bright side. At least it didn't get into the local paper despite that journalist being there.'

Sam decided not to tell her that maybe Laura had had a hand in that.

'That's true. But I do wonder who that other guy was sitting next to him at the hearing.'

Sam resumed his morning surgery and was able to absorb himself in his patient workload. He needed to break some bad news to a seventy year old man whose prostate cancer appeared to be spreading. It put Sam's problems firmly back into perspective.

Having made up his mind to contact the Medical Defence Society, as soon as surgery was finished he made the call. He was put through to somebody he hadn't dealt with before but was reassured that his adviser today had all the relevant information on the screen in front of him. Sam related the contents of the letters.

'Well that must be a great relief to you doctor knowing this is all over, thank you for telling us,' was the reply he had not been wanting.

'How on earth can you say that?' said Sam. 'The case hasn't gone away at all, it's just been filed for future reference. One more false, made up, complaint like that and, added to this one, my career would be over. The complaint needs to be thrown out and my slate wiped completely clean.'

'Yes I can understand you feeling that Dr Preston, you have my sympathies but the advice from the MDS here is that you should just put it behind you and move on. At least there is no prospect of you and the MDS being dragged into compensation litigation.'

'I think your concern should be about me,' retorted Sam. 'Not about any compensation your insurers might have had to pay.'

But Sam knew he wasn't going to get anywhere and angrily terminated the call.

He stormed out to Anita's office to offload his frustration but perhaps fortunately for both of them she had gone out to lunch.

Sam calmed himself down with some deep breaths and called Laura to pass on the news.

CHAPTER 20

Sam had been to Chelsea's home ground in South West London many times but had never come close to spending the large sums of money needed to invest in platinum hospitality tickets.

Laura of course had done her research well and knew she would have to glam herself up for such an occasion.

'This isn't really about the football,' she had told him. 'It's about looking good and impressing people.'

Naturally Sam strongly disagreed with Laura, having been a lifelong Chelsea fan. The day would be all about the football match for him.

They travelled by train, first class, from Brighton to London Victoria and jumped on a District Line train for Fulham Broadway. They exited the tube station for the short walk to the stadium. Crowds were starting to gather and the pubs were doing a brisk trade. There were the usual ticket touts selling and buying and a born again Christian preacher sharing the words of his God through an amplifier. They ignored the tempting smell of onions frying at the hot dog kiosk and made their way along to the ground floor entrance of the East Stand. The kick off was at 3 o'clock and they had arrived two hours early to enjoy the food and drink that was coming their way, apparently for free.

Hospitality was on the third floor and a gold mirrored lift was their method of transport upwards. They surveyed their reflections in the mirrors.

'You look really smart Sam, thanks for making an effort. New shirt and tie. If you're trying to impress me you have succeeded.'

'I'd rather have my Chelsea shirt on and be sitting in the Shed end, but thanks,' replied Sam. 'As for you, you look quite stunning.'

Laura could tell Sam meant what he had just said. She had put her hair up and invested in a new dress, making sure blue was the predominant colour, finished off with a linen jacket. Leather pumps had been chosen for both style and comfort.

She felt it appropriate to take Sam's arm as they exited the lift.

They walked along a thickly carpeted corridor to the reception desk. They had no tickets as such and Sam still wondered if they would be let in.

He need not have worried.

'Ah yes, Dr Sam Preston and partner. Welcome to Stamford Bridge,' said the receptionist. 'Let me take you through to Dr Thomson, I know he is expecting you.'

They were ushered in to the large sumptuously decorated hospitality area which was already thronging with people. There was a buzzing atmosphere of excitement and anticipation at the start of a new football season. Drinks had been flowing for some time.

Hugo spotted them as they made their entrance and left his other guests to come over and greet them.

'Sam, how good to see you again after all this time. Thank you so much for coming. How many years is it since we qualified?'

Sam resisted saying, twenty for me and nineteen for you.

'Must be about twenty years now Hugh, time flies.'

'Indeed it does, indeed it does. I'm Hugo now, to my friends, by the way.'

'So sorry to hear about Gilly but who is this lovely creature you have with you here. I hope you are going to introduce me.'

Sam was worried Laura might do her own introduction after that remark but a quick glance reassured him that she appeared to be happy playing her role as supporting actor.

'This is my friend Laura Anderson. Laura this is Hugh Thomson, or Hugo as he now apparently wishes to be known.'

'Come on over the pair of you. Let me get you some champagne. Best drink it now in case the team loses.'

'And best not say that too loudly in here Hugo,' advised Sam.

They were seated at the end of a long table. Hugo was entertaining several other guests for the afternoon, one of whom looked very familiar to both Sam and Laura.

A four course meal was being served, with matching wines for each course. The food was good but not exactly exciting. Not up to 64 Degrees standards. They were distracted from their eating when they noticed some members of the Chelsea squad, presumably those not being called into action for the afternoon, doing the rounds of the tables.

Laura glanced up, looked panicked and whispered urgently to Sam, 'I need the loo', and was gone. Sam wondered what had happened. Something she'd eaten?

Sam was readily granted a selfie with one of his heroes and was feeling very pleased with himself when Laura returned cautiously.

'Are you OK? What was all that about? You left in a bit of a hurry.'

'I'm fine, has he gone?' replied Laura.

'Has who gone?'

'Matt Bryant. He used to play for Brighton. I didn't realise he'd been transferred to Chelsea. Don't think he would have been too pleased to see me after what I wrote about him last year!'

A bell sounded. It was the 'Time to take your seats' warning.

Some of the guests didn't seem too bothered about finding their seats outside to watch the match, and that included Hugo and his familiar looking friend, but Sam hurried Laura out. He could hear the music and chanting as the teams entered the arena and it gave him a sense of excitement and anxiety. Watching his favourite team was often not a relaxing experience. They found their comfortable padded seats in the second tier of the stand overlooking the half way line. The view of the match couldn't have been better. The blue shirts of Chelsea and the red shirts of Liverpool shone vividly in the bright afternoon sun as the away side kicked off to start the match.

The referee blew the half time whistle. Chelsea were leading Liverpool by a goal to nil. Sam was a nervous but happy man.

They made their way back to the bar for further refreshments.

'How's it going Sam?' said Hugo, 'We heard at least one roar in here.'

'One up Hugo. You not watching it?'

'My principal interest today is in keeping my guests happy Sam. You may remember I couldn't even get in the thirds at medical school.'

'Let me introduce you to one of my other guests here. I'm sure you must have recognised him.'

'Giles. This is my old friend from Guy's, Sam Preston, and his partner Laura ....,' he hesitated.

'Anderson,' said Laura. 'Nice to meet you Mr Barrington.'

Of course, thought Sam. The Minister for Health.

'A pleasure to meet you Laura but please call me Giles. The press call me all sorts of things but rarely Mr Barrington. And good to meet you Sam. Hugo tells me you are a GP in Brighton. Thank you for your service to the NHS.'

As Hugo had intended, Sam felt flattered to be meeting the Health Minister even if his general impression of him as a politician had never been very favourable.

'Pleased to meet you too Giles. I didn't realise my old friend Hugo was moving in such lofty circles these days.' Sam tried, but failed, to make his words not sound sarcastic.

'Oh Giles and I go back a long way, we were at school together,' butted in Hugo. 'And of course we now have many shared interests. I'm a great supporter of our National Health Service.'

And so you should be thought Sam. The NHS spends a fortune on your drug.

Not surprisingly Giles was drawn back to Laura.

'And what do you do for a living Laura?' asked Giles, politicians naturally being excellent at remembering people's names. 'I assume you would be a nurse?' he added, rather letting himself down.

'Me a nurse? Goodness no. I'm a journalist. I work for the Brighton and Hove Herald.'

That jolted Giles back to attention and he tried to remember how many glasses of wine he had drunk.

'A GP and a journalist, an unusual combination. So how did the two of you meet?' he asked.

Laura had also had a glass or two of wine and said 'Oh Sam was accused by a patient of being a pervert and I was sent out to get the exclusive.'

Hugo suddenly looked very uncomfortable.

Sam hurriedly added, 'A totally false accusation of course that was completely without foundation. Wouldn't have minded having a bit more support from the NHS though,' pointedly looking at the Health Minister.

'I saw you on Newsnight last week Giles.' said Laura, keen to move the conversation on. 'I have to say I wholeheartedly agree with everything you said about social care funding. It's about time a government got to grips with that one. It's a subject very close to my heart. My mother has been diagnosed with dementia, she's only sixty, and is now being cared for in a dementia home. I have had to sell her house to pay the fees. Fifty thousand a year, and I don't know what I'll do when the money runs out.'

Giles had been staring at Hugo with an angry look on his face but seemed to take a genuine interest in what Laura had to say.

'Yes, yes I'm going to stake my political career on sorting this one out. I'm so sorry to hear about your mother Laura. Which care home did you say she was living in?'

'I didn't say actually, but she's in a nice place in Hove called Forever Autumn. Have you heard of it?'

'Goodness no, there are thousands of care homes, all doing a magnificent job looking after people in their golden years sadly suffering from the curse of dementia. But I'm always on the look out for suitable places to make political announcements, for the cameras you understand. Perhaps I can give you an exclusive sometime,' he joked.

The bell sounded again, the second half was about to start. Sam made their excuses and dragged Laura away from her conversation, back to their seats. He was ready to return to the real action of the day. The teams were welcomed back to the pitch by forty two thousand voices and the match restarted.

Back inside hospitality Giles was fuming. He glared at his host. 'You absolute bloody idiot. Look what you've done. For both our sakes I hope this doesn't backfire on us.'

The referee blew his whistle to end the game. There had been a very tense five minutes of added time due to injuries and Sam had been on the edge of his seat as his beloved Chelsea had managed to hang on for a narrow victory. A good start to the season. He and Laura joined the crowd returning inside eager to enjoy more of the hospitality and relive the highlights of the game.

Hugo was sitting alone in a corner with a large drink. No sign of Giles his Health Minister friend.

'That was brilliant Hugo, a great match, thank you so much.'

'Excellent, glad the team won of course.' It was clear Hugo couldn't care less about the result.

'Has your friend Giles had to leave?' said Laura glancing around.

'Yes he had some matters of state to attend to I believe. He doesn't have that much interest in football, more of a hockey man I think. But I'm pleased you had the opportunity to meet him, both of you. You never know Sam, he could be of some help in your career.'

'Let's get some more drinks in,' he waved across at a waitress who hurried over. 'Much better service here than at the old Guy's bar eh? I just wanted to take a few minutes of your time to reassure you about the safety profile of our drug Condrone.'

CHAPTER 21

Immediately after the death of Gilly, Sam and Ella had
continued to live in the old family home in the Kemp Town
district of Brighton. It had Gilly's decorative style all over it.
After her career as a nurse had been prematurely ended
by the arthritis she had thrown herself at the task of getting
the home exactly as she had wanted it. She had been both
design consultant and project manager, although because
her hands and wrists were so painful, the manual labour
had eventually been outsourced to a decorating company.
Gilly's taste had been Bohemian with choices of colours
reflecting not just the fiery tones of her hair but also her
lively outgoing personality. She had combined deep
greens with mustard yellows and vivid pink. She had loved
the paintings of Gaugin and prints of his work were
displayed on the walls of the living room. Exotic pot plants
had been loved and well cared for by Gilly but with her
passing many of the plants had died too.

At first it had been a great comfort to Sam and Ella to
continue to live in the style and colours of Gilly. They were
clinging on to the memories, trying not to let her go. But
after a few months, when they were starting to emerge
from the shock and the grief, they realised the vivid
colours were preventing them from making that move
onwards with their lives. They both knew they needed to
let go and make a fresh start. Old memories needed not
to be forgotten but stored away, available to relive when
the time was right. So they made the painful but necessary
decision to sell the old family home and move on.

It was now just the two of them and they had felt it
sensible to downsize. They quickly settled on a modest
three bedroomed terraced house not too far from the old

family home. Still convenient for Sam's work and easy access to school and then university for Ella. They even made some cash out of the transaction which was put aside for when Ella would need a deposit for a place of her own.

Without the inspiration of his wife Sam struggled with the issue of decor despite Ella none too subtly leaving out design magazines opened at pages with makeovers she approved of. He failed to take the hint and eventually professional help was sought with instructions given to avoid the style from the former home. Their place was now decorated less extravagantly but equally impressively in more calming chalky shades from the colour charts of Farrow and Ball. Sam was sure Gilly would understand.

They had settled in well and were comfortable. Sam was an easy going father and Ella a sometimes more than dutiful daughter.

Ella had realised with her mother's passing that it was now her role to keep an eye on her dad, it's what Mum would have wanted. She had not considered moving away to another city for university and had somehow left it too late to apply for accommodation in the university halls of residence. Sam knew what she was doing and hated to admit that he hadn't tried too hard to persuade her to leave home. But generally they had found a balance with Sam concentrating on his work and Ella on her studies.

A drawback to living in that part of the city though was the parking. It was street parking only, residents permits, one per household and even with that it was often hard to find a space close to home.

Sam had walked a couple of streets away today to his parked car and had driven off to collect Laura for today's mission.

They were both now in Sam's car, a bright yellow Citroen 2CV. He and Gilly had bought Joan when they first moved to Brighton. The name had been Gilly's idea, it came from the French word for yellow. So Joan had become the fourth member of the family.

They had driven west through Brighton and were heading up the hill out of the neighbouring suburb of Hove towards Forever Autumn. Today was the day for Sam to make the acquaintance of Laura's mother and for their plan to gain access to the medication records to be actioned.

During the drive they reflected on their day at the football which, especially with Sam's team having won, they had to admit had been enjoyable. Hugo had been very welcoming, if a little clumsy, but they both had the feeling he wasn't entirely to be trusted. It was also the second time Sam had seen Hugo and Giles together and their relationship seemed to him to be a little more involved than just as old school friends.

Sam had emailed Hugo after the match to thank him for the hospitality they had been shown and had received a reply almost immediately.

'Great to have seen you both, glad you had a good day. You are both welcome anytime. And just in case you have any further concerns about our arthritis drug Condrone please don't hesitate to give me a call. I would be very happy to meet again, introduce you to Peter White my chief scientist. He could show you the statistics and evidence behind our excellent safety profile.'

Hopefully that won't be necessary, thought Sam. He would prefer it if today's detective work was just going to provide them with reassurance. But he did need that reassurance and was prepared to take the, hopefully small, risk that today's mission brought with it.

Laura, of course, thought the opposite. The journalist in her was still in search of a good story. And potentially with a politician involved, getting better all the time.

Sam indicated and turned the car left into the sweeping driveway of the care home. He needed to remind himself not to park in the space marked 'Doctor'.

It was late morning and their visit had been timed to coincide with the second medication round of the day. There were no set visiting hours, relatives were welcome at any time. They would just have to put up with the smell of lunch cooking.

They signed into the visitors book. Laura Anderson, daughter and Sam Anderson, apparently a cousin down from London for the day.

Laura's mum's room was on the ground floor at the rear of the building and they made their way along the corridor. They passed a member of staff, wearing a nurses uniform, wheeling the drugs trolley around, carrying out the task of dispensing pills and liquids to the residents. She was referring to a collection of medication charts which were clipped together and attached by a thin metal chain to the side of the cart.

'Good morning,' said Laura as they walked past but the nurse was deep in concentration studying a chart.

Sam thought to himself that they were cutting the visit a bit fine and they would need to get a move on before the nurse had progressed too far on her round.

Laura knocked on her mum's door and as usual there was no reply, so she pushed the door open and they walked in. The poor lady was clearly not having a good day. She was slouched in her wing backed chair with her head bent to one side and she had been drooling saliva down her chin. Bits of what looked like scrambled egg were clinging to a bib round her neck, left there since breakfast. Her silver hair hadn't been brushed and was greasy and wiry causing her to have a wild unkempt appearance.

'Hello Mum,' said Laura. 'I've brought somebody to see you today.'

The elderly looking lady slowly looked up but there were no signs of recognition in her face.

'She gets days like this and they've been happening more and more often recently,' Laura said to Sam. 'Sometimes I can spend ages with her and still get the feeling that she thinks I look vaguely familiar but doesn't have a clue I'm her daughter.'

'It might be best, just for today, if you don't try too hard to convince her,' said Sam. 'We are, after all, here for a reason and the sooner we get it over and done with and out of here the happier I'll feel.'

'Relax Sam, it will be fine. Take a look outside the door and see where the nurse's trolley is.'

It was parked up outside, two rooms along, the nurse, he assumed, was with the resident in her room.

'How long are you going to be able to give me?' said Sam.

'I'm good at making a fuss. How does three minutes sound?'

'Should be ok but if I get caught the shit will really hit the fan.'

'You worry too much, let's get on with it.'

Sam slipped out of the door, the nurse was nowhere to be seen, presumably still with her patient, and he disappeared round the corner, out of sight.

'Help, help, somebody please help,' Laura called from the room, loud enough to be heard two doors down but not loud enough to bring any other staff members running. 'Somethings not right with my mum.'

The nurse came hurrying out of the adjacent room, nearly bumping into the drugs trolley. She had the presence of mind to shut and lock the medication compartment before darting into Laura's mothers room.

Sam instantly moved into action. His three minute window had started.

Laura had managed to work herself into a state of frenzy and was fussing over her mother as the nurse appeared by her side.

Laura was gently shaking her mum and calling to her.
'Mum, Mum are you alright, what's happening?'
She turned her attention to the nurse.
'I've only just arrived and I've come in and Mum didn't seem responsive. I was worried she might be unconscious or something and then she started to shake all over.'
The nurse quickly took charge. 'It sounds like you're describing some sort of fit, how long did it last?'
'It felt like ages but it was probably just a few seconds,' replied Laura. 'Is she OK, can you check her over please?'
'Yes of course, now stop panicking, your mother seems fine to me, she isn't having the best of mornings. Now let's just check her vital signs.'
Out in the corridor Sam was busy at work. He could hear Laura making her fuss and had to smile at how convincing she sounded.
He had his iPhone out and had put it in camera mode. With one hand he was flipping through the medication charts and with the other he was taking photographs of as many of the charts as time would allow. He continued to monitor the sound of activity from within the room.
He had planned to check each chart for a date of birth but he found it quicker just to take pictures indiscriminately, preferably of the whole lot. There were about thirty patients on the ground floor. He had taken about a dozen photos so far.
'What are you up to young man?' A voice from behind startled Sam and sent a shock wave of adrenalin through his system. He had been caught in the act. He turned, quickly trying to think of what he could say and sighed with relief when he saw it was a confused elderly resident who was doing the challenging.
'I'm the doctor, checking the medication is correct. Best you get to the dining room, I think lunch is just being served.'

She gave him a fearsome look and shuffled off along the corridor. Sam breathed deeply and returned to his undercover work.

Back in the room, the nurse had checked pulse and breathing and had now moved on to shining a light in each of the patients eyes. Laura was trying her best not to calm down. The exact opposite of what had been instructed by the nurse.

'Has she wet herself or bitten her tongue or anything,' she said when she was worried the exam might have been nearing completion.

'Let's just check shall we?' said the nurse shifting her attentions with the torch to Sue's mouth.

'Looks fine, certainly no blood anyway,' she said. 'And I'm afraid your mum is wet a lot of the time anyway.'

'Just going to check your pad Sue.' She took a look. 'Her inco pad seems to be dry at the moment though.'

'I think Mum is starting to look a bit brighter now,' said Laura. That was the signal she had arranged with Sam for him to get the heck away from the medication trolley.

Sam took one final picture then moved away quickly and locked himself in a toilet conveniently located just along the corridor. From his hiding place he could hear Laura expressing her gratitude to the nurse and apologising for having made a fuss.

'I get so worried about her. I can't seem to stop panicking. This is all so awful, she's so young, I can't believe this is happening.'

'Well right at the moment I think you might be the one who needs medical help more than your mother. Best you try and talk to somebody about it. Get some counselling. Your mum looks fine to me. The GP will be in on Monday, we'll get her checked over thoroughly then. Maybe she needs her medication increasing again.'

'Thank you, thank you so much,' said Laura finishing up.

The nurse went back to her medication trolley to resume her round and a couple of minutes later Sam rejoined Laura in the room. She was leaning over her mother.

'Sorry about all of that Mum but it really was all in a good cause.' But although Mum might have been listening she wasn't hearing, she was miles away, in another time.

Laura and Sam waited for a carefully considered amount few minutes. Laura kissed her mum fondly on her forehead and they left the room. They signed back out at the desk and were the picture of innocence as they returned to Sam's car.

'So how did you get on? How many records did you manage to photograph?' said Laura as they headed back down the hill towards town.

'I got the lot, about thirty I reckon. I just hope the light was ok and that they're in focus,' replied Sam.

'Don't worry, there's another medication round at five o'clock. I rather enjoyed that,' said Laura making the most of Sam's anxiety.

'As the nurse said, you need therapy.'

Sam's phone lit up, unknown number and he answered on his hands-free.

'Sam Preston speaking.'

'Hello Dr Preston, sorry to trouble you on a Saturday, it's Newhaven lifeboat here. We've had a shout to attend an incident at Beachy Head. The Eastbourne crew are already out and it's been put through to us. We're going to need some medical input. Any chance you can step in?'

Sam looked across at Laura who was nodding and raising her eyebrows. Of course it's ok to go, you don't need to check with me.

'Yes sure, of course. Give me twenty minutes and I'll be with you.'

'Sorry Laura, this happens occasionally. It's one of those weekends when I'm on standby duty. Can I drop you in town and we'll meet up later to go through the photos?'

'No problem Sam, the photos can wait, we've done the hard bit. Not sure I like the sound of an incident at Beachy Head though.'

Sam dropped Laura off near Churchill Square, the main shopping area in Brighton and headed off back along the coast to Newhaven. He knew that a call to Beachy Head was going to mean only one thing. A body had been found. It would be his job to confirm death, the law required it.

He journeyed east out of Brighton, past the Marina and through the pretty village of Rottingdean, before driving up the slope of the cliffs and eventually down again into the port of Newhaven. The lifeboat station was on the west bank of the mouth of the River Ouse, just opposite where the ferries for France departed from.

The lifeboat crew were waiting for Sam. There was no particular urgency to this kind of call, not like some they went out on. He changed into a bright yellow waterproof suit and boots and made his way onto the orange and blue lifeboat which was moored up on the wooden jettied bank of the river. No spectacular launching down a slipway here.

The lifeboat powered up and they left the protected waters of the harbour. Today the sea was calm, not that Sam minded bad weather days. In fact he rather enjoyed the roller coaster ride when the waves were high. He readied himself for the job in hand as he stood at the bow of the boat, enjoying the feel and taste of the salty wind on his face. The route took them along the same path he had followed during the scenic flight with Laura. Past Seaford Head, Cuckmere Haven and Birling Gap. Crowds of people were on the beach where the cliff was low enough for a metal staircase to have been built to allow access. A row of houses stood precipitously close to the edge of the cliff and looked as if they would be at the bottom, on the beach, before long. Nature was relentlessly unforgiving to the crumbling chalk line.

The story Sam had been given was that a man walking his dog at the foot of the cliffs had actually seen a body, a person, falling through the air from the top at one of the highest points of Beachy Head. He had decided not to get too close to the site of impact and had quickly put his dog on the lead. The emergency services had been alerted and had decided the most efficient way of retrieving the body would be from the sea.

There had been no reports of phone calls from witnesses at the top. The question, as always, would be, was it a fall or a jump? Sam knew that if it was a woman the clue would be in the handbag. Female jumpers invariably left their handbags at the top. If you slipped the bag went with you.

They were now abeam the lighthouse and Sam could see where they needed to go. A couple of police officers had made their way along the beach from Eastbourne to secure the area, which was also the site of a recent fall of clean white chalk.

Sam and two other crew members went ashore in an inflatable. The tide was high and most of the chalk rocks were covered. He jumped out as the craft hit the pebble beach and with a feeling of trepidation walked over. This was not going to be a pleasant sight. Sam was sure if people knew what human bodies looked like after falling five hundred feet and crashing on to rock they would choose another method to end their lives.

There was a popular myth that if you jumped you would be already be dead by the time you reached the bottom but Sam knew from painful experience this was not the case. Not all sections of the cliff are a sheer drop to the rocks anyway. Choose the wrong place to jump and you would bounce down long rough slopes or get stuck halfway in undergrowth. Occasionally an unfortunate soul will be found only nearly dead.

Sam's sense of anxiety was increasing as he got closer, it had been quite a day already. He greeted the police and introduced himself. He noticed they had covered over the subject of his imminent examination with a blanket. The dog walker was watching morbidly from a safe distance.

'I don't think there's too much doubt about the prognosis here Doc but shall we get on with the formalities?'

The Police sergeant started to pull away the blanket.

CHAPTER 22

Sam's sense of foreboding began to be realised as soon as he caught sight of the bright red Arsenal shirt. The last time he had seen one of those was back in his surgery a couple of weeks ago.

The corpse was lying on its front, still in the position where it had impacted against the rock.

'I'll just turn him over for you sir,' said the sergeant donning a pair of rubber gloves. 'Come on lad, give me a hand,' he said to the young PC who didn't appear too keen to help.

The police officers carefully turned the body over and Sam's worst fears were confirmed. Despite the damage to the face from the fall, the body was clearly recognisable as his old friend Richard. Bad enough to see your best friend dead, but like this?

Both legs had sustained compound fractures with jagged ends of femur and tibia protruding through rough gashes in the skin. His face was caved in and the nose flattened. But the worst injury had occurred to the torso where the force of the impact, at a velocity of a hundred miles an hour, had caused the abdominal cavity to explode open allowing Richard's intestines to escape onto the pebbles in long, grey, shiny coils. Flies were already swarming round attracted by the repulsive stench. There was very little blood which at least meant death was mercifully quick.

Sam stood there stunned. He was overcome with emotion and grief but tried to maintain his composure in the company of such hardy souls as police and lifeboat crew.

'Not seen a jumper before Doc?' said the Sergeant.

The young PC came to Sam's rescue and vomited his lunch onto the shingle.

Sam made a formal declaration of death and the rescue team started to unpack the body bag and equipment needed to transport Richard's body to the mortuary.

He couldn't look any more. The sight of his friend Richard disembowelled on the rocks would stay in his memory for ever. He averted his gaze and looked upwards to the top of the cliffs towering above them and wondered what the last few moments of his friend's life must have been like. Free as a bird for five seconds, dead as a Dodo forever.

Sam had vowed he would do his best to help Richard and yet it had come to this. A lonely and desperate end to a life only half lived.

Sam and Laura were now in Sam's living room back in Kemp Town, Ella was away, staying with a uni friend for a few days, in the North of England. Laura had come over as soon as Sam had made the phone call. She had been waiting at his door by the time he had got back from Newhaven.

'It's not your fault Richard's dead Sam,' said Laura. 'There's nothing you could have done to stop that happening. I just wish you hadn't taken the call from the lifeboat station, you shouldn't have had to see your friend like that.'

Sam had described in some detail what he had witnessed at the bottom of Beachy Head.

'Can you be sure it was suicide anyway? The cliffs are very fragile there and you did say he was laying right next to a pile of chalk from a cliff fall. Maybe he was just unlucky.'

'Thanks Laura, I know you are only trying to help but I think we both know that this was no accident. He had said in surgery, last time I saw him, to give him a pill to end it all when things got too bad.'

'Well I managed to do a quick bit of research and apparently of the fifty or so people that go off Beachy

Head every year, only half are recorded as suicide, the rest are accidents or people being stupid,' replied Laura.

'I'm going to need to speak with the coroner on Monday,' said Sam. 'I think I will definitely keep quiet about what Rich said to me, I made no mention of it in the notes at the time. You are right Laura, I know what happened but there's no reason for the rest of the world to know too.'

'I guess it's fortunate,' continued Sam. 'That his end was rapid. He didn't want the indignity of a slow death alone. He was married once, but only for a short time. Poor old Rich, he wasn't really the settling down type. I don't think he had any close family at all.'

'So unless he's left a suicide note, and bearing in mind there were no witnesses at the top and the recent chalk fall at the bottom, the coroner will probably record his death as an open verdict,' said Laura. 'That must be for the best Sam.'

'Let's open a bottle of wine Laura, I think we could both do with a drink after a day like that. I'd like to raise a glass to the happy times I shared with Richard, I bet that's what he would have wanted.'

They sat down with a bottle of cold Pinot Grigio. Sam felt that he was just starting to unwind.

'Well I suppose we'd better take a look at the photos I took earlier. Goodness that feels like a week ago.' said Sam.

'Sure you are up to it?' said Laura.

'I think it would be a good distraction for us both, keep us occupied.'

The photos had automatically been streamed through the cloud to Sam's iPad and he opened the Photos app and scrolled to the images he had taken earlier. He was relieved to see that the pictures were easily of good enough quality to read. He had taken twenty nine in all.

'Best I get a pen and paper,' said Laura. 'I can write down the details as we go through.'

'Just need to write down a date of birth and whether the patient is on Condrone to start with. No names,' said Sam. 'We should quickly be able to see if there is any pattern forming.'

The process didn't take long. The results saddened and shocked Sam. The same results shocked but secretly pleased Laura. She tried to hide her excitement when she saw how deflated Sam was looking.

'We have a total of twenty two patients over sixty five and eight of those are taking Condrone. Of the seven patients sixty five and under the whole lot are on Condrone,' Laura proclaimed. She waited for Sam's response.

'It doesn't look good does it. This is strong evidence, certainly enough for me to be very worried, but it's a tiny sample of patients and it doesn't prove anything of course,' replied Sam. 'Don't forget Condrone is a massively prescribed drug. It's become the treatment of choice for arthritis since it was launched. It has strong NICE approval, the lot.'

Laura couldn't hide her disappointment at Sam's response. 'Well one things for certain we absolutely have to do something. This drug has been poisoning loads of people including my mum.'

Sam couldn't disagree. In fact he agreed with Laura but knew that their new found knowledge needed to be used very carefully.

'Massive issues are at stake here Laura. It will be argued that Condrone has benefitted tens if not hundreds of thousands of patients, many of whom might have ended up like Gilly. And don't forget how wealthy it's made Hugo and his cronies, not to mention the huge amounts of tax the government has raked in from the sales.'

Laura had to agree. 'Yes we are not exactly going to be the bringers of good news are we. Hope you weren't looking forward to a return visit to the football Sam.'

Moving forwards they would need to tread very carefully. A new plan would have to be formed.

CHAPTER 23

Monday morning and Sam knew he had to make that
difficult call to the coroner. Suicides or potential suicides
always have to be reported and it was certain the coroner
would want to hold an inquest in order to establish a
method and cause of death.

It was usually difficult getting through on the phone after
a weekend, with three days worth of deaths waiting to be
notified. Sam eventually got his call answered by the
coroners officer, a serving policeman. Like all GPs Sam
knew PC Mick Wilson well from many similar calls. Sam
had decided he wasn't going to mention that Richard was
a personal friend. Just his role as GP and his duties as the
stand in lifeboat doctor on Saturday.

'Morning Mick, Sam Preston from Kemp Town Surgery
here. Sorry I have to trouble you again but the coroner is
definitely going to be interested in this one.'

'Good morning to you Sam but being a Monday I doubt it
is,' replied PC Wilson. 'What have you got for me this
morning?'

'A jumper, or I should say a suspected jumper, from
Beachy Head Mick. I've got a double interest here
because he was my patient and I was also on duty as the
lifeboat medic on Saturday when the body was found.'

'Poor you, never a pretty sight. Where is the body now
residing? Is it over in Eastbourne or here in Brighton?'

'The body's here in the city mortuary. He was brought
over here because it was the Newhaven crew who did the
recovery.'

'So any medical details you can give me Sam. As his GP
I mean, I don't want the other details just before lunch
thanks,' said the coroners officer.

'Well sadly you might have known him Mick. The body is that of Richard Davies, a former surgeon at the hospital. He was retired quite recently on health grounds. He had been diagnosed with Post Traumatic Encephalopathy as a result of repeated head trauma. He was a keen footballer in his younger days, told me he used to head the ball a lot,' said Sam with difficulty. He didn't add that he had always felt a personal responsibility for Richard's repeated injuries.

'I know the name,' said Mick. 'But I don't think I ever met him. Played rugby myself, much safer game.'

'He didn't react well to his illness or his career being ended,' said Sam. 'He became quite depressed and I was treating him with Prozac.'

'Did he ever express any thoughts of suicide to you Doc?'

'No never, none at all. I'm very shocked about it to be honest.'

'OK well leave it with me Sam, you are right, the coroner will be taking care of this one so no need for you to issue a death certificate. First thing of course will be to get the post mortem done.'

Sam thanked PC Wilson and hung up. He knew it was his duty, not only as a GP, but also as a friend to Richard that he would attend the autopsy. It was the least he could do and probably the last thing he would do for his friend.

Another person who had been busy that Monday morning was care home manager Mrs Prior. She had only recently been given instructions from head office to pay particular attention to any visit carried out by Mrs Anderson's daughter Laura. Her request to view other resident's medication records had not been welcomed at senior level. Prying relatives were never a good thing as far as head office was concerned.

So Mrs Prior had noted the visitors book record and as such had been reviewing CCTV images in and around the home from Saturday's recordings. Externally the cameras at Forever Autumn were obvious but less so inside the building and it would appear that the lunchtime visitors had been a little careless.

Interesting, very interesting, thought Mrs Prior as she watched the video of the man who had signed in under the name of Sam Anderson taking photos of her resident's medication records. These images were not going to be welcomed up at head office but she knew she had to send them anyway. And the duty nurse from Saturday wouldn't be returning to Forever Autumn any time soon.

CHAPTER 24

The Chairman and Chief Scientific Officer were having another of their unofficial meetings at Valerian HQ. Hugo, as usual was dressed in pin striped power suit and old school tie, Peter in his white lab coat. They were seated in functional but comfortable chairs in the scientist's immaculately tidy office adjacent to the main laboratory area.

'Thought I would just feedback to you about the situation with my old student colleague you spoke with Peter,' said Hugo to Dr White. 'Keep you in the loop as it were.'

'He and his companion, Laura I think she was called, a bloody journalist for goodness sake, were lavishly entertained at the football. Hopefully they will understand that if they want a repeat visit they will need to behave themselves. It was a good opportunity to introduce them to our business associate as well.'

'Sam Preston certainly seems to have a bit of an obsession about drug side effects and Condrone. I did my best to win him over, get him onside to coin a football term' continued Hugo. 'Old pals act, that sort of thing, but it was hard to gauge whether my efforts will prove successful. I rather suspect we will be hearing more from him, especially if he is being encouraged by the journalist. I think we need to find out a little more about that woman.'

'I've also just had a strongly worded message from Giles to the effect that he feels it necessary Dr Preston and his friend give us no more trouble. He said "on a long term basis". I think I got the message he was trying to convey.'

'Politicians don't like talking directly do they? They always prefer to be able to choose at a later time how their words should have been interpreted,' said Peter thoughtfully. 'But we have been quite reliant on his help recently.'

'Help for which he has been generously rewarded,' Hugo reminded him.

'We need to handle Giles carefully bearing in mind the project we have in preparation. Which reminds me, just how close are we to getting our new major advance to market?' he continued.

'Close Hugo, very close indeed. The trials have gone very well. I'm still amazed at how we managed to take advantage of that huge potential setback. We turned things around and discovered a mechanism for a novel drug that will be the biggest advance in medicine this century.'

'Excellent Peter, great for mankind and also great for the company's balance sheet. The new project has the potential to dwarf the profits we have made from Condrone. Sometimes the end does justifies the means.'

'A great move of yours to reduce the Condrone selling price to the NHS. Brilliant.' said Peter.

'And we are quite popular in a certain African country as well, even if Giles took most of the credit,' added Hugo. 'Giles will probably take all the thanks from the Chancellor as well, once all the tax revenues roll in from our new drug. Won't do his career any harm at all.'

This was the day Sam had been dreading. The autopsy on Richard was being carried out in the afternoon and he was sticking by his decision to attend in person. Maybe if he were there what remained of Richard would be treated more gently but he somehow doubted it.

Events had not gone well so far today. His mobile had rung late morning and he could see it was Laura calling. He had a difficult patient with him at the time and had been forced to decline the call. He had noticed a text message appearing on the iPhone screen almost immediately after. Laura was obviously upset about something. 'I'm feeling extremely pissed off at the moment, can you call me back

ASAP.' It was followed by another that said, 'Sorry know you are in surgery, not pissed off with you x.'

Well a kiss anyway, that's promising, thought Sam, but he was not especially looking forward to calling her back.

The patient got her prescription more easily than she was expecting and was happy to be dispatched quickly out of the consulting room door.

'Hi Laura, what's up, you sound very upset.'

'Sorry Sam I've calmed myself down now. Probably just as well you didn't answer,' she said. 'But I've just had a letter in the post from the manager at Forever Autumn. Mum's been given notice to leave, they've terminated her contract, they are saying she attacked a member of staff.'

'Crikey, that doesn't sound like your mum. In any case she has dementia poor thing, she's not exactly in control of all her actions is she. That doesn't sound right at all Laura.'

'Thanks Sam, no it doesn't sound right. I'm just on my way to the home to give them a piece of my mind.'

'Perhaps you mean to discuss how the difficult situation can be resolved?' suggested Sam trying and failing to be helpful.

He tried instead, 'Don't forget we can always contact Social Services and ask them to help us, that's what they're for.'

'Thanks Sam, you're right, I'll do my best but I have to wonder if this is anything to do with our visit on Saturday.'

'Can't see why it would be,' said Sam but he didn't feel quite so certain. 'Anyway we'll catch up later, we both have difficult afternoons ahead of us.'

The City of Brighton mortuary was situated in the grounds of a cemetery and two crematoria on a gentle hill a couple of miles back from the seafront. The dead centre of town.

Sam checked in at reception, his presence was expected and he was directed to a changing room to don scrubs and surgical boots. The autopsy was to be carried out by

Consultant Pathologist Dr Siddiqi. Sam had not met the pathologist before.

Suitably gowned up he pushed open the double swing doors and with trepidation stepped carefully into the chilly, white tiled, autopsy room. The smell of disinfectant was overwhelming, deliberately so in order to conceal the unpleasant smells produced by the post mortem examinations carried out in there.

One wall of the room was lined with what Sam recognised as the refrigerated storage drawers where corpses were kept prior to autopsy or transfer on to a funeral home. There were four white raised marble examination slabs spaced apart but only one was hosting a body today.

'Ah you must be Dr Preston,' said the pathologist, a distinguished looking gentleman with hair turning to silver showing from under his surgical cap. 'You are very welcome. It is not often a General Practitioner takes the trouble to attend one of my examinations. Do you have a special interest in this case?'

'Thank you for allowing me in Dr Siddiqi. I have to admit I haven't been to an autopsy in quite some time,' Sam replied. He decided honesty at this time was the best policy.

'I do have a particular interest here I'm afraid. The person on your slab today was not just my patient but also an old friend from medical school.'

'An old friend? I'm sorry to hear that. And which medical school may I ask?'

'We were both at Guy's. We played a lot of football together.'

'One of the better London schools in my opinion,' said Dr Siddiqi.

'Well we were certainly one of the better schools at football,' said Sam.

'It's just that I think the football has contributed to his death with all the repeated head injuries he suffered. He was diagnosed with PTE.'

Yes I am aware of that of course. I have read the medical records.' Dr Siddiqi was definitely in charge in his theatre.

'Well let's see if that diagnosis was correct shall we? Come on over and join me. Will you be alright? I am afraid your friend is in a bit of a mess.'

'I don't think he can look any worse than he did on the rocks below Beachy Head,' said Sam, before adding 'I was the lifeboat doctor on Saturday. We had to recover his body.'

Sam wandered over to join Dr Siddiqi who was being assisted by the mortuary technician, a tall slender black man who was introduced as George.

Richard's body was laid out on his back on the white marble slab, his head resting on a shaped plastic block. Gutters surrounded the slab to drain away the escaping body fluids.

Sam thought he actually looked more peaceful than he had at the foot of the cliffs.

Most of the prep work had already been done, with internal organs removed, inspected and weighed. The legs had been tidied up with rough sutures holding together the gashes caused by the fractures.

'Well the organ you will be most interested in then is the brain,' said the pathologist. 'George would you be kind enough to do the honours please.'

The technician took a large scalpel and incised the skin all round the upper forehead region and started to retract the scalp backwards to expose the skull.

'As you can see he has sustained a nasty fracture of his left parietal bone. That on its own would have been enough to bring about his demise but frankly there are so many injuries any one of them could have been fatal.'

He looked up and added. 'Subject to the usual toxicology and histology the cause of death will be multiple organ damage due to blunt trauma.'

'It is of course not my job to say whether he jumped or fell, that will be for the coroner to decide.'

George had now powered up a small circular saw.

'Best we stand back for a moment.'

The dome of the skull was swiftly and expertly cut through all the way round. The cut line passed straight through the fracture site and fragments of bone fell away. The top of the skull was removed and set aside.

'Now let's take a closer look at the macroscopic anatomy,' said Dr Siddiqi. 'With PTE one would expect to see evidence of multiple aged micro haemorrhages and scarring around the surface of the cerebrum.' He changed his glasses and peered more closely. 'Which in fact I see no sign of.'

He took a scalpel and sliced through the junction between the brain stem and the cervical spinal cord, just below the cerebellum. He used both hands to lift the freed brain out.

'The next step is to take slices through the brain to look for signs of more recent bleeding, which with a parietal fracture I am sure we will find.'

Sam found a morbid fascination in what he was watching as the pathologist took a slicing knife to the brain. The wide bladed knife cut easily through the brain tissue in slices a few millimetres thick. He surprised himself at how easy it had been to detach himself personally and remain in the role of interested physician.

However the pathologist was now inspecting the sliced surfaces a little too closely for Sam's comfort.

'See here, in these slices from under the fracture site, your friend sustained massive intra cerebral haemorrhage as a result of the blunt force trauma. He would have been rendered unconscious immediately and death would have been very rapid. I don't think Mr Davies suffered for very long.'

Sam felt reassured by that but mention of 'your friend' and 'Mr Davies' had brought the personal element sharply back into the reality of the examination he was observing.

Dr Siddiqi put the sliced brain down on the slab. 'We are finished here George, can you take the usual samples for histology then put him back together please.'

He turned to Sam. 'Well done, that can't have been easy for you. We will need to wait a few days for the histology but based on the gross examination I see no signs of Post Traumatic Encephalopathy. Is there any reason why he may not have been suffering from Alzheimer's type dementia to explain his symptoms? We are seeing increasing numbers of younger patients with that diagnosis you know.'

Sam suddenly felt as though he were in a vacuum, all external sensations had vanished apart from a weak unsteady feeling in his legs. He swallowed hard and tried to compose himself.

My God what if this is Alzheimer's. I had been prescribing Rich Condrone for at least two years for his arthritic knees. Please let this be PTE type dementia and not Alzheimer's.

'But the MRI scan had suggested the diagnosis was PTE,' he said. 'How could this turn out instead to be Alzheimer's?'

Dr Siddiqi replied, 'I think we both know that scans only assist a physician with diagnosis, they do not confirm a diagnosis. And with your friends history of repeated head trauma a conclusion of PTE would have been reasonable. But based on what I have seen today I think it might also have been wrong.'

'Will you be able to tell from the histology what sort of brain disease it is?' said Sam and realising the naivety of his question, 'Sorry of course you will.'

As an afterthought he added 'My patient was taking a drug that I am worried may be responsible for causing memory problems in some patients. It's called Piricoxib or Condrone, I'm sure you've heard of it.'

'Yes of course I've heard of it but not in connection with dementia. It sounds very unlikely to me.'

'Is there any chance with the histology of seeing if there is any special test or stain that can look for the presence of that specific drug in the brain samples?'

'I doubt that would be possible,' said Dr Siddiqi. 'But I will have a word with the National Poisons Centre at Colindale. They may be able to come up with something.'

'I'm grateful to you Dr Siddiqi, you have been very kind. Best you don't mention my worry to anyone else. I'm probably totally wrong.'

'Well we shall see won't we. I will give you a call in a few days as soon as the samples have been processed.'

'Good day to you Dr Preston.'

Sam left the room without turning round. He had already said goodbye to his friend at Beachy Head. Richard wasn't in this sterile, lifeless room.

They were sitting in the rooftop bar of Bohemia in The Lanes, competing with one another to see who had had the worst day. They were sharing a bottle of English sparkling wine. Laura was allowed the first competition entry.

'So how did you get on up at the care home,' enquired Sam. 'Any members of staff in plaster casts?'

'No sign of anything like that,' replied Laura. 'And no sign of Mrs Prior the manager either. I got to see the Deputy Manager, but she wasn't much help. I shouldn't have called in advance to tell them I was coming.'

'So what did she say to you?'

'Just that Mum had got cross while a member of staff was feeding her lunch. She apparently knocked the dinner plate over with one hand and gave the carer a backhander with the other. I was told she had a split lip. I did ask to see the member of staff to apologise but she is on sick leave, or so they say.'

'Why do I get the feeling you didn't believe what she was telling you?' asked Sam.

'Because it's just so out of character for Mum. I've never known her do anything like that before.'

'So did you get them to change their minds about kicking her out?'

'The deputy manager said it was totally out of her hands. An instruction had come down from head office. Something about a zero tolerance policy.'

'You would have thought that in an establishment like a care home, tolerance would be exactly what is needed,' said Sam. 'So how long have they given you to find some place else?'

' "As stipulated in the contract Ms Anderson, four weeks" was what I was told. It's so unfair, even if she did wallop somebody. It's not exactly Mums fault is it?'

'Well I think the next step is to have a word with Social Services. They have to approve and register care homes. They need to know how your mum has been treated and we are probably going to need their help to find an alternative. She will come with a reputation so it won't be easy,' said Sam.

'I'll get on with it tomorrow. Not a task I will look forward to. I don't think Mum will be able to understand why she has to move, it will just make her even more confused.'

She paused before asking, 'So how was your afternoon? Was it as bad as you thought it would be?'

'In some ways better and in another way worse. The autopsy itself wasn't too bad, it didn't really feel like my friend Richard laying on the slab, it was just another dead body and I'm well used to those.'

'But the part that worried me was when the pathologist, a Dr Siddiqi, said that by just inspecting the brain it didn't seem to look like Post Traumatic Encephalopathy. I think he reckons it might be Alzheimer's Disease. And the implication of that is terrible because I had been prescribing Condrone for Richard's knee problem for at least a couple of years.'

'Will they be able to tell which it is by looking under a microscope?' asked Laura.

'They certainly will and I asked the pathologist if it might be possible to look for the presence of Condrone in the brain samples. He said he would see what he could do. It will take about three days for the results to come back from London.'

'This is all starting to look really bad Sam. You have young patients with dementia on Condrone, there's my mum and her fellow inmates at the care home and now maybe Richard as well. And I think Mum being kicked out all of a sudden feels mighty suspicious too.'

'I think we could call today's 'bad day competition' a score draw Laura. Let's take a look at the menu.'

CHAPTER 25

It had been a tense and anxious few days waiting for the results of the histology to come through. Sam had been tempted to check on progress with Dr Siddiqi, but the pathologist had not seemed like a man to be rushed. Why the hurry when your patient is already dead?

The call came late in the afternoon as Sam was coming to the end of his working day.

'Hello is that Dr Preston? This is Dr Siddiqi from pathology speaking. Is it a convenient moment?'

'Hi Dr Siddiqi, how are you? Yes it's a good time. I've just finished with my last patient. Have you got some news about the histology?'

'Indeed I have. If you have just finished your surgery would you like to come over, there are some things that I think you will be interested to see for yourself. I am in my laboratory over at the medical school.'

Sam was in a state of excitement and anticipation as he drove a little too quickly, in his Yellow 2CV, out of Brighton towards Falmer, where the medical school of Brighton and Sussex was located. Just alongside the football ground, the Amex Stadium. He knew that his visit was not just going to be straightforward. If the diagnosis of PTE had been correct then surely Dr Siddiqi would have said so over the phone.

He parked up, hurried into the modern looking medical school building and asked at reception where to find Dr Siddiqi. He occasionally taught students at the university but had never visited the pathology labs. He was handed a visitors badge and given directions.

'I'll ring through and let him know you are on your way Dr. Preston,' said the receptionist.

The door with a 'Dr Ahmed Siddiqi' nameplate was already open. Sam knocked just as the pathologist pulled it open wider.

'Good to see you again Dr Preston, come in, come in. Would you like tea?'

'That's very kind but I'm fine thanks. My Practice Manager has been poisoning me with caffeine all afternoon, she likes me to stay awake,' Sam joked.

'Well I think you will have no trouble in staying awake when you see what I have to show you.'

That sounds very interesting, thought Sam as he followed the pathologist over to a bench equipped with a microscope connected to a large monitor. He had actually given up hoping that he and Laura would discover nothing untoward about Condrone, too much had happened, too many coincidences.

'The slides came through today along with some special stains that I managed to persuade a colleague at Colindale to have made up. They have been reported on but I knew you would want to see for yourself.'

Dr Siddiqi put a slide under the high power lens of the microscope and a fuzzy picture appeared on the monitor screen. He adjusted the focus on the lens and the image came into view more sharply.

'Wow, it's been a few years since I looked at a histology slide,' said Sam. 'Probably not since medical school in fact.'

'Well this is obviously brain tissue, as you would expect, with the standard silver stain technique. But these areas here and here are not what you would have expected if the original diagnosis by the neurologist had been correct.'

He pointed out some densely stained areas which he said were outside of but clinging to the neurones, the brain cells. 'These are plaques of an abnormal protein called beta amyloid,' he adjusted his point of focus. 'And these tangled structures within many of the neurones are called tau protein.'

'Oh my God, the microscopic features of Alzheimer's type dementia, unless I'm very much mistaken,' said Sam. 'Sorry about my language Dr Siddiqi,' he added.

'Not at all. I thought you might be surprised, it's why I asked you over. And congratulations on remembering something from your pathology lectures back at Guy's. The accumulations of both the beta amyloid and tau protein would interfere with the normal electrical messaging between the brain cells. Hence the symptoms of memory loss and confusion your friend was suffering from.'

'But the finding I think you will consider to be most interesting is yet to come,' continued the pathologist. He removed the slide from under the microscope lens and replaced it with another.

'What do you think you might be looking at here?'

Sam looked at the monitor closely. 'Well obviously I don't really know but I'm going to guess these dark areas with red staining through them are plaques of beta amyloid again. But I've no idea what the deep red colour represents.'

'This is the specially stained slide I requested from the poisons unit at Colindale Sam. These dark red stained areas, widespread through all the plaques of amyloid in fact, are caused by the presence of Piricoxib or Condrone as it is more commonly called. The question you posed me has been answered.'

For the second time in just a few days Sam was stunned. He couldn't speak because he couldn't breathe!

Fortunately Dr Siddiqi broke the silence and helpfully expanded. 'I have spoken to my colleague who prepared the slides and he seemed in little doubt that the presence of the drug is causing the beta amyloid to form more easily and indeed probably making it easier for the amyloid to adhere to the surface of the neurones.'

Sam struggled to find his voice again. 'I think what you might be telling me Dr Siddiqi is that the drug Condrone has poisoned Richard's brain and caused him to develop dementia.'

'As a pathologist that might indeed be what I am telling you Sam. But it's only a might. Clearly more investigative work would need to be done before reaching that sort of conclusion. If I value my career I shall certainly not be standing up at the coroner's inquest and making any wild accusations.'

'But if I were standing in your shoes I would be thinking that I have just seen the cause of my friend's dementia and death.'

CHAPTER 26

Laura and Sam were north of Brighton, walking along the crest of the hill just above the valley called The Devil's Dyke. Sam had texted Laura to see if she was free after his revelatory meeting with Dr Siddiqi. She had been busy in a conference with her editor and replied that she would be about an hour. That was fine. It had given Sam the chance to sit in his car at Falmer and gather his thoughts. He would not have been in any fit state to drive, his brain was scrambled.

They had views from the top of the Downs back across Brighton and out to the west as far as the Isle of Wight, silhouetted against the channel by the fiery colours of the setting sun. To the north they looked down over the Sussex Weald and in the far distance could just see aircraft making their final approaches into Gatwick Airport.

Sam had thought it a good idea to meet here, out in the open, as he absolutely didn't want any part of what he had to say to Laura to be overheard. He had agreed with Dr Siddiqi that the knowledge they had shared was best kept between themselves for the time being.

They strolled along slowly, listening to the sounds of the skylarks singing from above and enjoying the feel of the warm breeze on their faces. It was helping clear their minds.

'I could say I can't believe what you've just told me Sam but actually I can easily believe it,' said Laura. 'Poor Richard and probably poor my mum too. I know you didn't want to find out something like this Sam but if there was any doubt left in my mind then it's all completely gone now. We have to follow this through and expose exactly what's been going on at Valerian.'

'I completely agree with you Laura. The only question in my mind right now is whether Hugo and his scientists at the drug company have any idea what their drug has very likely been doing to patients. Surely they can't suspect anything or they would have withdrawn Condrone while it was being investigated.'

'And wouldn't they have been forced into action by that regulatory body the MHRA if other doctors had reported any suspicions?' added Laura.

'That's certainly true, but GPs are busy people and they're not all suspicious buggers like me, so I suppose there can't have been any other reports. Everybody knows dementia is much more common than it used to be and there have been so many different theories put forward as to why that might be. Maybe if dementia was a rare condition a doctor somewhere would have taken notice and reported it.'

Sam stopped walking for a moment and looked at Laura.

'Look Laura, Hugo's an odd sort of bloke but I think the right thing for us to do here is to go up to Cambridge and have a serious discussion with him and his chief scientist colleague. We can tell them we don't want to make a fuss officially but that we are sure they would want to know, so they can make absolutely sure their drug is safe. No drug company would want to think they are poisoning their patients. Would they?'

'That's true and the financial consequences to a company of not reporting something like that would be massive. But I'm not so sure about Hugo, I didn't take to him at all or his Health Minister friend Giles. But I can't think of a better idea Sam. And they know I'm a journalist, so they have to listen. They wouldn't want to see my story appearing all over the front pages of the Sunday broadsheets would they!'

'Remind me never to get on the wrong side of you Ms. Anderson,' said Sam feeling a little proud of his determined investigative partner.

The following morning Sam called the Chairman of Valerian Pharmaceuticals.

'Hello Hugo, it's Sam Preston. Is it OK to have a chat? You did say to call you if I had any further concerns about Condrone.'

'And I suppose the fact you are calling means you do have further concerns, that's a shame. I'm a bit tied up right now Sam, I'll have to call you back.' And the connection was cut.

Hugo wasn't doing anything in particular but he needed some thinking time and would certainly be making a couple of phone calls before he was ready to speak with Sam again.

A few hours passed by and Sam was still waiting for his call to be returned. Obviously Hugo didn't yet realise how serious this could be for him and his company. By four o'clock Sam had lost patience and called Valerian back. He was put on hold by the receptionist. Eventually Hugo's pompous voice sounded down the line.

'Sorry to have kept you waiting Sam. I was just about to call you back as it happens, it's been a rather full day.' Hugo wasn't exaggerating about that one. 'You mentioned you have what you called further concerns. Best you fill me in.'

'Hugo this isn't something that I think you would want me to talk about over the phone,' Sam replied. 'Let's just say some new and very upsetting evidence has come to my attention about your drug Condrone. It's best we meet in person.'

'New and upsetting you say? Sounds a bit dramatic to me. Well it's probably best you come up here to Cambridge then. Just the two of us?'

'I think you need to arrange for your Chief Scientific Officer to be present Hugo. It was he I spoke with initially if you remember. And I will be bringing my colleague and friend Laura Anderson with me, the journalist.'

Sam could hear a deep exhalation of breath at the other end of the line.

'Very well if you must. Let's see.' He consulted his diary, 'I can fit you in on Thursday at eleven then. I hope that's convenient.'

'Yes that's fine Hugo. I have a private pilot's licence so we will fly up to Cambridge from Shoreham. See you on Thursday.'

'I've spoken with Hugo,' Sam said to Laura, 'And we agreed that you and I will meet with him and his science chief in Cambridge the day after tomorrow. We can make a day of it. Valerian are on the Science Park and it's very close to Cambridge Airport, so I thought we could fly up in the Warrior.'

'Sounds good,' said Laura.'I've given my editor a vague idea that I'm working on a big story that will sell thousands of copies of his paper, so it won't be a problem getting away. How did Hugo sound on the phone?'

'I don't think he was exactly pleased to hear from me but that's not surprising. Somebody giving him hassle about a drug that's making him a fortune isn't going to be too welcome. He didn't return my initial call and when I phoned back later he sounded very cold.

'OK,' said Laura.'I think we need to be careful what we say. In fact we need to be careful full stop. But yes let's go and flying will certainly be much quicker.'

Sam had one last task to do for his old friend. It felt like the closing of the book on Richard's short life.

He had already attended the inquest held at Woodvale in Brighton. As his GP and as the lifeboat doctor Sam had been required to give evidence to the coroner. He had confirmed the date of his last consultation and had informed the coroner that the diagnosis given by the neurologist at that time had been Post Traumatic Encephalopathy. He was asked if the deceased had shown any signs of depression and Sam had confirmed that he was being treated with anti depressant medication.

'Had you considered referring Mr Davies for a psychiatric opinion regarding his state of mind Doctor?' Sam had found the question a little threatening, almost as if he had been negligent in not doing so. But it wasn't the coroners job to make accusations, just to collect the facts.

'And had Mr Davies expressed any suicidal ideation to you Dr Preston?'

'Definitely not,' Sam had replied. 'Had he done so I would have referred him urgently for a psychiatric opinion.'

The pathologist Dr Siddiqi had been called next to give evidence and gave his oath swearing on the Quran.

He confirmed to the coroner the autopsy findings. The correct diagnosis had in fact been Alzheimer's Disease as suspected at the post-mortem examination and confirmed by the histology slides. He was careful to make no mention of the special stains he had obtained from the poisons unit at Colindale.

'There being no effective treatment for Alzheimer's Disease the fact that the original diagnosis was later shown to be incorrect would have had no bearing on the eventual outcome,' the coroner had stated for the record.

The evidence having been considered, an Open Verdict was delivered by the coroner. There was no evidence to confirm suicide, no note, no expression of suicidal ideation. It could just have been an accident, misadventure.

Cause of death Part One. Multiple Bodily Trauma. Part Two. Alzheimer's Disease.

Case closed.

Sam and Laura were now at the Woodvale Crematorium where the short non denominational service was being held. Attendance was sadly sparse for a man who had done so much for so many people. A single family member was present. An estranged brother who had seen the notice of death in The Times. There were a few old colleagues from the hospital who had made the effort to attend. The hospital Chief Executive had sent a floral tribute. Sam read a heart felt tribute to his friend and felt relieved when the service was over.

Richard's body was to be cremated and Guy's Hospital had given permission for his ashes to be buried in a corner of the sports fields back at Honor Oak Park. Legal affairs and probate were in the hands of a local firm of solicitors.

Life closed.

CHAPTER 27

Sam and Laura felt reasonably well prepared for the forthcoming meeting but they were not going to be as well prepared as Hugo. Between and after Sam's calls he had been very busy. Naturally he had spoken with Giles and had been left in no doubt at all that this 'difficulty' as Hugo had described it needed to be resolved. Both immediately and permanently.

He had spent a long time with Peter White.

'How on earth could a mere GP have found out about the memory problem and Condrone?' Peter said to Hugo rhetorically. 'I thought we had made arrangements for our secret never to see the light of day. This could be a disaster not only for sales of Condrone but for our future product as well. We are so close.'

'If we had discovered earlier in the development of Condrone what was happening we might have just abandoned it, but we were too far down the line, too much invested.' said Hugo ruefully. 'And I really would have preferred not to have needed to enlist the help of a politician, never mind a devious bastard like Giles.'

'The contacts he had as Health Minister and the fact you were at school together in Hampstead made him the obvious choice. Anyway I have been thinking about how we should handle this meeting. With your agreement of course,' he quickly added.

Peter also had been preparing. The truth was that he had always dreaded their secret coming out and much of his preparation work was long in the planning. He presented Hugo with sets of very convincing data he had prepared. All genuine data of course, it was the detail that was missing that was important. And of course there had never been any concerns raised by the MHRA, surely that would be seen as very reassuring. Giles had been very helpful there too. He wondered how the medicines regulatory body's chairman was enjoying his new villa in the Algarve.

The meeting over, Hugo pondered over what Peter had said. It was going to be up to his chief scientist to confuse and convince with his impressive sounding statistics. But he felt sure an additional plan would be needed, an insurance policy. One that would keep Giles happy.

He took out his phone and scrolled through his list of contacts stopping at the entry listed as 'Dragan'.

It was not generally in Hugo's sphere of interest to get involved with the hiring and firing of staff. OK he had become involved with the hiring side of things once or twice when a new PA was needed. But only in terms of vetting photographs, nothing as personal as interviewing candidates. He had a whole department for that sort of thing.

But an incident had come to his attention a few months previously when an employee had become a little too involved in a situation of conflict with a colleague.

The employee in question was working for Valerian as a delivery driver. He was a recent immigrant to the country having arrived in England, apparently in something of a hurry, from his home country Albania. In the short time he had been working for the company he had developed a reputation as somebody it was best not to get on the wrong side of.

It had been something to do with who would be given the job of carrying out a few hours of double pay overtime and the employee's unfortunate colleague had been put in a condition whereby he wasn't in a fit state to carry out any kind of work for several weeks.

There had been medical bills to settle and a generous compensation package had needed to be hastily arranged in order to avoid a law suit and the adverse publicity that would accompany it.

Hugo, always happy to benefit from somebody else's misfortune, had immediately spotted the hitherto untapped talent in his delivery driver. For some time he had been looking unofficially for a suitable person to carry out the sort of tasks that were sometimes necessary in business. Those tasks that had an element of persuasion about them, useful in such a competitive market. So many secrets of one's own to protect and so many secrets belonging to others to discover.

He decided to invite the delivery driver to a private interview, no need for Human Resources to be involved, and Hugo had been quickly impressed by the man. Naturally the usual background checks had to be carried out and the services of a suitable investigation firm were retained. Their delicate enquiries revealed the delivery driver to have been involved in similar work back home in Albania. His deliveries had consisted of trafficked human organs for transplantation and his employer was a notorious mafia family. It was thought possible by the private investigator that the odd organ or two had gone missing in transit, hence the hurried relocation to the UK.

Background checks having been carried out entirely to Hugo's satisfaction a new post was formed at Valerian Pharmaceuticals. Head of Security, and it was filled by Dragan Kastrati, a fresh faced young man.

'Good morning Dragan. Come to my office now please. You are going to be given an opportunity to demonstrate your mechanical skills.'

Sam and Laura were at Shoreham Airport again, with a flight plan filed for Cambridge. They needed to avoid some highly restricted air space around both Gatwick and Stansted Airports. Sam had explained that they were not going to be able to fly above two thousand feet. His flight plan took them to the east of Tunbridge Wells, across the Thames and then overhead Southend Airport before keeping well to the east of Stansted in order to make their approach into Cambridge. Sam had calculated the journey time at about seventy five minutes. They planned to take a taxi from the airport to the Science Park.

All the usual safety checks had been completed, the plane fuelled and they took off in a north easterly direction from runway zero two, back over the main coast road.

The airspace was busy but Laura had taken over control of the plane for a few minutes early in the flight, she had found it surprisingly easy. 'It is easy,' Sam had said. 'When you're up in the air. It's when you want to come back to the ground it gets more complicated.'

The journey had become less smooth than the last time Laura and Sam had flown together. The air pressure was changing and the plane was buffeted by the turbulence of an unsettled atmosphere. Laura had been pleased her harness was fastened tightly as she had felt the plane lurching up and down, leaving her stomach behind. She sucked on Polo mints which at least distracted her from the feelings of nausea. Sam had reassured her that light aeroplanes easily keep on flying in unstable conditions but he was a little concerned about the weather prospects for the return journey to Shoreham. There was the possibility of a lowering cloud level later in the day. He hoped the meeting would not be unnecessarily long.

Apart from the turbulence the flight was uneventful and Sam landed the plane, safely but not gently, in a gusting cross wind and they taxied to the parking area on the grass by light aviation. Laura was relieved to have touched down safely and took a few deep breaths as she unbuckled her harness. They climbed down across the wing of the Warrior and made their way through the small terminal. There was no sign of waiting taxis outside and Sam had to make a call to summon their ride to Valerian.

It was a short ride, less than ten minutes and featureless. They were north of the main part of the old city. Laura felt it was a shame they had no need to pass though the historic centre with its ancient brick colleges along the banks of the River Cam. Another day perhaps.

The taxi dropped them off right outside the main entrance of what Hugo had referred to as his 'UK Headquarters of Valerian'. Perhaps he was making grand plans for the future.

The building was large, modern and of individual design. An inverted U shape, constructed from glass and steel for the administration block, with more functional looking buildings to one side. Presumably the labs and manufacturing units.

They entered the building through a double set of revolving doors and reported to the long open reception desk. They were a few minutes early, perfect timing. The receptionist, dressed smartly in green and cream company colours, handed them the customary visitors badges and requested they wait while Dr Thomson was informed of their arrival.

Laura and Sam sat down on the comfortable semi circular seating and surveyed their surroundings. The reception area was very light and high roofed. The glass enclosed atrium was air conditioned and the humidity had been controlled to enable the planting of a variety of species of tropical trees and plants. The sound of water trickling through the indoor rain forest made for a relaxing sensation.

Their inner calm was disturbed by the arrival of the Chairman.

'Sam, Laura. So good of you to come to see me at my place of work. How are you both? How was your flight up?' As was usual for Hugo he wasn't allowing much time for answers before he moved on to the next question, but he did seem interested in their journey. What route had they taken, exactly what kind of plane had they flown in?

'Always been interested in the thought of flying myself, but I think I would need a jet. Nothing fancy, a Lear or a Citation, something like that. Valerian is going to be expanding into Europe, we have a very exciting development taking place.'

'Let me take you on a tour of my building. I worked closely on the design with the architect. State of the art you know. Same firm that designed Wembley Stadium. This has all been possible thanks to the success of Condrone you know. It really is a most wonderful drug. I'm sure when you talk with PW a little later you will understand just how good and safe it is. Quite remarkable.'

Sam and Laura obediently followed along behind Hugo on his ego boosting tour. The facilities certainly looked impressive and included a gym and swimming pool for Hugo's co-workers but really they were not that interested. Laura had a feeling the tour was just being used as a means of distraction away from the reason for their visit. A demonstration of how successful and important Hugo was. Not to be messed with.

Eventually the tour group arrived at the most luxuriously appointed space in the building, Hugo's office. It had a sign on the door, 'Chairman', no name being necessary. He ushered them in and closed the door. 'We have complete privacy in here. You can be reassured there is no covert video or recording, there is no need, my security is very tight, pharmaceutical secrets are extremely valuable.'

'I can come and go as I wish, I have my own private staircase down to the car park.' He indicated a set of double doors on the far side of the room.

They looked around the spacious room. One wall was entirely of tinted glass. A large modern design wooden desk, it looked as if it was constructed from walnut, sat in front of a wall adorned by what looked from a distance to be photographs of the chairman at various official events. Laura looked behind her and saw two large canvases, they looked like originals, and she recognised them as being the work of Jackson Pollock. The floor was deeply carpeted apart from the wooden flooring around the desk.

Hugo gestured them over to a circular low level table. Sam and Laura were placed in low slung comfortable armchairs. They were not going to get out of them in a hurry.

Hugo returned to his desk and buzzed a message through to his scientist.

'Peter will be joining us very shortly. Now let me order you some refreshments.'

Hugo pulled over seating for himself. A much lighter and more practical club chair. His bulk would have prevented him from getting out of one of the armchairs.

Coffee and pastries arrived through the office door, brought in by one of Hugo's personal assistants.

At the same moment the double doors opened and into the room stepped a serious looking, middle aged man in a clean starched white lab coat.

'Ah Peter, perfect timing. I believe you have spoken with Dr Preston here on the phone but you won't have had the pleasure of meeting his companion Ms Laura Anderson.'

Laura was surprised Hugo had remembered her name and grateful not to have been described as 'a creature' this time.

They both stood and shook hands with Peter White as the introductions were made. The scientist seated himself next to Hugo. Coffee was poured and pastries declined.

'Well it's pleasant enough to have you both here but I expect you would like to get down to business,' said Hugo. 'You mentioned on the phone, Sam, you have what you described as new and upsetting evidence. You make it sound as if you have been carrying out some sort of private investigation but I am sorry it has caused you to be upset. Please enlighten us.'

'Thank you Hugo,' said Sam. 'No, not an investigation, just a genuine concern for patients and relatives. We have reasons to strongly suspect that your drug Condrone is leading to the development of memory problems in some patients, many of whom have gone on to develop early onset dementia. I want you to understand at the outset that I have no personal animosity towards you or your company. We both felt that you and Dr White here would want to know at the earliest opportunity if your drug were to be suspected of causing a previously unrecognised side effect.'

Laura chipped in. 'I'm sure your company would not want any adverse publicity if the information we have were to leak out through any other channels. We felt it best to come directly to you.'

Hugo seemed to take on board the veiled threat from Laura but he didn't immediately rise to the bait. Sam gave Laura something of a sideways look that said. 'Hang on, slowly does it.'

'I hope I can rely on our relationship of mutual trust that you will not be publishing any unsubstantiated allegations about our drug Ms Anderson,' responded Hugo.

'Don't worry Dr Thomson, my paper would never allow that,' she said continuing the formality that Hugo had introduced.

'And neither would my legal team,' retorted Hugo.

'So what reason do you have to believe Piricoxib is causing the issues you have mentioned,' enquired the scientist, eager to proceed with his presentation.

'You may remember that I have a particular interest in monitoring drugs new to the market through my membership of the Post Marketing Surveillance Group,' replied Sam. 'Hugo here will fully understand why I have an especially keen interest in anti arthritis drugs. My wife died as a result of a GI bleed caused by such a drug.'

'I am indeed familiar with your tragedy Dr Preston and I am sorry for your loss but it is exactly for that reason that Condrone is such a wonderful drug. No gastrointestinal side effects.'

'But that's not the same as no side effects at all is it. Anyway, I was asked by the group to take a particular interest in Condrone and I called in for review a sample of my patients on repeat prescriptions for the drug. Part of my examination was to assess mental state and memory function. I noticed a much higher incidence of early cognitive impairment than should have been happening purely by chance.'

Laura's turn now. 'Dr White, Hugo. My mother is aged only sixty and she has developed advanced dementia, Alzheimer's Disease. She has been taking Condrone on a regular basis virtually since the day the drug was launched.'

'But my dear...'

But Laura was on a roll and not to be interrupted. 'She is now a permanent resident in a dementia care home in Hove and I noticed there were a large number of other residents who, like my mother, seemed very young. I can tell you that all the patients there under the age of sixty five are taking your drug.'

Hugo managed to get a word in. 'And I'm sure they would have been on many other drugs as well. Tell me Ms Anderson, how did you come about such information, surely medical records are confidential?'

Sam felt it was time to step back in. This was starting to feel like a good cop, bad cop routine.

'It's not relevant to our conversation today how the information was obtained Hugo. We felt you would be pleased that we came to you. We thought you would want to carry out your own investigations. Suspend use of the drug in the meantime.'

'Of course I am pleased you have come to us Sam, that is the right thing to have done,' said Hugo. 'But naturally we are not pleased to hear that you think our drug may be causing a few patients to develop dementia. As for suspending the sale of Condrone? You really need to remember how much benefit many thousands of patients are gaining from it. Are you only interested in adverse effects? Perhaps the tragic death of your wife has caused a loss of sense of perspective. I think it's time to put your minds at rest, because naturally Condrone has been rigorously tested and monitored pre and post launch. I will ask Peter to go through some facts and figures with you.'

The next hour was spent looking at the huge white board connected to Dr White's laptop. Chart after chart, multiple graphs, reassuring reports from the MHRA, trial data, efficacy data. There were specific slides showing, proving, that no study had ever linked the use of Condrone with any sort of decline in mental function. A few skin rashes, constipation, the usual things, but no adverse neurological effects. Peter's brief had been to confuse and convince; he had done plenty of the former but not much of the latter.

'There Dr Preston, Ms Anderson I hope that shows you firstly that there is absolutely no evidence of any link between Condrone and memory function. And secondly how careful we are at Valerian to monitor our product for safety. Patients are our prime concern. In addition, as you would well know, if other doctors had shared your concerns, then the MHRA would have received reports to be passed on to us. There have been no such reports.'

'You say no evidence Dr White but Laura and I have just presented you with evidence,' said Sam, his frustration starting to show. 'What action do you intend to take as a result?'

'Evidence? Evidence? You call what you have told me evidence? I thought doctors were meant to be scientists. But of course you are only a GP. You have a few patients from a tiny insignificant sample, that's all. It's nothing.' Peter White was feeling cross his persuasions had not been accepted and he was starting to lose control of himself and the situation.

The discussions were not going in the sort of direction Hugo had hoped and he was beginning to feel his plan B would be be required. Dragan needed to be told to make the arrangements.

'Peter, Peter it's fine. I'm sure Sam and Laura here are just showing their genuine concern. They are clearly very anxious.' He turned to Sam. 'Do you any feel better now that you have reported your concerns? We will of course add your comments to our database and I can offer to send out questionnaires to all doctors participating in our in-house safety monitoring scheme. We will specifically enquire about the possibility of early memory problems. How does that sound?'

Once more Hugo didn't wait for a reply before continuing. 'You mentioned something about being upset. Was that in relation to Laura's mother, terrible for you of course, or was there something else on your mind?'

Sam sat as upright and as forward as his armchair would allow and said, 'Hugo do you remember Richard Davies from medical school?'

'Of course, football friend of yours. So what?'

Sam related the story of Richard's decline into dementia ending with his suicide at Beachy Head. He described the scene at the foot of the cliffs in vivid detail.

'Hugo, I was Richard's GP and I had been prescribing Condrone to him for over three years.'

Hugo paused for just a moment before saying,

'Well I'm sorry to hear about your friend but of course the story is no different from the other anecdotes you described earlier.'

'Yes it is Hugo. Just listen for once and take notice. I was present at Richard's autopsy. I was there when his brain was sliced through and samples put in jars for histology. I was there with the pathologist when the slides were inspected. I was shown the huge amounts of beta amyloid plaque coating his brain cells and the tangles of tau inside the neurones. And I saw the specially stained slides that showed massive quantities of your drug, Condrone, within those amyloid plaques. The pathologist told me that your drug was the cause of those plaques sticking to the neurones. I saw with my own eyes, in his brain tissue, evidence of the drug that killed my best friend.' During the last sentence Sam had not been able to stop himself jabbing his finger in the direction of Hugo's face.

The resulting silence was ended with Peter White getting out of his chair and leaving the room. He didn't bother with any polite formalities.

Hugo's face remained impassive, showing no emotion or empathy. He gathered himself.

'I am very shocked at what you have just said. Please excuse me for one moment, I will be back shortly.' He left the room via his private staircase.

Sam and Laura were alone. Laura put a finger to her lips and an ear as if to say 'Someone might be listening. You never know.'

Sam heaved himself out of his chair and walked around the office. He inspected Hugo's ego wall, for lack of anything else to do. Mainly photos of Hugo with various politicians, even the current Prime Minister. He wandered over to the tinted glass windows overlooking the car park. He glanced down and saw Hugo in animated discussion with a baby faced man who looked of Eastern European origin. A face that looked strangely familiar to Sam. Where on earth had he seen him before?

Hugo returned soon after to his office and appeared to have recovered much of his composure. He absolutely insisted on Sam and Laura staying for lunch and led them out of his office to an adjacent private dining room. They spent an awkward hour with Sam repeatedly looking at his watch and Hugo not seeming to take the hint. Conversation was stilted and limited to reminiscences of their days at Guy's. Neither Sam nor Laura were feeling hungry and it was a waste of probably very good lobster.

They eventually managed to depart in a taxi for the airport. Hugo had been very cold to them since Sam's outburst and they wondered why he had bothered entertaining them for lunch. Sam turned round and looked at him standing there motionless, watching, until the taxi turned a corner and Hugo had disappeared from sight.

Sam and Laura were later leaving than they had wanted to be for their return flight. Sam took out his phone and checked the aviation meteorology report for their journey home.

'The weather is not looking that brilliant for our flight back Laura. The cloud base at Shoreham is lowering. It's currently down to fifteen hundred feet. The circuit height is only just under that, at eleven hundred. No way can we fly in cloud, we have to stay in sight of the ground. We need to get a move on.'

Sam had to forget about what had been said during the meeting for now. He had to concentrate on getting airborne as quickly as possible and returning to Shoreham, before the clouds came down and covered the tops of the hills.

CHAPTER 28

The returning pilots hurried through the terminal and out to the Piper Warrior on the grass. Sam had a brief look round the aircraft.

'Let's get on our way Laura, we don't want to get stuck in low cloud at Shoreham.' They climbed over the wing into the cabin, took their seats and Sam started the engine.

Permission to taxi for runway zero five was given by Cambridge Tower and Sam steered Sierra India to the holding point before being given permission to line up and depart. Full throttle, sixty five knots and rotation. They were given the OK for a right hand turn at six hundred feet and they made their way in a southeasterly direction to skirt back around Stansted. Sam levelled the plane off at two thousand feet and changed the radio frequency to London Information as instructed by Cambridge Tower. He wanted to check again on the cloud level at Shoreham.

'London Information this is Golf Papa Romeo Sierra India, a Piper Warrior out of Cambridge bound for Shoreham, currently two thousand feet, ten miles north east of Stansted. Can you give me an update on cloud level at Shoreham please.'

'Roger Golf Sierra India, hold please. The current cloud level at Shoreham is thirteen hundred feet.'

Laura could detect Sam's concern and began to feel anxious. 'You said we have to stay in sight of the ground Sam. What happens if the hills around the airport are covered in cloud. It sounds a bit dangerous.'

Sam didn't reply immediately and his silence informed Laura that cloud covered hills spelled trouble.

Eventually Sam said,'No need to worry Laura, we will sort something out, we could always divert to another airport.' But he didn't really have a plan for where they could divert to. He knew their only alternative would be to stay below cloud level, follow a river and get out over the English Channel, no danger of crashing into unseen hills over water. Fortunately with Shoreham Airport located right on the coast this was always an option, but a risky one.

He carried out the usual in flight safety checks and was relieved that all seemed well. He relaxed a little and smiled at Laura to reassure her.

Laura could see well off to her right, Sam's starboard, the buildings and runway at Stansted Airport. They were flying at well below the altitude for commercial airliners. Already the sky above them was thick with menacing gunmetal grey cloud.

'Might get a bit murky as we approach the Thames estuary,' said Sam. 'We need to keep a good lookout.'

Sam changed radio frequency again. To Southend Approach this time. He requested and obtained permission to overfly the airfield at two thousand feet. They were about three miles north of Southend.

Suddenly the engine stuttered and the propellor slowed. The engine fired up again, and then stopped altogether, as did the propellor. It went terrifyingly quiet inside the cockpit.

'Shit, what on earth's happened,' said Sam.

Laura looked horrified, 'Sam, Sam, the engine has stopped.'

They were in a situation all pilots are trained for. Sam had even been tested for a 'fan off' scenario in a simulation during his final flight exam. But this was the real thing.

Sam quickly turned on the electric fuel pump and changed fuel tanks from the port to the starboard wing. He turned the key to fire the starter, the engine turned but didn't fire. It looked as though fuel was not reaching the carburettor. He pulled out the "carburettor heat" knob to melt any potential ice in the fuel intake. He tried to fire the engine again. No difference.

Instinct as well as training took over.

'Laura, I don't think the engine is going to restart, tighten your seat belt, I'm going to put the plane into glide mode. I'm hoping we might be able to reach Southend Airport.'

'Mayday, Mayday. Southend Approach this is Golf Papa Romeo Sierra India, a Piper Warrior. We have total engine failure, repeat total engine failure. Establishing glide, request clearance for emergency landing.'

'Roger your Mayday Sierra India. Cleared for emergency approach. Rescue services being informed. All other traffic to divert.'

With a total absence of power the speed of the plane was falling and as a result the lift from the wings was being lost. Sam knew he had to lower the nose of the craft quickly to regain speed and generate lift. If he didn't the plane would stall and fall from the sky.

Keep the plane flying. He could almost hear the instructor's voice in his ear.

He pushed the control column forward and watched as the airspeed indicator needle came back up. He trimmed the elevator out for a speed of 70 knots for maximum glide distance. Did they have enough altitude to allow a glide as far as Southend Airport. No formalities of lining up on the runway for final approach, just get the plane over the airfield and get it down. Runway or grass, it didn't matter.

They could see the airport clearly through the front screen of the plane but they were losing height too quickly.

Sam tried another turn of the starter key, nothing.

The airfield was appearing to move upwards in the view through the windscreen. It was a clear sign they were not going to make it. Sam knew he couldn't pull back on the controls, they would lose speed and stall.

'Sierra India is not going to make the field. Will attempt emergency landing north of the field.'

'Roger Sierra India, emergency services on their way. Good luck'.

Sam looked ahead at the rapidly approaching ground. They were at just five hundred feet and losing altitude. Where could he try and land the plane? He needed some flat ground, preferably grass, with no obstructions. And he needed to attempt the landing into the wind if possible to reduce the ground speed.

He spotted a golf course just to the right and in front of them. A wide fairway seemed as good as anything.

'Laura, you need to brace yourself, we are going to land on the golf course down there. It will be fine, just hang on tight.'

Sam chose his landing point target and turned the plane to the right and lined up with the cut grass swathe of fairway. A golfer below looked up and saw with alarm what was happening. He shouted at his playing partners. They abandoned their clubs and ran for the safety of trees.

Two hundred feet, fly the plane as slowly as you can but don't let it stall. He lowered the flaps to give more lift. The improvised runway came into sight. The plane bled off speed. Down to fifty knots. Stall speed is forty knots. Don't stall, keep flying. Don't run out of grass, hedge at the end. The stall warning alarm was shrieking, the plane started to judder with the imminent stall.

Nearly down, control column back, lift the nose, keep your nerve.

The main wheels hit the grass hard followed too quickly by the nose wheel. The ground outside was rushing past.

Sam pushed as firmly with his feet as he could to apply the brakes. Don't skid, don't run out of fairway, don't hit the hedge. No space left. Sam kicked the rudder pedal hard and the plane careered round to the right before sinking its wheels deep into the sand of a green side bunker.

The plane stopped abruptly, the propellor pitched forward into the ground.

Laura and Sam were held firmly in place by their harnesses and for just a second were too stunned to move.

'Are you OK Laura?' She didn't know. There was no pain, she could move her legs, she could breathe. She nodded.

'We've got to get out quick.' He reached across and released her seat belt before doing the same with his.

'That handle there Laura, push it down.'

The door opened and Laura scrambled out onto the wing, followed immediately by Sam. They jumped down onto the sand and ran clear of the craft. They could hear the distant sirens of the emergency services fast approaching.

CHAPTER 29

'Pilot error, that's what they're saying.'

Sam and Laura were reflecting on the events of their ordeal over an early evening drink a few days later. 'I'm not sure what I'm supposed to have done wrong.'

They were discussing the aftermath of their forced landing at Southend. They had been checked over by paramedics at the scene of the crash and taken to Southend University Hospital to be examined. Remarkably and at least partly down to Sam's success in carrying out an emergency landing, they had escaped with remarkably little in the way of physical injury. Bruised ribs were inevitable where the harnesses had restrained them and Sam had a sprained left ankle but that was about it.

The mental injuries might take a little longer to heal and Laura was not at all sure she would get in a light aeroplane ever again. Sam was eager not to lose his confidence and was keen to fly again but his flying licence was temporarily suspended while the cause of the crash was being investigated.

The preliminary findings had been of water in the fuel tanks. Had Captain Preston visually checked the condition of the fuel by draining into a measuring cylinder prior to take off? Well he had before the outward flight at Shoreham but hadn't really thought it necessary for the return flight. And there was the urgency to return home before the cloud level came down. 'Normal, usual and safe practice Dr Preston,' he had been told. So pilot error then.

'I just don't see how enough water to cause the engine to stop could have accumulated in such a short period of time,' he said.

Laura didn't know what to think. If he should have checked the fuel then he should have checked the fuel. On the other hand what Sam had just said made good sense. And he had shown such calmness and composure in safely crash landing the plane. Looking at it that way he had saved her life. But had he endangered it in the first place?

She had trusted him before and now was not the time to doubt her trust. She had nearly died with this man. A shared experience, defying death, had started to create a strong bond between them. She was happy about that, and she sensed Sam felt the same.

'It does all seem to be too much of a coincidence Sam. We fly to a meeting in Cambridge, piss off a really powerful man and our plane crashes on the way back. How can the authorities prove that our plane wasn't tampered with?' said Laura.

'Exactly, they can't, that's my point, but without any evidence we can't just blame Hugo Thomson. Who's going to believe that?'

'He did seem to deliberately delay our departure by insisting on lunch at his offices.'

'Yes and I saw him talking to that guy in the car park. Nasty looking character. He looked so familiar but I just can't recall where I've seen him before.'

'I said we needed to be careful. If Hugo did try to have us killed then he has failed. The trouble is he would probably try again.'

'Would Hugo really risk trying to have us killed just because we have told him we think his drug is causing side effects?' said Sam.

'Huge, huge sums of money involved Sam. And a politician. Where the two of those go together there is going to be corruption. I smell a huge rat. And I sense a massive story. He would stop at nothing to prevent that story getting out.'

'I can't help feeling that you're right Laura but a massive story is only of any use to us if we're still alive,'

They weren't too sure what they should do next. It was clear Hugo wasn't going to take their concerns seriously. He just wanted to shut them up, probably by any means. They couldn't go to the regulatory authorities because they were suspicious that the MHRA might be complicit in what was happening. After all Condrone had the reputation of being much safer than the old fashioned anti inflammatories with all their gastro side effects. And they couldn't go to the police. Any evidence they had was circumstantial at best, and some of it had been obtained by probably illegal means.

As it turned out further events took place which made their decision easier.

Laura had been called into an early morning meeting with her editor.

'Welcome back to work Laura. How are you feeling?' said Tony, her boss.

'Fine thanks, it only hurts when I laugh and I'm not laughing much at the moment,' replied Laura.

'Well I'm glad you are alright. We have been concerned about you. A plane crash on the way back from Cambridge. Why is it I think your trip to Cambridge might in some way be connected with that big story you've been working on? We tracked your work mobile and you seem to have spent the day at the HQ of Valerian Pharmaceuticals. There are some powerful people involved in the pharmaceutical industry Laura.'

'You tracked my phone?' Laura was furious.

'Indeed we did with you having been involved in a plane crash. Call it journalistic instinct Laura. We have every right to do that, check your contract.'

'Have you called me in this morning to enquire after my health or to give me a good bollocking?' asked Laura.

Her editor paused for a moment.

'Bit of both really,' he said. 'I took a phone call from the paper's owner yesterday, my boss and your boss. I have been instructed to inform you that you will no longer be continuing with any investigation involving Valerian Pharmaceuticals. Not if you want to carry on working here anyway.'

'But why would you say that? You've no idea what the story is even about. I'm telling you my story could be massive, really make your name as editor.'

'Well if you were to carry on with your story I wouldn't be the paper's editor anymore and you would be out of a job. It was made that clear to me. I wasn't given the exact reasons but I suspect the owner is terrified of getting sued by such a rich and powerful company as Valerian. I understand they have connections through to the heart of government.'

'Dead right they do, that's why the story is potentially huge.'

'And presumably that's why the risk is also huge. Look I'm sorry Laura but you need to get back out there and find some more misbehaving footballers to write about or your time here is done.'

There was nothing more to be said. Laura stood up, shoved her chair to one side and left the room. She didn't bother to close the door.

Sam's day was no better, it was a case of déjà vu, only worse. A letter had arrived by recorded delivery with the sender on the envelope marked as "Department of Health". He had that sinking feeling, similar to when a letter is received with "HMRC" printed on the outside. The contents of the letter were not going to be delivering good news.

He tore the envelope open. It was brief and starkly to the point.

Dear Dr Preston,

I have been instructed by the Department of Health to carry out an urgent investigation into your prescribing habits which may well affect your licence to continue to practice.

It has been reported to the Department that your level of prescribing for opiate type drugs far exceeds that of any other doctor in your local area. You do not currently hold a Home Office licence to treat drug addiction and it would appear you are therefore in breach of your terms of service as a General Practitioner.

An enquiry team has been established and I have been appointed as its chairperson. The team will be visiting your practice in the very near future to further its investigations.

This is regarded as a very serious matter by both the Home Office and The Department of Health and you are therefore suspended from practice until our enquiries have been completed.

We are in contact with your Practice Manager to ensure adequate arrangements for the care of your patients are put in place.

Yours sincerely

Thomas L Evans

Under Secretary

Department of Health

Sam's mobile rang. It was Laura.

'How did you know I needed to speak with you right then?' asked Sam.

'Well I phoned because I needed to speak with you right now. Something rather awful has happened over at the office. Have I disturbed you with a patient?'

'For the foreseeable future, there will be no patients for me Laura. Can we meet for coffee? How about the pier? I need some fresh air.'

CHAPTER 30

The weather was like their mood, dark and somber. The sea was grey and angry, foaming onto the beach. Seagulls were screaming at each other as they wheeled in the gale force winds. Bad conditions for swimming or sunbathing but good conditions if you need to have a private conversation.

They stopped off at a take away coffee shop on the forecourt of the pier. Double shot latte for Sam and Americano with a dash of hot milk for Laura. At least the strength of the wind had ensured that the smell of doughnuts cooking was less intense than usual. They wandered onto the pier, which by normal standards was virtually deserted. They walked along on the eastern side, sheltered from the worst of the wind and could almost feel the force of the giant waves erupting over the marina wall a mile to the east.

'So I'm nearly out of a job and you're completely out of a job,' said Laura. 'What a complete mess.'

'We are at least alive and I think it's time to start kicking,' said Sam. 'I'm done with trying to think the best of Hugo Thomson and his friends. Let's have a think about where exactly we are right now and we can work out what we should do next.'

'Shall I do the journalist thing and write my piece as we walk?'

'Please, yes, let's try and get things straight in our minds. It all feels confusing but there's going to be a reason we are where we are.'

'OK well here's what's happened so far. You have several patients far too young to have dementia who are on Condrone. There's my mum and the others at the care home who are in a similar position. Then there's Richard who we can prove had dementia and whose brain was stuffed full of Condrone. We got to look illegally at records at the care home and shortly afterwards my mother is given notice to leave, for no apparent reason. You talk with Valerian's scientist Peter White about your concerns and a week later you are the subject of a completely false allegation that threatens your career. We fly up to talk with Hugo and Peter White and they are either not interested or hiding something. The plane crashes because of water in the fuel on the way back. We know that Hugo is well connected at high levels through his school friend Giles the Health Minister. We are not killed in the plane crash and a few days later I'm warned off my story or face the sack and you are suspended from your job by the government department Giles is head of.'

'Good summary, that's it in a nutshell,' agreed Sam. 'So we either accept all these events are coincidental or we have stumbled on a massive conspiracy. The only part that doesn't really fit at the moment is, why would your mum be evicted? So there are two questions I would ask based on your summary. One, who owns the care home and two who owns your newspaper?'

They had reached the end of the pier. Most of the outdoor attractions and rides were not operating due to the poor weather. A couple of anglers were trying their luck, or risking all, depending on how you looked at it.

'Well this is not coincidental is it. Circumstantial but not coincidental,' said Laura. 'I agree, we need to find out what the connections are with Forever Autumn and the Herald. I somehow don't think we are going to find out they are owned by Hugo. Why would he bother with small businesses like those?'

'Can you do some digging, see what you can find?' asked Sam.

'Shouldn't be a problem. A search through Companies House records ought to do the trick. I suddenly don't have much else to do and you have absolutely nothing to do. Why don't we head back to your's and start our research.'

Laura was stationed in front of Sam's iMac in the spare room and Sam was laying down on the sofa suffering from a headache. Too much stress and too much caffeine. He was hoping the four hundred milligrams of Ibuprofen would kick in soon. In any case Laura was best left alone, she was the investigative journalist with a degree in computer science.

It didn't take long for Laura to find out who the owner of her paper was, it was common knowledge revealed by a simple Google search. A man called David Mulligan. He looked to be in his early forties and the Herald appeared to be one of a number of businesses his name was associated with.

She did an image search on Mr Mulligan. There were hundreds of pictures of him at various official events, sometimes with minor politicians, but none of him with the Health Minister or Hugo. She did however notice a photo of him taken from the Ham and High, the local newspaper for the Hampstead area of London. He was awarding an achievement prize at the Hampstead Boys School to a smartly dressed young student. According to the caption Mr.Mulligan was on the governing body of the school.

I wonder?

Laura walked through to the living room to find Sam laying on the sofa with his eyes closed. 'I know you're not asleep Sam so don't bother pretending. I need you.'

Sam sat up. 'What have you found out?' he asked.

'Do you happen to know which school your former friend Hugo attended before he got into medical school?'

'As a matter of fact I do. He was one of those types, full of himself, you know much too confident, who had been to an exclusive public school. He was at Hampstead Boys

School. It's where he knows Giles from. In fact I think Giles is Chair of the governors. Why do you ask?'

'There's our connection with the paper then. The owner is a character called David Mulligan. I found a picture of him online presenting a prize at a school where he is a governor, Hampstead Boys School.'

'Nice work Laura. So Hugo has used the school's old boy network to ask his old mate Dave for a favour.'

'Judging by the look of his photo I very much doubt his friends call him Dave, but yes I guess that's what happened. Either that or Giles made the call. They must see each other frequently, at governor's meetings.'

'That's the other slightly odd part of this,' said Sam. 'I can see that Hugo has been supporting Giles' political career, but what has Giles been doing in return for Hugo?'

'Did you say that the medicines regulatory body the MHRA is a government controlled authority. That part of the government that's maybe the Department of Health?'

'Wow that would be corruption on a massive scale. If we are right about all of this Laura it's no wonder somebody has tried to kill us,' replied Sam.

'And while I was laying there doing nothing, in your obvious opinion, I was able to let my mind wander off under the influence of my self medication.'

'I remembered where I have seen that baby faced Eastern European guy before. He was sitting next to your journalist colleague at the patient complaint hearing. Just after I had first spoken with Peter White.'

'The implication of that being obvious then,' said Laura. 'The guy works for Hugo and he set you up with that false allegation. The complaining woman was probably just an actor.'

'Exactly, that must be it. I suppose Hugo just doesn't want the truth about Condrone to come out. Laura, he must have already been aware his drug was causing problems and he has been deliberately suppressing data to make sure his profits keep rolling in.'

'And maybe Giles has been keeping the MHRA quiet for him.' said Laura. 'I'm off back to the computer to see what I can find out about Forever Autumn.'

CHAPTER 31

'Everything is in place for our announcement Hugo,' said Dr White. 'We have enough in house trial data to declare that our new drug is both highly effective and safe.'

'I still find it amazing how you managed to almost stumble on this one Peter. Just when we were trying to find out how Condrone was causing dementia and you came up with this.'

'It often is the case Hugo that when you find the mechanism of causation of a disease you come up with a treatment for it as well,' replied Peter, with a sense of pride in his voice.

'It is going to justify the decision I made not to abandon production of Condrone. I think this is a good example of the end justifying the means,' said Hugo.

'It's going to do a massive amount of good for patients all round the world. Especially in that grateful African country.'

'Yes, quite, but one aspect we must remember is the effect our announcement may have on our business associate,' said Hugo. 'I don't think he is going to be too pleased. But he has outlived his usefulness to us. He can hardly complain after all we have provided for him.'

'Do you think it wise to alert your security man to the possibility of trouble? I know he was unsuccessful with his last task but those two were extremely fortunate to survive a plane crash.'

'I have already spoken with him. He knows what action to take if our associate turns up here unannounced looking threatening.'

Hugo continued. 'So have we set a date for the press conference? I assume all the major news and media outlets would wish to be present for such a game changing announcement.'

'It's set up Hugo, thank you for giving me the responsibility to handle all of this. It's for the day after tomorrow, 5pm in our Education Theatre. Good timing for the lead story in the early evening news programmes.'

'It should be your moment of glory Peter, you deserve it.'

'No glory for me thank you Hugo. This sort of thing is what you do best. I'm happy to be there to answer questions but the headlines will belong to you.'

That was the correct response and one Hugo had been expecting.

CHAPTER 32

Laura had not had any luck in trying to establish ownership of the Forever Autumn care home. She had found out that the home in Hove was just one in a large national chain of similar facilities. There were over fifty Forever Autumns across the country, with an excess number scattered through the southern counties.

Searching the Companies House website had revealed that the ownership of the chain was in what appeared to be a shell company called Winter of Content. The shell company was registered offshore in Jersey. Why on earth would a company owning care homes need to be so secretive? What were they trying to hide?

There was no way she could access information about an offshore company legally but she knew somebody who could. Time to give her brother down in Cheltenham a call.

'Sam, I'm going to take a short trip down to Cheltenham,' said Laura.

'You've spoken with your brother Tim, then,' said Sam. 'What is it exactly he does for a living?'

'He quite probably kills people for all I know,' joked Laura. 'He's always said it's best I don't know too many details of what he gets up to. He works for the security services and seems to travel a lot. I spoke with him on the phone but as soon as I started to give him a few details of our concerns and activities he stopped me and said it was high time I paid him a visit. I'm off down there tomorrow.'

Sam's daughter Ella had finished her first year at Sussex University and was enjoying the long summer break. She had taken a job in a bar on the seafront, she was saving up some money to go off travelling at some stage. She had turned down the chance of a travelling gap year after school because she hadn't wanted to leave her dad at home on his own.

She had just finished a four hour lunchtime shift and was making her way home. She thought she might catch up on a little sleep as she was planning a night out with friends later. It was a thirty minute walk from the seafront bar back to home and she was enjoying the feeling of the late August sun on her back.

In view of everything that had happened, Sam had felt it wise to tell Ella to keep an eye open for anything unusual. Sam had actually tried to persuade her to finish with her job for the summer and take a break with her grandparents in the South of France, but Ella was having none of it. She was not prepared to leave her father or her friends. She assured her dad she was quite capable of looking after herself. She was strong willed, something else she had inherited from her mother, along with the fiery coloured hair.

She was particularly aware this afternoon. She had noticed in the bar, a man drinking alone who seemed to be paying very close attention to her. She was of course well used to the close attention of men but this was different. He was older and she thought a bit strange looking. She had taken the precaution her father had suggested earlier, he definitely hadn't noticed.

But now she was aware of him again and she was sure he was following her. What's more he didn't seem to be too concerned if she was aware, it was almost as if he wanted her to know he was there, watching, following.

It was mid afternoon and there were plenty of people about so she didn't feel particularly threatened. He was probably just some weirdo. She quickened her pace and crossed the road. Her follower was about two hundred yards behind and appeared to be walking with a purpose. She wondered if she should dive into one of the little shops or cafes but unless there was an exit route out of the back doing that wasn't really going to help.

She was walking along Edward Street but would soon have to turn off left into a maze of smaller and quieter roads. She then usually took a short cut through Queens Park en route to home. That didn't seem like a good idea today and she kept walking alongside the busy road.

Behind, her stalker was still there, about the same distance away. Perhaps she should just stop, turn around and confront him, tell him where to get off. She reckoned that's probably what her mother would have done. But she remembered what her Dad had told her and he had said, 'Just get to a place of safety or shout for help if you are worried.'

Ahead on the left she saw the uninspiring blend of old and modern buildings that made up the Royal Brighton and Hove Hospital. She had been to the hospital on several occasions and knew the layout of the buildings well. She hastened on and turned left into the forecourt of the hospital. She looked behind, the man started to run as he saw where she was going.

She pushed the main doors open and found herself in the entrance foyer. She quickly looked around for options. She saw a flight of stairs on her right and dashed on up as far as the second floor. Her follower would have no way of knowing which way she had gone. She left the stairs, ran along a lengthy corridor and looking back over her shoulder was relieved to find there was no sign of him. She saw a notice on her right giving directions to the Accident and Emergency department at the rear of the hospital and she continued her run. She nearly collided with a patient on a trolley being pushed by a porter. 'Sorry,' she shouted behind her.

Late afternoon, it was quiet in A&E. She slowed to a fast purposeful walk and passed straight through the department, out of the exit doors and back into daylight.

Unless her follower knew the hospital well, which she thought unlikely, then she would be in the clear. But what if he knew where she lived? He would just lie in wait for her there. Phone Dad, he'll know what to do.

Dad probably would have known what to do but unfortunately for Ella he wasn't answering his phone. Straight through to voicemail, probably switched off, or battery run out. What should she do? That guy looked as if he meant business when he ran after her into the hospital. He would probably guess that she would try to find another way out of the building. What if there were more followers than just the one that had been obvious? Somebody could be watching her now waiting for a chance to pounce.

Was this just unwanted attention from a strange looking man or was this connected in some way with the situation her dad had got himself involved in? After all he had warned her to be very careful. And if so what were the man's intentions towards her? Was this an attempt to frighten her or was she being threatened with real harm?

Ella quickly worked out that where there were people she was probably safe and she reasoned it was quite likely they, whoever they were, knew where she and her dad lived.

She looked around. An ambulance had just arrived and a stretcher was being lifted out of the back. A taxi had just offloaded a young mum with her little boy, he looked to be about six. He was crying and holding his arm. No sign of anybody watching as far as she could tell. But this person, these people, were likely to be professionals.

She took the decision to head back into the Casualty Department. She would ask for help. The receptionist would understand. They would keep her safe until she could talk with her dad. Why wouldn't he answer his phone?

She passed through the single walking wounded entrance door to casualty and walked inside. She looked around, fearful of what she might see.

Standing right by reception, looking straight at her, was her stalker. He was smiling, smirking. His face was saying. You are stupid, I am clever, you can't just run away from me.

Ella put a hand to her mouth and suppressed a scream. She turned round and ran back outside. Her stalker was hurrying after her.

She escaped through the door of A&E just as the taxi was starting to drive away. She waved and shouted frantically at the driver to stop. Her luck was in, the taxi driver saw her and noticed how frightened she looked. Ella grabbed the handle of the taxi door, jumped in and said. 'Drive please quickly, anywhere, just get me away from here.'

She sounded very convincing and with an agitated man in hot pursuit the taxi driver quickly decided that she wasn't a mental health patient doing a runner. He accelerated the taxi down the slip road leaving the stalker watching as Ella was driven away to safety.

'Thank you, thank you so much,' said Ella. 'You probably think I'm a mad person but that man back there was following me and I was terrified.'

'Well you certainly looked terrified. Glad to be of help. Where would you like to go? I could take you to the police station if you like?'

'Just drive for a minute please while I have a think,' said Ella.

She took a few moments to consider her options then instructed the driver to take her home. They could do a drive by and see if Dad's car was parked up nearby. That would mean he might be at home. There was no way, Ella reasoned, that her stalker could get to her home before she did. If the car wasn't there then she could either return to the bar and hide in a back room or maybe go into the

Churchill Square shopping area in the centre of town. She would be safe where there were people, she thought.

'OK love but I still think the police station is your best bet.'

They drove along the street past her home and Ella was elated to see her dad's Yellow 2CV parked right outside. That didn't mean he was at home of course, but there was hope.

'Just stop here please and can you wait while I check to see if my dad is home?'

'Sure but you need to pay me first if you don't mind love.'

Ella looked in her purse and handed over a twenty pound note before getting out of the taxi.

She walked to the front door and pushed her key in the lock.

Having been paid and having delivered her home, the taxi driver decided he had fulfilled his side of the bargain and sped off.

'Thanks a lot mate,' said Ella and just hoped her dad was at home. She entered the house, shut the door behind her and bolted it.

'Dad, Dad, are you in?'

She opened the door to the living room to find her father sleepily getting up from the sofa.

'Just been having a nap Ella. Everything OK?' he asked.

'No Dad, everything's not OK. Why haven't you been answering your phone? I've been calling you. I've been followed Dad, I've been stalked. It was horrible. I needed you.'

Sam guiltily admitted he had actually turned his mobile off.

'I just needed to get some rest darling. I'm so sorry. Tell me exactly what's happened. It's fine now, you're home. You say you were being followed. Are you sure about that?'

'Absolutely bloody positive Dad,' and she related the events of the afternoon. 'Do you think it's connected with that drug company thing, your plane crash and everything? This is getting scary, you really need to go to the police.'

'I know Ella, I know, but I can't. The police wouldn't listen to me, I have no firm evidence and Laura and I have sailed a bit close to the wind as far as the law is concerned.'

'We are safe in here, in our home, so just try and relax while I sort out what to do next. It will be fine I promise you.'

The house was actually relatively secure. He and Ella had moved to the three bedroomed terraced house when it had been time to move on after Gilly's death. One door at the front led onto the street and one at the back into a fully enclosed courtyard garden. Access to the back of the house would be very difficult. Any intruder would need to cross through the fenced off gardens of several other houses in the terrace. At the front the entrance door was solid oak and well secured with locks and bolts.

'Any chance you were able to take that precaution we discussed?' he asked.

'Of course Dad, I'm my mothers daughter.' She reached in her bag for her iPhone.

'I managed to take a selfie. Me and one of the other girls at the bar. Reversed the camera lens and got a full frontal of the guy sitting on his own.'

She scrolled through her photos and showed the 'reverse selfie' to her dad.

Sam pinched the screen with his fingers and enlarged the image of her stalker's face.

He was not surprised to see the familiar baby face again.

'Do you recognise him Dad?' she asked.

'Things have suddenly got a lot more serious Ella. This is the guy who works for the drug company, you know the one who was at that complaint hearing. I have a nasty feeling he was behind the plane crash as well. I think this afternoon he wanted to send me another message. I'm so sorry you were chosen to be the messenger.'

Ella didn't object when her dad made arrangements for her to go on holiday to France the following day.

CHAPTER 33

When her mother had been moved into the care home there had been no choice but to sell the old family home to pay for her care. Laura had been told by Social Services that they would only provide funding for her mum's dementia care once personal savings and all other assets were virtually exhausted. This had seemed very unfair to Laura. After all, she had reasoned, if you suffered from other medical conditions like multiple sclerosis or you'd had a stroke, the NHS would pay your care costs. How could it be fair that dementia was regarded so differently? It was a disease of the brain just like many other conditions. But dementia had always been regarded as just a process of normal ageing, so not really a disease at all. Absolute nonsense. Well, Laura thought, we will soon find out if the Health Minister is as a good as his word. She hadn't liked him personally but maybe he wasn't so bad if he was genuinely determined to get dementia care funding sorted out once and for all.

Laura, because she shared the home with her mother, had at least been allowed to keep some of the money from the house sale to use towards buying herself an alternative. Property doesn't come cheap in Brighton, a trendy place to live by the sea and only an hour on the train to London.

But she had managed to find herself a one bedroomed flat near Preston Park, just north of the centre of Brighton. The apartment was on the fourth floor of a modern block and had views to the north, towards the Downs. It was also reasonably secure, which was a comfort to Laura bearing in mind the situations she and Sam had got themselves into recently. And the block of flats also had locked secure parking, a major benefit in a city like Brighton.

It was through the gates of her apartment block that Laura now drove her Audi TT. She turned right onto the A23 London Road before joining the coast road and heading off westwards on her journey to Cheltenham to visit brother Tim. It wasn't often she had an opportunity to take her car out for a longer drive and she was looking forward to putting her foot down and hear the TT's engine roar.

She travelled on past Shoreham Airport and her heart raced as she was reminded of the horrors of the plane crash, still very fresh in her mind. She wondered if she would ever fly again. She guessed it all depended on how things worked out with Sam.

The journey took her on through the sprawl of Lancing and Worthing before she was finally able to put her foot down on the dual carriageway taking her towards Arundel and it's imposing castle built on the side of the hill.

It was late August now and she noticed some of the trees, chestnuts probably, were just starting to show the first colours of autumn. Would she even be around to see winter? Her life seemed decidedly uncertain, she hoped her visit to Tim today would provide some clarity.

The A27 became the M27 and a little speed became a little more speed. Her car packed a punch when she asked it to.

She left the motorway just as it was ending, turned to the north and headed towards the ancient city of Salisbury, famed for the cathedral with it's tall spire. Then across Salisbury Plain, a high exposed area of land chosen by the druids centuries ago to place their monument, their celebration of the sun, Stonehenge. And chosen also by the British Army to blast the heck out of the place during their tank training exercises. The clouds were down today giving the plain a moody, mystical and deceptively calm feel.

The proximity of the Salisbury Plain training ground may have been one of the reasons her brother Tim was currently living in this part of the country. The other being the large doughnut shaped building known as GCHQ, Government Communications Headquarters, located in Cheltenham.

Laura knew her brother's work had something to do with the security services but he had always been vague when she had asked about it.

She had arranged to meet Tim at his home. He had bought a flat in a converted old Georgian townhouse in the Pittville area of Cheltenham, just south of the racecourse, famous for it's spring festival of horse racing.

She had spoken with Tim on her hands-free just a few minutes before and he was waiting to greet her outside his home.

Since Dad had died and Mum been admitted to the care home they hadn't seen too much of each other and Laura had been really looking forward to spending some time with her younger brother. She jumped out of the car and Tim warmly embraced her.

'Hello big sister. How's life as a journalist suiting you?' he said.

'A lot better than a pointless job in the city thanks. How's the world of spooks?'

'No idea. You'd need to ask one,' replied her brother.

Tim took Laura's overnight bag and deposited it in the spare room. His apartment was decorated very tastefully with furniture and antiques gathered while on his travels to various parts of the world. The boy had taste, she had to give him that.

They had thought it best for their discussions to take place in the comfort and security of Tim's home. They did however pop round the pub, Tim had said he was desperate for a beer and Laura didn't need much persuasion. They chatted about life in general, about Mum in a non specific way and reminisced about the old childhood days back in Brighton. Happy days.

As well as having a good taste in antiques and artwork Tim also had good tastes in food and had gone out of his way to prepare something special for his sister. Lamb with chilli and juniper cooking slowly in the oven. A dish he had discovered in Italy.

'Best drink up Laura, we need to head back, don't want supper to burn. And I have a nice bottle of Chianti open and waiting for us.'

After supper Tim said, 'So Laura, what on earth have you got yourself involved in? Your phone call was unexpected and surprising to say the least. I know you have ambitions to be an investigative journalist but what you hinted at on the phone sounded worrying.'

'And we're quite free to talk in here by the way, my employers have this place swept regularly.'

'Nice of them to send in the cleaners,' said Laura, knowing what Tim meant.

'So you'd best fill me in, tell me what's been going on.'

It felt like a relief to be able to talk freely with her brother, to not hold anything back. She knew she could be completely open with Tim, he wasn't likely to be shocked by anything she said.

She described meeting the doctor, Sam, and even mentioned the complaint by the fake patient, because she was convinced that was a part of what was going on. She talked about their mum's dementia and the surprising number of younger people in the care home. Nothing of significance was left out.

'Oh and there was also a little episode where the light aeroplane we were flying in, back from the meeting in

Cambridge, was sabotaged and we had to make a crash landing.'

She was wrong about Tim not being shocked by anything. He was shocked, having already been concerned when she had mentioned the likely involvement of Giles Barrington, the Health Minister.

'Well that's some story. But surely any reputable drug company would want to take action if they were told their drug was causing something like dementia,' he said. 'But from what you have said, at best there is a cover up going on and at worst? Well if the Health Minister is involved there is some serious shit happening.'

'Exactly,' said Laura. 'But you can see why we can't go to the police or any government authority about this. Not until we have a lot more to go on. Which is why I'm down here telling you all this. Any more wine? The bottle appears to be empty.'

'So what do you want me to do?' asked Tim as he poured her another glass from a fresh bottle. 'I'm guessing you must know I've got various skills and contacts that could be of use to you.'

'Spare me the details Tim but yes there is something I think you can do that I can't, not legally anyway.'

She continued. 'Part of the puzzle we can't solve is where the dementia care home, Forever Autumn, fits into it. I know it's part of a very large chain of similar homes and they seem to be hiding ownership behind a company called Winter of Content.'

'Wow they like their corny names don't they?'

'And Winter of Content appears to be a shell company registered offshore in Jersey. And that means I can't access any details about who the owners and directors are.'

'It just seems to me to be too much of a coincidence that our mum is being chucked out of her home while Sam and

I are being warned off. It feels like another threat to add to a pretty long list.'

'Yes I can see where you are coming from on that one. In my line of work there are no such things as coincidences. Not until you have excluded all the other possibilities anyway.'

'So do you think you can help us?' said Laura.

'I definitely could, accessing company details in most offshore tax havens isn't a problem. Might need to get a little clearance from above but in view of what you've told me I would need to be very discreet.'

'And this meeting was purely to discuss the future care of our mother. To whom we should raise our glasses.'

Sam was speaking on the phone to Laura. They were both driving. Hands-free of course. He was on his way back from Gatwick Airport having dropped Ella off for her flight to Toulouse and Laura was driving back from Cheltenham. She felt surprisingly clear headed despite last night's Chianti.

'Hi Laura, where are you?' said Sam.

'On the M23, just left the M25, traffic's a bit heavy.'

'You're about twenty minutes behind me then,' said Sam. 'I've just dropped Ella off at Gatwick, she's having a break with her grandparents for a while.'

'That was a bit of a change of heart then,' said Laura.

'Our baby faced friend changed it for her. I'll tell you more when we get home. Might be best if you come back to mine.'

'Just as well I've got my overnight bag then,' replied Laura.

Sam smiled at the thought. What a strange way to have met someone, and what a journey they had travelled together on in the last few weeks.

'We should just about make it in time for some late afternoon TV viewing. I heard on the news earlier that

Valerian Pharmaceuticals are making a big announcement at five o'clock.'

'Interesting. OK, we'll talk later. I'll tell you then how I got on with Tim.'

Laura didn't have her own key to Sam's house, although that might be about to change with Ella being safely tucked away in France. She rang the bell and Sam opened the door to let her in.

She gave Sam a quick kiss on the cheek as she walked past him through the doorway.

Sam said.'It's been a bit of a couple of days. Let's have a cup of tea and catch up with where we are. You can tell me how your brother was. Very protective of his sister I imagine.'

'I think you probably know by now that I don't need protecting but yes he's always looked out for me. And he was fine thanks.'

'But before I tell you about Cheltenham I can't help but notice Ella isn't here. You said she is with her grandparents?'

Sam filled Laura in about the stalking by the man he now presumed was Hugo's henchman and the subsequent agreement for Ella to go and stay with her grandparents.

'It's all become very personal hasn't it Sam. It's acceptable to take risks for yourself but when your family is threatened that's a different ball game entirely. But all of this isn't just going to go away on its own, we have to see it through. I had a good discussion with Tim and he thinks he will be able to help us with the Forever Autumn ownership issue.'

'That's great news, tell me more in a while because I think we need to turn the TV on. That announcement by Valerian is due any moment.'

They could have chosen any one of several channels to tune in to as most of the major broadcasters were carrying

the news conference live from Cambridge. They chose
Sky News.

CHAPTER 34

'And I'm being told that the news conference from Valerian Pharmaceuticals is about to start,' said the TV anchor. 'Over to you you at Cambridge Abbi. Anything happening yet?'

'We are just about to start John, here's Dr Hugo Thomson, Chairman of Valerian Pharmaceuticals.'

'Thank you, thank you ladies and gentlemen of the media. I am going to make an announcement regarding a major breakthrough by the research team here at Valerian. My statement will be followed by the opportunity for you to ask questions of my Chief Scientific Officer, Dr Peter White, who is the real hero of the story this afternoon.'

He continued from behind his lectern. 'The commonest form of dementia, Alzheimer's Disease, is currently afflicting nearly one million people in this country. That represents approximately one in fourteen of our population aged sixty five and over. And those numbers have been increasing rapidly over the last few years for a variety of reasons, some known, some unknown. Until now, until today there has not been an effective treatment for this terrible condition. There have been many false dawns for various medications in the past but today is a day of real hope, expectation indeed, that this curse on the elderly of our society will soon be ended.'

'Today, here in Cambridge, at the headquarters of Valerian Pharmaceuticals I can tell you that we have produced a drug, a medication we have named Mementum, that will not just slow down or halt the progress of dementia but that will reverse the pathological changes found in the brains of patients with Alzheimer's Disease. Mementum will rid the brain of beta amyloid and untangle the tau. Messages of life rather than death will once more flow between brain cells. Ladies and gentlemen we have developed a cure for dementia.'

He paused for this breathtaking news to sink in.

'Mementum has already successfully completed early phase trials conducted in-house by my company and the results both in terms of efficacy and safety are astounding. This is the story of a great British success by a great British company.'

The last sentence wasn't on his teleprompter and hadn't been agreed but Hugo couldn't help himself. The world stage today belonged to Hugo Thomson. He just hoped the Dean from his days back at Guys was paying attention.

Hugo stood to one side basking in his own glory with a ridiculous self satisfied smile on his face.

Dr White took his place behind the podium to a gesture of applause from his boss. The media, totally unprepared for an announcement such as this, asked a series of vague and easy questions for Peter to bat off.

The real questioning would come later but he and Hugo had nothing to fear. Their drug was genuine enough and safe enough. It was just the exact route to its discovery that would need a little creativity in explaining.

'Well there you have it John,' said Abbi. 'A major breakthrough in the treatment of dementia. Back to you in the studio.'

'Many thanks Abbi, astounding indeed. I'm pleased to say that we have managed to find the Minister for Health, Giles Barrington over in the House of Commons. Minister, thank you for joining us. Have you managed to listen to the stunning announcement from Cambridge this afternoon? I imagine as Health Minister you must be very excited.'

Giles was the picture of seriousness and sincerity. He looked directly into the camera.

'Indeed I have John and thank you for having me on the programme,' he said.

'So what did you make of it Minister? Great success by a great British company? That's what the Chairman of Valerian Pharmaceuticals has just claimed. Is he right?'

'As you know John I have always championed the care and treatment given to those poor unfortunate people who suffer from dementia. My own mother died of the condition only last year. I would like to think that at least some of the claims made by Dr Thomson this afternoon will come to fruition. But he was right to talk of false dawns. Much more trial work is going to be needed and of course this new drug, Momentum was it?'

'Mementum I believe Minister.'

'Yes, Mementum, would need to be approved by my colleagues on the MHRA, assuming satisfactory performance in the trials of course.'

He continued, keen to hammer home his government's policy. 'My main focus will continue to be in providing adequate funding arrangements for those patients with dementia who are in long term residential care. It is only right and proper that dementia is funded in the same way as other brain diseases. Thank you very much.'

He shared his smile with the nation and was gone, in an important hurry.

Probably for a stiff drink in the member's bar.

'Well what do you make of that?' Laura asked Sam.

'I feel a bit speechless to be honest, unlike our friend Hugo. I haven't really absorbed it yet. Not something I or I guess anybody else was expecting.'

'Hugo had hinted to us about a new drug and expansion into Europe.'

'Yes but a treatment for dementia of all things, when another drug he already produces is causing the condition.'

'Oh my God,' exclaimed Sam as he started to realise the implication of what he had just said.

'Surely not, no surely not,' he looked at Laura for her reaction.

'And the Health Minister didn't seem too happy did he?'

CHAPTER 35

Meeting Laura had been a happy twist of fate for Sam. It was six years since his wife Gilly had died and life had been busy and eventful since that terrible day. But in another way life had also been quiet and empty. There had been his health problems to deal with and they had led to him leaving his old medical practice under something of a cloud. And having to start up something new on his own, albeit with Anita's help. But his new practice had been a success. A success now being threatened by a Department of Health investigation approaching rapidly in his rear view mirror.

Sam's main focus as a single parent had been on raising Ella. Not easy at the best of times for two parents to guide, advise and sometime control a growing daughter. Those teenage years, a cycle of being a child one day and a fully grown adult the next, never anything in between. Sam had to admit that on occasions it had been a struggle. No fault of Ella's of course, goodness she had her own grieving to do, never mind all the usual teenaged angst to deal with. But there are some things only a mother can help a daughter with. Sam was good enough at being a father but sometimes had to admit defeat in his efforts to be a mother as well.

He loved Ella deeply, there were so many parts of her that reminded him of Gilly. Not least the fiery red hair. But it was her determination and intellect that made her a fierce combatant in any situation of family conflict.

He had been shocked and was now feeling guilty that his involvement in the investigation of Valerian had dragged Ella into danger. He was at least relieved she was now safely in France, probably being spoiled rotten by her grandparents.

Her absence of course gave Sam the space to spend time more freely with Laura. He didn't know where things were heading with her. He knew he was happy to be in her company. She made him feel relaxed and she made him laugh. Their relationship had started based on a shared interest, the finding of a common foe. And you don't have experiences like those they had shared without some kind of bond forming.

Ella having been at home had given Sam the excuse to take things slowly but circumstances had now changed. Indeed Sam wasn't sure it would be safe for Laura to return to her flat on her own. In the short term they had agreed she move in with him.

Was there to be a longer term?

With a little awkwardness last night's sleeping arrangements had found Laura in the spare room and both of them feeling a little lonely.

These were all issues to be dealt with. Circumstances were forcing him, and probably Laura too, to consider how they felt about becoming more involved. Perhaps romantically involved. Sam hadn't felt like committing to any kind of long term relationship since he had lost Gilly, but perhaps it was now time to move on. What would Gilly have advised him to do?

Sam found himself in a place where he often went when he needed his wife's help. Somewhere he could sit quietly and order his thoughts, bring clarity to his mind. He was not a believer in God or religion and had never understood what people meant when they claimed to be spiritual. As a doctor he had always felt that when somebody dies, that's it, they've gone, there is no ghostly presence living on as part your life.

But then, he reasoned, it's the memories of lost loved ones that remain inside your mind. And those memories strongly experienced can feel as real as if those imagined events were actually happening, as if your loved one was still with you. Maybe that's what being spiritual meant.

A simple wooden bench on the hills above Brighton, by the side of the race course, used to be a favourite spot for Sam and Gilly. They had spent time on their own talking, making plans or just taking in the views and enjoying the silence that joined them together. Often they had been there with Ella, eating a picnic, flying a kite, being a family.

And it was near this spot that Sam had buried the ashes of his wife. She had been too young to think about making detailed instructions in the event of her death. She hadn't even made a will. Death had been so unplanned. But Sam had decided she would be happy here. The thought of that at least brought him comfort and it now provided an opportunity for him to talk with Gilly, seek her counsel. He could still hear her voice, that infectious laugh, it made him feel happy not sad.

What have I got myself into Gilly? What should I do? I'm so sorry to have put our daughter in danger. But I've found out something that I can't ignore and I think I have to carry on and find an answer.

Sam knew that Gilly would never have given up on anything she believed in without a fight. She was there sitting on the bench beside him again, and she was telling him not to let somebody like Hugo get the better of him. What was it she had called him that night in the colonnade at Guys? Little fat shit, that was it. He smiled at the memory, an accurate summary.

And Gilly, I will always love you but I think I might have met somebody who I could be happy again with. What should I do? Is it OK with you if I just let my feelings go to wherever they choose? Her name is Laura and I think you would like her if you met her. She has the same determined streak you had and her laugh is quite like yours. But you will always be my redhead, my only redhead.

Sam thought he knew what Gilly's answer would be if she really was sitting next to him. She would want Sam to be happy and she would tell her husband that soon their little girl would spread her wings and fly. Maybe she might even need a little push out of the nest to help her on her way. And if Ella knew her dad would not be alone then she could be free to make life choices for just herself.

Sam felt more relaxed at that moment than he had in a long time. He concentrated on the feeling of the sun on his face and the wind blowing through his hair. He felt a fresh determination to move his life forward in whatever direction fate took him. And he knew he could not move on unless he had dealt with Hugo and his criminal activities on a permanent basis.

CHAPTER 36

Following his sister's visit Tim had thought it wise to tread very carefully. Based on what Laura had told him he had a strong suspicion that the likely corruption reached up to the highest levels.

Levels that had very close connections with his own employers.

It looked as though it would be a fairly simple task to carry out what she had asked of him. He just needed to obtain confidential information about the ownership of a company registered overseas in Jersey. He knew that nine times out of ten when a company hides information about itself in this way that some form of corruption or criminal activity was taking place.

Tim certainly didn't have security clearance just to access any information for whatever reason. Such activities needed to be as part of an authorised investigation. He would be putting his own career at risk if he was caught hacking into a company's database without the required permissions.

This was a task he was going to need to be very discreet about carrying out. Certainly not something he would be doing in any official capacity. And if the results of his enquiries turned out to be as shocking as he suspected then his sister was going to have to be very careful in the way she used any information he revealed.

But he owed his big sister, she had always looked out for him when they were kids and he thought she was in real danger. He would get answers for her and he reckoned he could probably help her decide how best to sort out the mess she had got herself involved in.

Laura meanwhile was having difficulties of her own. Her repeated requests to the management of Forever Autumn not to evict her mother had been ignored. The same old reply every time.

Our hands are tied, Head Office have told us your mother must be moved on. She had been given the vague excuse of "something to do with insurance" once or twice.

Social Services had been contacted and Laura had visited their offices for a discussion about her mum. She had been told that it was most unusual for a care home to terminate a resident's contract just because of a single episode of alleged aggression. The social worker was very sympathetic towards Laura's plight, she had even checked through the resident's contract with her. Unfortunately it seemed the care home had every right to terminate Mrs Anderson's contract, with one months notice, for no reason at all. Social Services would certainly keep a note of what had happened for future reference but there was nothing they could do to put pressure on the management to alter their decision.

Laura was provided with a list of other dementia care homes in the area and it was suggested to her she should visit a few of them and see where she felt her mother might be happy. This was a task Laura had hated when she had inspected Forever Autumn for her mum.

She found the attached price lists daunting. Sixty thousand pounds a year seemed to be the current going rate. Her mum's money was running out fast and then she would be at the mercy of the government. She hoped the Health Minister would be as good as his word and sort out the funding issue soon. But somehow she doubted it. Maybe nature would take its inevitable course, Mum did seem to have been sinking of late despite the medication. Or maybe because of it. Laura's eyes had been opened to the harsh realities of medicines and their side effects since she had met Sam.

And Sam of course was the other issue immediately on her mind. She too wasn't sure where they were heading. Had Sam really got over the loss of his wife? Sometimes she thought he hadn't. And maybe this entire case they were working on together was actually about Gilly. Was Sam trying to gain some sort of revenge on the drug companies? She shook that thought from her mind. Don't be ridiculous, just look at all the things that had happened to them.

But Laura wished she knew how Sam felt about her. She hadn't even been introduced to his daughter Ella. Maybe with Ella safely in France things would become clearer. She hoped so and she hoped that she and Sam had a chance at a future together. Just a few days ago it had felt as if there would not be any future at all. So much had happened. The threat of losing her job seemed the least of her worries right now and she certainly wasn't going to stop her investigation because she had been threatened by the owner of the newspaper.

I just hope Tim comes up with an answer for us that allows all the pieces of the puzzle to come together quickly, she thought.

The pressure was building on Sam too. His practice was in the hands of a locum doctor and the reports he had been receiving from Anita had been none too favourable. Apparently he was not popular with the patients, several of them had left and were now re-registered with Sam's former practice. And of course the drug addiction clinic was no longer functioning, but the addicts were still demanding their regular medication. Rather too forcefully for Anita's liking.

She had called him earlier because there had been news of the investigation into his prescribing of controlled drugs. The computer records of the relevant patients had already been released to the Department of Health at the insistence of the Under Secretary in charge of the case.

Patient consent was not even needed. She had been told the records were the property of the department.

The practice inspection, at which Sam was required to attend, was scheduled for a week's time. It seemed Sam had a lot of explaining to do and he didn't feel as if he was on very firm ground. He had done what he had thought to be right and in his patient's best interests but he had also broken the rules about carrying out work for which he did not have specialist doctor approval.

Sam knew in his heart that the inspection was directly connected to his digging the dirt around Valerian. Hugo was well connected and had demonstrated he would stop at nothing.

The answer to all the difficulties he and Laura found themselves in was to expose Hugo and his associates as the criminals they obviously were.

But how to do it? Maybe Laura's brother would have an answer soon about ownership of the care home. Sam felt all the pieces were nearly in place to expose a scandal. Perhaps Laura should just write her article. Publish and be damned! But he seriously doubted any newspaper would take the risk of running with such an explosive story unless there was concrete proof of wrongdoing.

An idea formed in his head that just might work. Highly risky for both himself and Laura but they were in this so deeply that they had to accept the risks. To do nothing now was not an option, careers even lives were in danger. Events out of their control were chasing them into a tight corner and time was running out.

CHAPTER 37

Tim had bought himself a new laptop specifically for the task in hand. He would dispose of it afterwards, he wanted to leave no evidence of his involvement in what, off the books, was a highly illegal activity. He was using a VPN and had camped himself in a corner of the local Starbucks, logging on to their wifi system. He was prepared to buy as many coffees as it took but with his knowledge he didn't think it would take too long to answer the question Laura had presented to him. He booted up the laptop and got down to work.

Sam and Laura were feeling tense. They were expecting to hear from Tim at any time and after the incident with Ella they felt constantly on edge. They were safe enough at home, the doors and windows were securely locked and Sam had invested in a DIY home security system. The back and the front of the house were covered by CCTV. So far they had seen no sign of anything out of the ordinary.

But life had to carry on, they couldn't just lock themselves away and hope things turned out alright in the end. Sam didn't seriously think an attempt on their lives would happen on a street in Brighton in broad daylight but there was a lot at stake. If the conclusions they had come to were true then Hugo Thomson stood to lose everything and Sam knew from painful experience that the Hugh he had known was not a good loser. Maybe they should go into hiding, check into a hotel somewhere, until they had decided how to get proof of Valerian's shady activities.

Neither Sam nor Laura had ever run away from a challenge, there was no way they were going to start now.

Laura's mobile rang, breaking the tension in the room. It was a FaceTime call, the screen indicated an unknown caller. Laura answered the audio only call and immediately recognised the voice of her brother.

'Hi Sis, it's me. Sorry about calling you anonymously like this but as you know everything we send and say is monitored. I don't want you to say anything to me now. I have had success with the task you asked of me. I'm going to send you an encrypted WhatsApp message in a minute which will tell you what I have discovered. Just reply to the message if you have any questions.' And he was gone.

Laura and Sam waited anxiously for the promised message to arrive. Would this show that Hugo after all was secretly behind the ownership of the care home chain of Forever Autumns?

The message arrived a couple of minutes later with a ping. It was concise and to the point.

Ownership of the shell company registered in Jersey has been established. Several names are on the register, most of which I think will not be of interest to you. Apart from one. Giles Barrington MP. I suspect you won't be too surprised. This information can never be attributed to me. Be very careful how you use it. He is a powerful man. Come and visit again if you want to discuss.

The conspiracy was deeper and more shocking than they could ever have suspected when they started out on their investigation. Not just a drug causing side effects that it's manufacturers had chosen to ignore.

'Surely as Health Minister that can't be right,' said Laura. 'No wonder he has been all in favour of his government sorting out funding for residential care for dementia patients. He's just trying to get all the beds in his care homes paid for.'

'Well before we jump to the obvious conclusion,' said Sam, 'Let's look up the Register of Members Financial Interests online. I'm sure that sort of thing is freely available. Members of Parliament are obliged to declare all other income outside of their MP's salary. To avoid conflicts of interest.'

'Sounds like "conflict of interest" might be a massive understatement,' replied Laura. 'Let's check'

It was no surprise that Giles Barrington had not declared an ownership in the Forever Autumn chain. In fact he had nothing to his name at all, quite unusual for an MP. How could he maintain his lifestyle on seventy thousand a year?

'So it looks like we have our answer Sam. It's as bad, probably worse, than we had thought. We always wondered quite what Giles was getting out of his deal with Hugo, and this is it.'

'Yep, Hugo has been supporting Giles' political career and his party and that's legal and above board so long as it's declared. But he can't just give him money,' said Sam. 'Tell me if you think I'm wrong but it looks as if Hugo has known for a long time his drug Condrone causes dementia and has tipped off Giles to invest heavily in ownership of a national chain of dementia homes. The Forever Autumn chain has expanded rapidly in the last couple of years and no wonder. Giles knew the beds would be filled by those people being poisoned by Hugo's drug.'

'Yes people like my mum. So rather than withdraw his arthritis drug when he found out about the dementia side effect he has carried on lining his pockets as well as those of his mate Giles.'

'You are right Laura and it's become worse than that. I suspect Hugo's scientist Peter White has used his knowledge of how Condrone is causing dementia, to come up with a cure for it. Do you remember that announcement a while back about cutting the price the NHS pays? That was nothing to do with helping the NHS or allowing more people with arthritis to be treated. He has just been increasing the size of the market for his dementia drug.'

'And poisoning a few million people in Africa as well,' added Laura.

'Bloody hell, what have we got ourselves into Laura? Were you expecting this kind of story when we joined forces? I know I wasn't.'

'A bit of a scandal, some corruption maybe. Usual bad company stuff. But something involving the government, the Health Minister for goodness sake, absolutely not.'

'I think we could do with some fresh air. We'll check the CCTV and take a walk out. I think we need to clear our heads and try and work on a plan.'

CHAPTER 38

'Well I may have grabbed the headlines at the media conference but you have been pretty busy on TV and in all the newspapers ever since,' said Hugo to Dr White.

They were sitting in a corner of the bar in the basement of the Institute of Directors in London's Pall Mall. It was only a short walk from Hugo's private members club in St James' but Hugo preferred to meet at the IOD. He didn't feel that his club was suitable for Peter White, he was just a scientist after all, he had no sense of power or importance. In any case Hugo didn't want to run the risk of bumping into Giles any time soon. He had heard nothing from the Minister since the media announcement of the development of Mementum. He wasn't sure if that was a good thing or a bad thing.

'Yes our announcement has generated huge public interest, just as we expected,' replied Peter, taking a sip from his pint of Stella.

'It's been relatively easy dealing with the media, they don't require too much detail for their viewers and readers,' he added.

'And how about your colleagues in the scientific world. I bet we've ruffled a few feathers there?' Hugo was sniggering over his very large vodka and tonic.

'Not a laughing matter Hugo. As you must know it's always controversial making public announcements before publication and peer review in one of the scientific journals.'

'But we have good and genuine data do we not? No need for the adjustment of figures you had to do during the launch of Condrone.'

'I note your use of the word "you" just then Hugo. I think the adjustment was a responsibility we both shared. But yes the data is all strong. I just need to be careful to avoid any questions about the way in which we first came to realise how we could develop a treatment for dementia. After all our reputation has been built as a company specialising in rheumatology.'

'Yes it wouldn't be a good thing for anybody to make a connection with Condrone,' said Hugo.

'Which reminds me. That bloody Sam Preston problem is still lurking. He is the potential fly in the ointment here. He and his journalist friend have been remarkably resilient to being silenced. I will have to find another way. Trouble is I can't just have them done away with. Guess who'd be the first suspect?'

'In the way you leave the science to me Hugo, I very much leave that side of things to you. As you said before it's part of your special skill set. But, yes of course, he and his friend need to be dealt with.'

'Changing the subject slightly Hugo,' continued Peter. 'But have you given any more thought to the idea of our company becoming entirely legit after that issue has been sorted. It's never sat comfortably with me that we are basically poisoning people.'

'Best keep your voice down when you say things like that. Plenty of big ears in here. The trouble with you Peter is that you can't see the bigger picture. The hundreds of thousands of patients who have benefitted from Condrone. And don't forget it is an excellent treatment for arthritis. The money saved by the NHS through not having to fit prosthetic joints. The huge amounts of tax we have paid to the exchequer.'

'I think the trouble might be your total lack of conscience Hugo but I do understand what you are saying of course,' said Peter.

'And what we had always considered to be the slight downside with some of the punters going on to develop dementia before their time has turned out to be the driving force behind the greatest medical development this century. You see Peter those unfortunate patients who have suffered as a result of Condrone's side effect will now be cured. So in my book that's a win win all round.'

'Well I'm not sure the MHRA or indeed the legal system would see it that way,' said Peter. 'What if Giles were to spill the beans about the way he has held influence over the leadership of the medicines regulatory body. We'd be totally fucked then wouldn't we.' The lager was starting to go to Peters head, he was not a regular consumer like his drinking partner of the moment.

'Giles has far more to lose than us. We have always had a policy of mutually assured destruction. He will keep his mouth shut.'

'Well let's hope so Hugo. So once we have Mementum up and running and the profits are rolling in surely Condrone will become almost an irrelevance. How would you feel about withdrawing it from the market at that stage? It would be my preference, we would be totally legitimate then as a company.'

'Ah your conscience ruling your mind again Peter. How on earth could we explain away deliberately choosing to deprive arthritis patients of such an effective drug. There would be a national outcry. People, scientists would wonder why. Questions would be asked and you can be sure it would be you who would be answering them.'

'No, we carry on full steam ahead with Condrone and Mementum. The benefit to mankind overall is the only thing that matters here.'

'And my glass appears to be empty.'

With that, Peter assumed this particular line of conversation was concluded.

CHAPTER 39

The fresh sea air was doing them both good. The news about Giles hadn't been overly surprising, they had known he must have been involved in the conspiracy somehow. It made them realise how high the stakes were and why an attempt on their lives had been made as well as several efforts to discredit them.

They were walking along the lower promenade heading west away from the pier, in the direction of Hove. Out at sea the wind had whipped up some white tops on the waves and kite surfers were taking advantage of the conditions. The parachute like kites were pulling the surfers several feet clear of the water. Free as birds. Sam felt envious that some people were allowed to be care free, no worries. But that wasn't fair of course and probably not true either. It's just that he and Laura were trapped. No way to go except forwards, no escape, no turning back.

There were no obvious followers and so what if there were. What could they do? Nobody was going to try anything down here with all these people about.

'You know what Sam, in a funny sort of way it could be a good thing that Hugo is still trying to put pressure on us both. You with the drug clinic investigation and me with the threat to my job. As for my mum and the care home that's just Barrington being vindictive. Stupid really because he just drew attention to himself. Typical politician, not as clever as he likes to think he is.'

'How can it be a good thing that we are both about to lose our livelihoods Laura?' said Sam. 'It sure doesn't feel like a good thing to me right now.'

'Well I can understand Hugo wanting us both dead. He would hope that might solve his problem. But even that is only a might. I could easily have filed my story with a paper to be used in the event of our untimely demise.'

'That's not such a bad idea at all, you should do that anyway,' said Sam.

'Well I'm certainly in a position to do that. The story isn't written but all the important facts are documented.'

'But what I mean Sam,' she continued. 'Is that if he is trying to apply pressure to us then he must think there is still a possibility that we will back off, change our minds, leave him well alone.'

'Yes that's a good point. I would like to think you are right. Being pressured is definitely better than being terminated,' said Sam.

They continued walking deep in thought, the smell of fish and chips hardly being noticed on this occasion.

'Hugo seems to have been using a carrot and stick approach since we went to his company with our concerns,' said Laura. 'The sticks are obvious, but he was quite nice to us initially. Trips to the football, a tour of his company HQ in Cambridge.'

'Following on from what you said Laura, how about if we offered Hugo the opportunity to present us with the sort of carrot that he thought we wouldn't be able to refuse.'

'How do you mean?' said Laura.

'Did I ever relate to you the story about how a difficulty for Hugo at medical school was managed? Let's say Hugh, as he was then, and I came to an arrangement to our mutual benefit.'

'Are you talking about the time when Hugo walloped you and got reported to the Dean. And you got your student loan paid off?'

'Not my finest hour I will admit, but yes that's the one. The carrot approach worked well for Hugo then.'

'You aren't trying to tell me you are prepared to accept a bribe to keep quiet are you? I certainly hope not. I can tell you now that I'm not taking money to keep quiet. How could you even think of such a thing?'

  'And what about my story?' she added as an afterthought.

  'What type of person do you take me for Laura Anderson?' said Sam taking mock offence. 'In any case I would want a lot more money than he gave me last time.'

  Laura could see the smile on his face. They had both been trying to lighten the atmosphere a little.

  'So your plan is clearly a little more cunning then.'

  'Well we are both apparently in a bit of a fix aren't we? All thanks to Hugo, and he will be pretty pleased with himself about that. Potentially we have no jobs, no money, we have bills to pay, least of all the care home fees for your mum. That's what he has been trying to achieve, so it's just possible he might bite.'

  'I think I can see where you are going with this Sam and the intrepid journalist in me rather likes it,' said Laura.

  'If we can get ourselves invited up to Cambridge again. You know give Hugo a bit of a sob story, tell him it's all got a bit out of hand, what a wonderful new dementia drug he has, by the way could we have a free advance sample for your mum. Things like that. We go on up, fully prepared, wired up and get Hugo to confess all by gloating about his victory.'

  'And we get the proof on record, the evidence, the confirmation we need in order to go to the police and be taken seriously,' said Laura. 'I get it. I like it.'

  She added, 'Would it be a good idea to run this past Tim do you think. It's kind of his field.'

  'Based on what you've told me about your brother I expect he wouldn't mind. He'd probably do anything for his big sister but I think he has risked enough already.'

  'OK well we have the makings of a plan then. I feel much better now, back in control. Two more things Sam. The fish and chips smell great and can we not fly to Cambridge next time?'

CHAPTER 40

They needed to be able to secretly record the meeting they were planning with Hugo. They had in fact had an exchange of WhatsApp messages with Tim regarding this and his advice was to keep things simple. He could gain access to highly sophisticated concealed equipment but he sounded a little reluctant to dig his personal hole any deeper. He had also been more than a little worried that if Hugo ordered his Head of Security to search them, and such equipment was found, then their trip to Cambridge would be a one way journey.

So they had searched online and were surprised at how easy it was to buy all kinds of listening devices. They opted for a simple pen device for just under a hundred pounds. It functioned perfectly well as a pen and would pass a quick visual inspection without difficulty. It could sit openly in the inside pocket of a jacket worn by Sam. Hopefully it would provide them with enough evidence, along with all the circumstantial evidence, to incriminate Hugo.

The next step of course was to persuade him to invite them up to Valerian HQ to discuss the deal that would solve everybody's problems. It was going to need another phone call to Cambridge. At least Sam now had a mobile number for Hugo. He had shared it with him during the arrangements for the match at Chelsea. Sam knew he had to be careful, it was more than likely Hugo would record all his mobile calls.

Sam tried to steady his nerve and called Hugo's number. He felt his heart racing, his palms were clammy. Laura laid a reassuring hand on his shoulder.

The ringing tone sounded for thirty seconds and then Hugo's voice message kicked in.

'You have reached the messaging facility of Dr Hugo Thomson, Chairman of Valerian Pharmaceuticals. Please leave a message if you wish or contact my PA through the usual channels.'

Pompous arse.

Sam declined to leave a message and terminated the call.

'That went well then,' said Laura.

'I suspect he has seen it's me and declined the call,' said Sam. 'But that's fine, the fact I've called will give him food for thought. We should let him stew on that for a while.'

Hugo had of course seen the call, 'Preston' had come up on the screen of his iPhone. He had been giving much thought as to how he was going to deal with the Preston problem. He had tried to warn him off, he had tried gently to buy him off with the trip to Chelsea and he had instructed Dragan to bump him off in a plane accident. But he knew he couldn't just kill Sam and Laura, he would be the obvious suspect and what if that journalist had lodged her story with somebody to be used in the event of her dying prematurely. He decided she probably would have done that, she seemed smart.

So he hadn't taken the call just then because he hadn't worked out a strategy. But, like Sam, he hadn't forgotten the deal they had come to back at medical school. He thought if the price was right then a repeat deal was a possibility but he wasn't so sure about the girl. He would take a call from Sam when he was ready, on his terms.

Laura very sensibly had decided to listen to her own advice. She had collected all her notes together and was in the process of writing her story. Bad enough to contemplate being killed but the thought of that bastard Hugo getting away with his criminal activities was just too much to bear.

She included everything. A big story, but once the Health Minister was featuring this could be something that could even bring down a government. Suddenly she felt relieved that her brother had decided not to share what she had told him, with his superiors. Bad enough Hugo and his henchman pursuing them but the thought of MI5 calling by for a chat was not something she wanted to contemplate.

She had discussed with Sam what they should do with her story and he had suggested that maybe a good choice would be to ask Anita if she would mind taking care of the manuscript. She had after all been involved right at the start of Sam's renewed acquaintance with Hugo and was well aware that Sam's life was currently in turmoil.

They both called in to see Anita at the surgery. This was not a matter to discuss on the phone.

'You do realise that you've been banned from the premises don't you Sam,' said Anita. 'I have been given instructions by the Department of Health that you are not to set foot in here until the practice inspection. I think they are worried you are going to try and change the patient records.'

'Sorry Anita I'm a little hard of hearing this morning. I didn't catch what you just said.'

'I said nice to see you Sam, and nice to finally meet you Laura.'

'Thanks Anita it's good to meet the person who has supported Sam so much over the last few years.'

'As if my life wasn't already interesting enough,' Anita replied.

'I notice the waiting room is looking quiet today,' said Sam.

'Well it would be wouldn't it. The locum doctor has gone off sick, so at the moment we have no doctor at all. The patients have all been directed to your old practice, CCG instructions.'

'Brilliant! I'm probably not even going to have a practice to come back to once we've got this mess sorted out.'

'In fact it's about the whole mess that we're here Anita. We had better spare you the details but let's say Laura and I have been investigating what's been going on with all those young dementia patients and it's threatening stuff.'

'Is it connected with your little forced landing incident in any way?' suggested Anita.

'Almost certainly but it seriously is best you don't know.'

'Sam and I are not out of the woods by any means Anita. I have spent some time writing the story up. And it's a story that needs to be told if something like a plane crash were to happen again, if you follow me.'

'And we can't think of anybody more trustworthy or responsible to hold the story for us than you Anita,' added Sam.

'Trustworthy? Yes. Responsible? Sometimes,' said Anita. 'Of course I'm happy to help in any way I can.'

They agreed that it would be best for Anita not to read the story and they decided it would be preferable if Laura printed out the story and sent it by post to Anita's home address, recorded delivery.

'And if we've both been bumped off Anita, sell the story to the highest bidder and retire to Tuscany.'

'I think I might just put it towards a little private surgery I'm contemplating,' she said.

The following day Sam was considering what his next move should be when his phone pinged and a WhatsApp message appeared. He read it.

'I note your call of two days ago. If the purpose of your call is to put an end to your difficulties you may call me back on the following number 07864655321. I remember coming to a sensible arrangement with you in the past. H.'

Sam showed Laura the message.

'Well that sounds promising. Perhaps Hugo is coming to the same conclusion that we have. He is in more trouble than us after all.'

'Yes I think so but he's a devious bugger. I expect the number he's given us is for a burner phone. I can understand why he wouldn't want to talk on his usual number or the company's landline.'

'A sensible arrangement is what two decent people should come to. The trouble is only one of you is decent. Sounds like things are heading in the right direction but I would trust Hugo about as far as I could kick him.'

'Your kick's likely to be better than Hugo's. He couldn't even get in the third eleven.'

'Best give him a call then. Are you going to stop shaking or shall I do it?'

Sam dialled the new number he had been given. This time it was answered almost immediately.

'As nobody else has this number I assume that would be you Sam. Thank you for calling again. I am sure you understand why I could not take your call the other day.'

'Hello Hugo I trust you are well. Is this call being recorded?'

'Thank you for asking. I'm fine and I'm certainly not stupid enough to record our conversation. Which incidentally I feel is best kept vague and non specific. Let me ask how I can help you?'

'You mentioned an arrangement in your WhatsApp message Hugo. We did come to an arrangement in the past to our mutual benefit and maybe we should talk about how we can help each other again,' said Sam. 'I think everything has got way too far out of hand. My career is at stake. I'm about to lose everything.'

'It sounds as if finally you are coming to your senses Sam. Come up to my office tomorrow at 11am. You had better bring your journalist friend with you. She is in as much shit as you are. Enter using my private staircase. I will send you the code via WhatsApp.'

'That's fine Hugo. Yes I will bring Ms Anderson and you should be aware we do of course have an insurance policy if our talks do not go well.'

'Of course you do, I would expect that. I will see you tomorrow at 11.' He ended the call.

The code arrived shortly after.

With perfect timing the door bell rang. Laura checked the CCTV and saw it was the expected delivery from Amazon. The pen styled recording device had arrived.

'We need to discuss tactics,' Laura said to Sam. It was only 4pm and Sam was breaking one of his strictest self imposed rules. They were having a gin and tonic to try and settle their nerves.

'Well I guess if I can get through all of this without totally falling off the wagon I can cope with anything,' said Sam.

'Yes, not falling off the mortal coil feels more important than the wagon right at the moment,' said Laura taking a hefty slug of her drink. 'But it will be just the one!'

'So I think we need to use Hugo's massive ego to our advantage during the meeting,' said Sam. 'Make him feel like he is winning a victory over us. Let him see how much damage he has inflicted on us through his schemes.'

'I doubt very much he will start feeling sorry for us. He would still prefer it if we were dead don't forget.'

'Yes he would but I think he understands that's not an option for him. Especially with our insurance policy in place.'

'Hugo gets to buy our silence,' said Laura. 'And in doing so involves us in the conspiracy as far as he's concerned. That's his insurance policy I guess.'

'I fear his back up insurance policy would be that if we reveal the truth to the world then he has lost everything and a man with nothing to lose is very much to be feared.

That baby faced guy that works for him has got 'assassin' written all over him.'

'We will just have to cope with that one,' said Laura. 'I don't see we have any other choice. So there's only one other question remaining. How much do we ask for and where do we put it?'

'Think of a number and double it! It has to be enough to make Hugo think we are deadly serious. And money is nothing to him.'

'Well I was working on five million,' suggested Laura.

'Ten million it is then.'

'We could retire to Barbados on that.'

'That could very well be what Hugo demands. It's certainly an attractive thought Laura.' And his smile was the sign Laura had been hoping for.

'As for where do we put the money,' said Laura. 'We can hardly ask him to transfer ten million into the local branch of HSBC can we? It wouldn't exactly convince him we were being serious.' She thought for a moment.

'I've got an idea,' she said. 'When my dad was in business he certainly made a few bad decisions which eventually caused his company to collapse but he did open a bank account for Mum and him in Geneva. They were able to hide away some of their savings. The account is still active and as I have Power of Attorney for Mum I am able to use it. Let's get Hugo to transfer the money there.'

'Wow, that will impress him Laura. A Swiss bank account will make us seem as devious as him.'

'I'll take a written note of the account details with us,' said Laura.

'One last thing,' said Laura enjoying the electricity that had sparked between them. 'Seeing as you made such a mess last time of getting us to Cambridge and back in one piece. I'll do the driving.'

Hugo was equally pleased with the outcome of the phone call. He knew this was going to cost him. Sam had driven a very hard bargain in order to get the Dean off his back last time. But he didn't care about the cost. Once Mementum was in production he would be fabulously wealthy. More importantly the entire world would be grateful to him. The entire world except maybe one person. There might be a price to be paid there as well but he was confident he could handle that. Money as the solution to everything was his mantra.

He just had one more WhatsApp message to send. The Health Minister needed to know that the Sam Preston problem was about to be solved permanently tomorrow morning.

CHAPTER 41

Neither of them had slept much during the night. Sam had woken with feelings of dread and Laura with feelings of excitement. If everything went according to plan she was about to get the biggest journalistic scoop of the decade. But it was a very big if. And if everything went according to whatever Hugo might be planning.... She stopped the thought process. Today was not going to be a day for negativity.

Laura had calculated the journey time from Brighton to Cambridge at just over three hours at that time of day. And there was the Dartford Crossing to make. That was always a bit unpredictable. So they made an early start at 7am, they could always stop off somewhere. It didn't feel like a meeting they should be late for.

They had spent a little time wondering what to wear. Sam of course had to wear a jacket as a vehicle for the pen device. They knew that Hugo would be dressed formally. He always was, that was his style. So they decided he should be allowed the upper hand and they dressed casually. In any case Sam hardly had a wardrobe to compete with Hugo. Jeans and trainers were the order of the day and just a small clutch bag for Laura. In the backs of their minds comfort and mobility seemed more important than style today.

They stopped off at a service station just outside Brighton and filled the Audi TT with fuel. The car might be getting on a bit but Laura knew how to make it shift when she wanted it to. But she would be careful with the drive today. They didn't need any unwanted attention from the traffic police. Sam grabbed himself a breakfast sandwich and Laura snacked on a muesli bar.

Despite the traffic being heavy on the M23 they made good progress, just a short hold up around the turn off for Gatwick Airport.

'Are you sure you don't want to clear off to Barbados right now Sam,' joked Laura.

It felt that once they had got today out of the way a feeling of freedom might just return. But only if things went well.

Sam had been quiet during the early part of the journey. Laura had been as good as her word the evening before and the gin and tonic had remained at just the one. So it wasn't that. In any case Sam had spent a lot of time on Skype with Ella and Laura had visited her mum. They both knew what they had been doing and it had been unspoken between them.

Sam was quiet because he was rehearsing in his mind how he thought things would play out. As a doctor he had learned, been taught, to be risk averse. Always take the safe option, be defensive. They were on the attack today, taking matters into their own hands. Regaining control, it gave him a strange sense of comfort. Rather like when you know you have to have an operation and today's the day and best just get on with it. And there was no safe option to take anyway.

Traffic flowed smoothly under the Thames at the Dartford Crossing and they were soon turning off the M25 onto the M11. Laura pulled the TT in at Birchanger Services by Stansted Airport and they filled up with caffeine. Not that they needed any more stimulation, nervous systems were already in overdrive. A visit to the facilities and they were on their way again, past the RAF museum at Duxford. The journey was rapid but it felt as if everything happening in slow motion, as if they were observers.

Cambridge Science Park, where Valerian HQ is situated, is on the north side of Cambridge and they exited the motorway on the A14 to head the short distance east to their destination.

Laura drove them into the parking area around the glass building and found a spot to park adjacent to the entrance to Hugo's private staircase. She reversed into the space which was also about where Sam had seen Hugo talking to his Head of Security at their last visit. Sam looked around wondering if anyone was witnessing their arrival. Were they being filmed? He assumed they were. The time was 10.50.

Hugo had also spent the morning preparing. He wanted nothing to go wrong but of course he didn't trust Sam. As for the girl? Well you would never trust a journalist. He had called Dragan into his office for a discussion.

'Today Dragan we are finally going to deal with the problem once and for all. Preston and the girl are going to accept a bribe which will make them just as complicit in my activities. They are asking for money and once it is transferred into their bank account we will be in the clear. Provided of course everything goes according to my plan.'

'Your plan is good boss,' said Dragan. 'But you have me here for if plan goes wrong I think. Best have more plan just in case.'

He continued. 'And I am not happy about other man, politician man, you need back up. I have present for you.'

Dragan placed a bag on Hugo's desk.

'In here, take look please.'

Hugo unzipped the bag and lifted out the item wrapped in cloth. It was heavy. He unwrapped it. Dragan had provided him with a gun. A Glock 22 to be precise. Favourite of the US police forces.

'Is for your defence boss. It fire fifteen bullets, keep press trigger, have fitted silencer for you. Very quiet, very accurate, easy to use.'

'Hmm very thoughtful of you Dragan, let's hope I don't have to use it but you are quite right, best to have a back up plan.'

'I have fired handguns before but I'm not sure I have ever fired one of these.'

'Easy boss. I take off safety catch, you keep in desk drawer here. Just pull trigger, bang.' He made a gun like gesture with his index finger.

Hugo took the gun in his hand and immediately loved the sense of power it gave him. The choice of life or death over your enemies that a gun gives you. He placed it in the top drawer on the right side of his desk.

'Thank you for that Dragan. Where did you get it from?'

'Best you not know boss, I have contacts. Gun untraceable, you not to worry.'

'Well Dragan, we have our two guests due here at eleven o'clock. They are coming by car this time.'

'They come in green Audi TT or yellow Citroen?'

'They didn't share their travel plans in any detail with me. I want you to position yourself in the car park and observe their arrival. Call me as soon as they are here. I have told them to enter using my private staircase. This is not a meeting that is ever going to have happened.'

'And as we discussed before, you know what to do if the politician man were to turn up. Not that I am expecting that to happen.'

'That's all for now Dragan. Thank you.'

The only other task Hugo needed to carry out was to make a phone call to his private banker in Zurich.

Dragan was positioned in the car park behind the wheel of his company car, an all electric black BMW i3 and had immediately seen the green TT arrive. He had been expecting the Citroen, but it was the girl who was driving. He sent a WhatsApp message to his boss as arranged. He observed them sitting in the car, he thought they looked nervous.

And so they should be. Did they really think they could fix a deal with his boss and get away with it? He felt frustrated that his attempts to stop them had, so far, failed. He would like to kill them, he would enjoy killing them. Maybe he would get another chance today.

'Well this is it Sam. Time to make our move,' said Laura after an anxious ten minute wait. 'Have you got the code for the door handy? Is the recorder in the pen switched on?'

Sam checked the pen device. All seemed in order. They climbed out of the car and made their way to Hugo's private entrance. Laura glanced around but could see no sign either of cameras or of being watched.

There was a key pad to the side of the door and Sam punched in the entry code. They pushed on the door. It opened with a click and they walked in.

Having watched them enter, Dragan exited the BMW and made his way round to the main entrance at the front of the building.

Sam and Laura made their way up the plain concrete staircase to the first floor of the building. They waited, feeling stupid in being unsure whether to knock on the door or just walk in.

Their indecision was interrupted by the door being opened from the inside by Hugo. Of course he would have known exactly where they were.

'Sam, Laura, do come in. I trust you had a pleasant journey. I believe you drove this time around, much safer for you.'

They walked into Hugo's office. Despite the reflective glass on the windows the blinds were drawn.

Hugo ushered them into chairs on the other side of his imposing power desk.

'I would order you both drinks but this is not a visit I wanted to advertise. Hence you being allowed to use my private entrance.'

'We are also very happy for our visit today to be discreet Hugo,' said Sam.

'And we are fine for drinks anyway,' added Laura.

The main office door behind them opened and a familiar figure walked in.

'Ah Dragan, thank you for joining us,' said Hugo. 'This is my Head of Security, I don't think you have met before.'

'Not exactly met, no, Hugo. I think we have been quite close a few times though.'

Hugo ignored the pointed remark and continued. 'He just needs to carry out one or two checks to make sure our meeting is completely private.'

'Dragan, please.'

'You stand please and put all items on desk, then I frisk,' said Hugo's security chief.

Sam looked at Laura. They were not entirely surprised but were both thinking, here we go!

'Mobile phones, keys, money any other items,' said Dragan gesturing towards the desk.

Laura emptied the contents of her purse. She had deliberately not brought much with her. Mobile phone, credit card, lipstick, car key. She had deliberately used her spare Audi car key, a simple all metal uncomplicated affair.

Sam added his iPhone and a credit card, house key and with a little reluctance his pen.

Dragan surveyed his bounty and separated it into two piles. He picked up the pen and clicked it once or twice. He checked the settings on the phones after demanding the passwords.

'You no have writing pad?'

Sam shook his head, 'No.'

'Why pen then?'

'I'm wearing my work jacket and it's the pen I use to sign prescriptions.'

'No prescription here.'

Dragan returned just the credit cards and the car key. He pointed to the remaining items on the desk.

'I give back when you leave.' He gathered them together and put them in a brown leather bag.

'Now I frisk,' he said.

Hugo stepped in having seen a certain look in the eyes of his security man.

'Thank you Dragan. That won't be necessary. You may leave us for the time being.'

With a look of disappointment on his face he took the bag and left the room.

Sam thought. Well that part of the plan has been blown out of the water already.

There was no choice but to proceed anyway. They would have to work something else out.

Sam and Laura gave each other a reassuring smile despite the setback and they sat back down.

Hugo took his place behind the desk determined to stay in control of the meeting.

'So we have made mention of an arrangement Sam. Perhaps similar to the one we came to all those years ago back in medical school. Tell me why you think I would wish to come to an arrangement with you both?'

Sam looked at Laura who nodded. She was very happy for him to take the lead in discussions.

'Back at Guys you had a problem which could have involved the police and I had a problem due to my financial circumstances. We came to a sensible agreement then. I think the situation now is not so different.'

'You think I have a problem now that could involve the police Sam? I know you have had concerns about our drug Condrone, but the police? You had better tell me what you think you know.'

Sam and Laura had discussed the question of how much they should tell Hugo of what they knew. They had decided on the bare minimum needed in order to achieve their objective.

'Look Hugo we are not here to repeat loads of accusations. We both wanted to come to an amicable solution with you,' Sam said. 'You know what we have discovered about Condrone. We have very strong evidence that the drug is causing dementia. Now a responsible drug company would have taken that evidence on board and carried out detailed investigations. They would have suspended use of the drug and they would have reported the concerns to the regulatory authority. It's obvious you haven't done any of those things.'

'Continue. I am listening,' said Hugo.

'It's clear to us that you have known about Condrone causing dementia from a very early stage but you have continued to market the drug and you have deliberately covered up any information about the side effects. Do you not think the police and other authorities would be interested to hear about that?'

'Anything else to get off your chest Sam? Is that it?'

'Isn't that bad enough?' replied Sam.

'So as usual Sam you appear to have got yourself into financial difficulties again and by the sound of it you have dragged this woman into your situation as well. Spending it all on booze again are we? I am informed your drinking did not stop with graduation. I imagine that clinic in Wiltshire was very expensive and probably not very successful either. You had better tell me about the extent of your problems before we discuss any way in which I might potentially assist you with your difficulty.'

Sam wasn't sure how Hugo knew about the rehab clinic but he let it pass. It was time to present the sob story and he was expecting some contribution from Laura. She seemed keen to have her say.

'We are both in trouble Hugo.' Sam continued. 'To be honest I'm not sure any of it is of our own making. You might have a word with your security guy sometime. I expect you know most of it already and no, it's nothing to do with drinking.'

Laura had been quiet for too long. She needed to talk to ease her tension and she had actually been looking forward to this day. Shame about the pen but press on anyway.

'I think as a result of our enquiries, my job is now at risk Dr Thomson. I have been told in no uncertain terms that unless I stop our investigation I will be fired. It really didn't take too much digging to establish a clear link between you and the owner of my newspaper. You were at school together. Something you may not be aware of is that my mother is being evicted from her dementia care home. Have you any idea how much the fees cost? And the money is about to run out. Wouldn't you want your mother to be properly cared for?'

Hugo felt relieved that she and Sam did not appear to have made any connection between his illegal activities and the business arrangement he had with Giles. And he didn't particularly care about either Laura's mother or his own for that matter.

Sam continued the hard luck story.

'I am being investigated in my practice, again,' he added for effect. 'This time for alleged over prescribing of opiates to drug addicts. I stand to lose my business, my livelihood. My daughter has had to go away abroad as she has been followed and threatened. Our lives are in a mess. So yes we are keen to do a deal and move on with our lives. Put all of this behind us.'

Hugo had thoroughly enjoyed hearing the tales of woe from Sam and his friend. All self inflicted, they should have just minded their own bloody business. The meeting was going well in his opinion and he wanted to enjoy his moment of triumph to the full.

'Poor Sam Preston you must think you are so clever. You have always hated me haven't you. Jealous of all the success I have achieved. You were pathetic at medical school. Passing exams, good at sport, popular with the girls.' He paused for a moment, probably not a good idea to irritate him too much. Didn't want any violence. He glanced at his desk drawer and decided to continue.

'But you two don't know the half of it. Of course we suppressed the safety data. We had known about the side effect profile of Condrone from a very early stage. Do you really think I should have just allowed such a magnificent drug to not benefit humanity in the way it has? It's all very well for you and those bloody people at the MHRA concerned about side effects but what about all the benefits? Pain relieved, joints saved, no gastrointestinal bleeds. You ought to understand that one at least.'

Sam did not respond, he wanted Hugo to carry on. If only all of this was being recorded.

'You just don't understand the reality of the pharmaceutical industry, either of you. Hundreds of thousands of patients get treated all the time for conditions they will never develop. Don't you know you have to treat a hundred and fifty people for five years with a statin drug just to prevent one death? That means a hundred and forty nine are taking a drug with well known side effects for no reason at all. And what about vaccinations? We vaccinate the entire country to prevent just a few thousand old people dying from a virus just a couple of years before their time. So what's the difference here then? None, it's exactly the same.' He paused to judge the effect he was having.

Laura butted in. 'Perhaps you are right Hugo, but it's society's place to judge complex moral issues like that. Not a judgement to be made by the person who is going to benefit financially. That's why the MHRA is there I understand.'

Hugo had thought of more ammunition.

'And through benefitting financially as you have just put it, we have been able to plough the profits into developing a new drug, a cure for dementia that will change the world. And don't you see, even those patients adversely affected by side effects will be able to be cured by Mementum. Surely that's fair, a decent trade off.' He had a further thought.

'With regard to your mother Laura. I will personally arrange for advance supplies of my new drug to be made available immediately for her. She will be back to the person she once was within a few months.'

'Well I have to admire you Hugo,' said Sam. 'You have done a great job in justifying to yourself what you have done but I'm guessing you are not stupid enough to think that the authorities are going to listen and say "Well done mate that sounds fair", are you.'

Laura added. 'And have you given any thought at all about how it's going to feel to a dementia patient to get better, be cured, just like that. All the family money spent on care home fees, house been sold. The life they had won't just come back you know. For an intelligent man that's pretty naive of you.'

Hugo managed to calm himself down. 'Some of what you say could be regarded, by some people, as being correct. People with no vision, no insight, no ambition. And that of course is why we are here this morning. Me with all those qualities on this side of the desk and you on the other side purporting to represent the righteous views of the world. But enough, you have no morals, you just want a share of the spoils. The only question I need ask of you is how much are you going to ask for?'

'But before answering me you will need to understand that once you have accepted my money you will be as complicit as I am. The trail of money into your account can always be revealed. You would also need to know that any future act of betrayal would lead to a further and final visit from my colleague Dragan. He has full instructions of what to do in that event. I assure you it would be pleasant for him but not so nice for you.'

'We do have a figure in mind Hugo. You have to understand also that both of our careers are about to be lost. In addition to needing to find funding for Laura's mother's care we have to have enough money to last for the rest of our lives. We will probably never work again. I certainly will not work as a doctor again and you know, I think, how much that means to me.'

'So the figure is ten million Hugo,' said Laura. 'Ten million for us to go away, disappear from your life forever. Ten million for my written story to never see the light of day. Sounds like a bargain to me.'

Hugo couldn't believe his luck. He had been expecting, and prepared, to pay far more than that. Did these stupid people not realise how much profit he was going to make from Mementum?

'And you would also have to promise to withdraw Condrone from the market Hugo. We could not agree to you continuing to poison people,' said Sam.

Despite what he had said to Peter White that also wasn't a problem for Hugo. He had already decided that if his slate could be wiped clean and if Valerian could become a legitimate company then that would be the best way forwards to achieve the greatness to which he aspired.

'As before, you drive a very hard bargain to which, as before, I am inclined to accept. I will withdraw Condrone as soon as practical and I am happy to transfer the funds to you with immediate effect if that would be your wish.'

Sam and Laura smiled at each other. 'Well it looks as though we have a deal Hugo. We have come to you today prepared for a mutually satisfactory outcome,' said Sam.

'Laura will give you the details of an account we have at a bank based in Geneva.'

Hugo was impressed. 'Well prepared indeed. Give me the account details and I will arrange the transfer online straight away.'

Laura passed a piece of paper with the account details written on it, across the desk to Hugo.

He turned to his keyboard and monitor and started tapping away. 'Should only take a few minutes, please excuse me.'

They waited while Hugo sent his instructions. 'There all done, you are now two very wealthy people. Congratulations, I am so pleased you were able to see the benefits of coming to an arrangement with me.'

'And now we must celebrate!' he said.

Hugo got up and wandered over to a cabinet. He opened a door, behind which was concealed a fridge. He took out a bottle of Dom Perignon along with three chilled glasses and returned to his seat behind the desk.

He took great pride in carefully easing the cork from the bottle. He took a sniff of the cork. 'Magnificent, one of my favourite vintages, 2003, and entirely appropriate for the occasion. 'Just a small glass for you Sam?' he said with unnecessary sarcasm.

He poured the champagne and raised his glass in a toast.

'To the future success of Valerian Pharmaceuticals and long, comfortable lives far away from me for the two of you.'

He drained a large mouthful from his glass.

The double doors to his right, from the private staircase, opened and into the room walked Giles Barrington.

CHAPTER 42

'It looks as if I am just in time to join in with a celebration. Perhaps the three of you have come to some kind of agreement. Is there a glass for me Hugo?' said the Minister for Health.

'Giles what on earth are you doing here,' said Hugo.

'Your WhatsApp message sounded like an invitation Hugo. I had imagined you would not wish to agree any sort of deal without involving your old friend and business partner.'

Hugo wished Giles would shut up. He didn't want to discuss any of their previous business arrangements in front of his very newest business partners. There was a good chance they were not aware of his dealings with Giles. He didn't want his recently completed deal to be wrecked, especially as he had just transferred ten million pounds from his personal account.

Giles sensed Hugo's discomfort.

'What is it Hugo? I'm getting the feeling you haven't mentioned our business dealings to these two people here. Do you really think they don't know exactly what you and I have been doing for the last few years. You must be even more stupid than I had thought.'

Sam had watched the arrival of Giles with horror. This was definitely not part of today's plan. This had changed everything. The stakes had been raised to a highly dangerous level.

But Laura was defiant. 'Of course we know exactly what you two have been up to. Your relationship always seemed too cosy, too convenient. Hugo could never have arranged a cover up like this without a lot of help from a person with influence. Who better than the Minister for Health to ensure that the side effect data was suppressed before reaching the MHRA. Bet you have plenty of friends there don't you Giles.'

Laura was on a roll. 'And Hugo isn't the only stupid person in here either. You couldn't help yourself could you,' she said addressing Giles. 'You just had to have my mother kicked out of her care home. Didn't you wonder if I might think that to be more than just a coincidence?'

Sam joined in. 'We know you are behind the company that owns a whole string of dementia care homes across the country. You invested heavily in Winter of Content about the same time as Hugo here was realising what his arthritis drug was really doing to people. You knew thousands of young people were about to develop dementia and you could make vast profits. You provided the beds and Hugo provided the means to keep them full at fifty grand a year. Did you really think you would get away with it?'

Giles ignored the rhetorical questioned fired at him and turned his attention back to Hugo who was now realising today's meeting was not going to turn out well. Such a dreadful waste of champagne.

'So how much have you paid them for their silence Hugo. And did you consider if that silence would include me as well? Probably not. Our arrangement was going well until you, my friend, became rather too greedy. Wasn't it enough that with my help you were making vast profits from Condrone? How much do you think I was making from a few nursing home beds in comparison to what you were raking in? And now all that is about to go thanks to you curing all the bloody patients in the care homes. But I wasn't greedy. I just needed enough money to pay my bills so I could carry on serving my country to the best of my abilities.'

'Serving your country? Don't make me laugh Giles. The only thing you've ever served is yourself,' retorted Hugo.

'Well my career is as good as over thanks to your greed,' said Giles. 'You, however, are now a national hero in waiting, thanks to you finding a cure for dementia. News of our association is bound to leak out, even if you have paid off your friends here. You might survive such a leak but I would not. You do realise I would be facing a long prison term don't you? I risked everything for you and my reward is to be double crossed.'

Giles paused, almost as if he was considering his options. He seemed to make up his mind quickly.

'There is only one option for me Hugo, I have no choice to make. My life will be over if I go to prison. It's proper pay back time now. You have made massive profits with the assurance of much more to come. You need to buy my silence. I need to be properly rewarded. I will have to make a new life for myself, far beyond the reach of the British legal system. The price for my silence is one hundred million pounds and it's non negotiable. That's nothing to you.'

Sam and Laura sat in quiet amazement at what they were hearing and waited for Hugo's response.

Hugo took a large swig of champagne, looked at Giles and started to laugh.

'You've taken leave of your senses Giles old fellow. All that power in government has gone to your head. You just don't get it do you? I don't need you anymore. You have outlived your usefulness to me. That's all you ever were, by the way, useful. You and I have never been friends, not even at school. A relationship of convenience that's all it's ever been. And Giles, it's just not convenient anymore. I don't have to pay you money to send you to South America, you've got to go anyway. Tell you what, I'll buy your plane ticket for you. I'll even make it business class, one last favour.'

The trouble for Giles of course was that Hugo was right. Giles had put all his eggs in one basket and that basket had just been taken away. Valerian Pharmaceuticals was about to become a legitimate company producing a drug already being hailed in the press as a life changer. In Giles' disturbed mind Hugo would be forgiven for not having paid proper attention to some side effect data, but he, as a corrupt politician, was finished.

Giles was now realising how stupid he had been. Stupid to have trusted Hugo, stupid to have taken his money, stupid to have become a bloody MP. He stood there watching Hugo drinking champagne with a smug grin on his ugly, fat, fucking face and suddenly all self control left him.

He had never been so angry, he had just lost everything and the person he had thought of as a friend was mocking him. He was going to take that bloody smile off his face.

He moved forward quickly, his hands shaking, his voice cracking. 'You cunt, you absolute fucking cunt, you're not going to get away with this. If I'm going down you're going down with me.'

He grabbed hold of the champagne bottle from the table and raised it to strike at Hugo's fat, squat, bald head. He leaned forward, he brought his arm down violently and the bottle crashed into Hugo's walnut vanity desk. Remarkably it didn't shatter.

Hugo had taken evasive action and moved to one side as quickly as his body would allow. The wheels on his swivel chair went the other way and Hugo crashed out of the chair onto the floor,

Giles was onto him in a flash. He tried to pin him down with one hand and crush his head with the bottle in the other. Champagne had spewed out of the bottle and as Giles swung it once more it slipped from his grasp and clattered away across the room. The two men started wrestling on the floor, Hugo was desperately trying to claw Giles' eyes out while keeping the other mans hands from his throat.

Somehow Hugo managed to roll over and push Giles away from him. He saw he was right next to his desk drawer. With his left hand he grabbed the handle and pulled the drawer open. He picked up the concealed Glock with his right hand.

He grasped the gun unsteadily out in front of him and pointed it at Giles with the expectation it would stop him in his tracks.

It had the opposite effect. Dangerous is the man with nothing to lose and Giles knew his life was practically over anyway. He launched himself straight at Hugo, straight at the gun. The bravest act the Minister for Health had ever carried out.

And a final act also. Just not a final act for Giles. The impact caused Hugo's weak wrist to twist round and the lightning impulse of pain caused his finger to spasm on the trigger. The gun discharged its bullet and Hugo instantly collapsed backwards with blood pumping out of a large wound in the centre of his chest. His body convulsed heavily for a few seconds, blood stained froth splattered from his mouth and then he lay quite still.

Sam and Laura meanwhile, had taken evasive action at the moment it had become clear that violence was inevitable. They had shielded themselves behind the huge desk. They saw Giles standing over Hugo, stunned at what had just happened. They eased themselves towards the staircase doors and watched with horror as Giles picked up the gun, knowing they were going to end their lives in this shitty office in Cambridge.

Giles said, 'You never should have been Head Boy, you bastard.' And he quite calmly shot Hugo again, straight through the centre of his forehead.

They were not interested in hanging around to survey the damage. They pushed the double doors open and rushed through, almost falling over each other in their desperation to get out and down the stairs. They needed to take advantage of the few precious seconds before Giles realised that Sam and Laura would need to be silenced permanently.

CHAPTER 43

Giles stood there, as if paralysed, for a few seconds. His body was frozen but his mind was in overdrive. What to do now? Members of Parliament make plenty of decisions but it's not every day they face the consequences of shooting somebody dead.

He rapidly realised that the GP and his friend needed to be stopped. He had killed once, so two more didn't matter. Yes, catch them, kill them and get off to Heathrow Airport as soon as possible. He had some money in overseas accounts, he would start a new life in whichever country the first long haul flight would take him to.

He looked around the room and of course they were gone. He glanced out of the window and saw the pair getting into a green Audi TT across the car park.

He rushed off down the stairs in pursuit. He felt amazingly calm. He was surprised by the feeling of ecstasy he had experienced when he had killed Hugo. He might come to regret the second bullet though.

Meanwhile Dragan, having witnessed Giles' arrival, had completed the task Hugo had given him in that eventuality. He had not seen Laura and Sam making their hurried exit but was now about to open the downstairs door to creep up and check on the meeting's progress. He laughed to himself at the thought he had left a gun for his boss in the desk drawer. He had thought maybe his employer might need to use the gun on himself if the meeting ended badly.

The door was flung open by Giles striking Dragan full in the face and knocking him to the ground. He was momentarily stunned but recovering quickly he wiped away the blood pouring from his nose and saw Giles getting into the bright red Porsche 911 Carrera that he, Dragan, was familiar with.

This did not look good at all. Should he go upstairs and check on his boss or should he follow the Porsche? The spatters of blood on the face of the politician made his mind up for him. This didn't look good but if his boss was still alive he would want him to follow anyway. He hurried behind the wheel of his black BMW and drove off trying to remain in visual contact with the Porsche.

Sam and Laura had no specific plan. Get the hell out of there, as far away and as quickly as possible from Valerian HQ. They knew Giles would be chasing them as soon as he had regained control of his mind. He had killed Hugo, he had even less to lose right now!

They hadn't needed to discuss who would drive. Laura had jumped into the drivers seat. Sam would be navigator. They didn't need to worry about the traffic police, in fact they would be more than welcome.

Laura accelerated away quickly. The TT had four wheel drive, there was no wheel spin. 'Just get out of the science park.' Sam said. Then, 'Turn left here Laura, to the north, we don't want to head down into the city centre. We need to get onto the open road.'

Sam adjusted his door mirror so he could see what was happening behind. He didn't know what sort of car Giles would be driving but he reckoned they would find out soon enough.

They sped to the Milton Interchange, a huge roundabout junction with the A14. Traffic light controlled but Laura ignored the red lights and shot out, narrowly missing a white van. The driver of the van sounded his horn aggressively as he swerved to avoid a collision.

'Go right here Laura, it's dual carriageway. Hopefully Giles won't see which way we've gone and we'll be in the clear.'

Sam glanced in his rear view mirror. A bright red Porsche was approaching rapidly from behind and driving with about as much attention to safety as Laura.

She put her right foot down hard and the little TT responded by accelerating away. She joined the dual carriageway by undertaking a large articulated lorry and moved over to the outside lane. Their speed was up to ninety miles an hour. The TT was capable of speeds approaching a hundred and forty, but was it as fast as the Porsche? Sam thought probably not.

Laura was weaving the TT left and right overtaking then undertaking. The Porsche was a few hundred yards behind but clearly visible. It was driving in a similarly erratic manner.

'I don't think we are going to be able to outrun him Sam,' shouted Laura. 'He's gaining on us. What's he going to try and do.'

'Probably he'll try and force us off the road, make us crash, or at least to stop. We have to assume he's got Hugo's gun. He's a killer.'

They had merged with traffic coming from the south on the A11 and the road was even more congested now.

Sam took note of a large road sign they were approaching.

'Laura, there's a junction coming up in a couple of miles, a slip road. Ease off the speed and let Giles get close behind. Then leave it as late as you can and swing off to the left. Hopefully he won't react quickly enough and overshoot the turning.'

The Porsche was now only two hundred yards behind and they were fast approaching the slip road. Laura eased off the accelerator and allowed Giles to draw up behind them. The slip road arrowed off to the left and at the last possible moment she pulled the steering wheel hard over and the TT careered over the white hatched lines to join the exit road.

Giles had been expecting some sort of move. He knew they had to do something different because it was obvious he was in the more powerful car. He had detected the Audi's speed slowing and was prepared. He swung his Porsche violently to the left crossing over the grass verge, momentarily causing the Porsche to leave the ground, before finding its path on the slip road.

'Shit!' said Laura. 'He's followed us over. We're never going to get away from him. What can we do Sam?'

They had joined a single carriageway country road, it was empty, no other traffic. Their manoeuvre had got them back to about two hundred yards in front of the Porsche. The road ahead was straight with what appeared to be a sharp bend to the right half a mile or so in front. They were in open, flat farmland and there was a small collection of trees surrounding the road at the corner ahead.

'Just keep going as fast as you can Laura, that's all we can do. You are doing great. We'll think of something.'

Behind, in the Porsche, Giles was feeling exhilarated. The road was quieter, nobody about, and his car was definitely faster. They had no way of escape. He would force them off the road and finish them off with Hugo's gun. Adrenalin was flooding through his system, his heart was pumping, he was excited at the thought of using the gun again. He was gaining rapidly, his foot hard down on the floor, as the two cars powered towards the right handed corner.

Laura left it till the last possible moment before braking into the corner and her four wheel drive TT shot round as if on rails.

Giles saw the TT's brake lights flash on and moved his right foot off the accelerator to hit the brake pedal hard.

He slammed his foot down. His foot went straight to the floor.

'What the fucks happened to the brakes,' he shouted.

The red Porsche shot on, failing to slow. Giles had to attempt to take the corner but he was going way too fast. He lost the back end of the car, it swung round and hit the kerb of the road. The momentum of the car carried on in a straight line. It left the road. Giles screamed. The car somersaulted over and over and crashed into one of the tall pine trees standing on the corner.

Laura had seen in her mirror exactly what had happened. So had Sam.

'Bloody hell. He hasn't taken the corner. He didn't slow down at all. His brakes must have failed! Stop the car Laura, we need to see what's happening.'

Laura pulled the car over onto the grass verge. They got out of the TT and cautiously made their way towards the scene of the crash. Surely nobody could have survived an impact like that.

They stopped fifty yards short of the Porsche. It was upside down on its roof. The front of the car was completely caved in against the base of the tree. They could see Giles, trapped by his seat belt and detonated air bag. He appeared to be still alive.

With a blast that almost knocked them off their feet the bright red Porsche exploded in a ball of flames as the fuel tank ignited. They could see the body of Giles engulfed in the inferno. He appeared to be trying to scream but his efforts produced no sound. He thrashed around in agony for several seconds before the appalling image disappeared behind a screen of smoke and flames.

There was nothing they could do except stand and stare and wonder what on earth had happened. Just a short while ago they were concluding a meeting, champagne was being opened and now two men were dead.

They were still standing there, stunned, when a black BMW i3 arrived at the scene. It had dark tinted windows. The driver's side window lowered and a baby faced man of Eastern European origin looked out and smiled thinly at them. He reached across inside his car and took out a brown leather bag. He threw it gently in their direction. He raised an arm in acknowledgement and drove away as silently as he had arrived.

EPILOGUE

They were sitting where they had begun. Brighton Pier. Summer had been blown away by autumn and Sam and Laura were dressed to repel the cold winds whipping in off the sea. Once again they were doing battle with the seagulls for ownership of a fish and chip lunch.

'Some things never change do they?' said Laura as she waved her free hand firmly in the direction of one of the more persistent gulls.

'And some things have changed for ever since we last sat here,' said Sam. He cuddled up closer to her. 'One or two of which have definitely been for the better.'

The spark of attraction had become the flame of love. Shared triumphs and disasters cementing the bond that had been forming over the past few weeks.

Ella had returned from her grandparents in France and was not surprised to see that Laura had not returned to her flat in Preston Park. The spare room didn't appear to be in use either. Ella was happy to at least share some of the responsibility she felt for her father. With gentle encouragement from Dad she had even applied for accommodation in the university halls of residence. Time for you to fly Ella. Gilly had been right about that. Just a little push from the nest.

In the aftermath of the events in Cambridge, the police had been all over the crime scene and Sam and Laura were interviewed extensively and separately. They had held virtually nothing back. After all, the truth is easy to tell, even if sometimes hard to believe.

It had been of no surprise to Sam and Laura to find they were not the only ones at the fateful meeting to have planned a secret recording. An SD memory card had mysteriously arrived at Sam's home in a package bearing an Albanian stamp. It would be kept for use only if needed.

The full extent of Giles' involvement became known to the police and unsurprisingly the security services had taken a close interest. Also unsurprisingly Laura's brother Tim had disappeared on one of his overseas trips.

So one cover up became covered up by another. It was a question of what was in the national interest. Evidently this was not a good time for a government to be brought down. It was somebody's job to make decisions like that.

The conspiracy never made it to the front pages and it never would. A shroud of secrecy was thrown over the whole affair. The sudden death of the Minister for Health was a great loss to the country according to the Prime Minister.

There was no need to cause alarm to those many patients who were being treated with Condrone. The drug was withdrawn from use for 'commercial reasons'. It would probably reappear at some stage in the future once the side effect issue had been engineered out.

Peter White was cooperating with the investigation in his attempts to deflect all the blame onto Hugo. He had hoped to bargain his knowledge of the wonder drug Mementum to make a deal for immunity. But his research was taken away from him and given to his old employer, Smithson Pharmaceuticals. A wrong had been righted.

Although the dementia drug, with a past to forget and a morally fraught future was too good to lose its inventor was not. Conspiracy to murder topped the list of charges.

Valerian Pharmaceuticals had been shut down and the company's assets seized. The police were having less success with tracking down Hugo's personal fortune.

The Department for Health investigation into Sam's prescribing had not just gone away as he might have hoped. But with Anita's unwavering support Sam had retained his licence to practice. On condition that he would not prescribe controlled drugs to addicts. Not until he had Home Office approval anyway.

And with Sam's support Anita was about to embark on some life changing surgery. Another wrong to be righted.

'Shame I don't get to publish the story,' said Laura. 'It would have made quite a name for us.'

'And it might have made quite a few enemies for us too,' said Sam.

'So there's only one question left to answer Sam. What are we going to do with our ten million quid?'

****

Side Effect

Printed in Great Britain
by Amazon

17268211R00165